HELL IN A HANDBASKET
SIN DEMONS

MILA YOUNG

HARPER A. BROOKS

Hell in a Handbasket © Copyright 2020 Mila Young & Harper A. Brooks

Cover Design by Jervy Bonifacio | Phoenix Design Studio
Editing by Dara Horcasitas of Refined Voice Editing
Proofreading by Nic Page and Robyn Mather

Visit our books at
www.milayoungbooks.com
https://harperabrooks.com

All rights reserved under the International and Pan-American Copyright Conventions. No part of this book may be reproduced or transmitted in any form or by any means, electronic or mechanical, including photocopying, recording, or by any information storage and retrieval system, without permission in writing from the publisher/author.

This is a work of fiction. Names, places, characters and incidents are either the product of the author's imagination or are used fictitiously, and any resemblance to any actual persons, living or dead, organizations, events or locales is entirely coincidental.

Warning: the unauthorized reproduction or distribution of this copyrighted work is illegal. Criminal copyright infringement, including infringement without monetary gain, is investigated by the FBI and is punishable by up to 5 years in prison and a fine of $250,000.

DEDICATION

For Spanking Girl
-Harper A. Brooks

For Limo Girl
-Mila Young

CONTENTS

Sin Demons Series — vii
Hell in a Handbasket — ix

Chapter 1 — 1
Chapter 2 — 12
Chapter 3 — 24
Chapter 4 — 41
Chapter 5 — 50
Chapter 6 — 67
Chapter 7 — 77
Chapter 8 — 99
Chapter 9 — 107
Chapter 10 — 128
Chapter 11 — 142
Chapter 12 — 159
Chapter 13 — 178
Chapter 14 — 192
Chapter 15 — 208
Chapter 16 — 225
Chapter 17 — 249
Chapter 18 — 266
Chapter 19 — 281
Chapter 20 — 296
Chapter 21 — 306

Night Kissed — 323
Death Wish — 325
About Mila Young — 327
About Harper A. Brooks — 329

SIN DEMONS SERIES

Playing With Hellfire
Hell In A Handbasket
All Shot To Hell
To Hell And Back

HELL IN A HANDBASKET

See no evil. Hear no evil. Speak no evil. Sleep with no evil... If only it were that easy.

Between being kidnapped by a psycho dragon-shifter, influenced by ancient relics, and fighting for my freedom, I'd say my hands are full. But really, my troubles have just begun.

Cain, Dorian, and Elias are wickedly dangerous, scorching hot, and all too tempting. They're devils in disguise. Literally.

I don't know why they're collecting these relics, but it looks like I'm not the only one with secrets. Despite all the risks, I might be falling for the three of them. But there's a good chance this Hellish relationship ends up being the death of me.

To make matters worse, there may be something more to my shadow than I originally thought. Something evil that's set on taking over me entirely if I let it.

With each passing day, I find myself falling deeper into its darkness and further under the demons' deadly charms.

There's no other way around it... Things are quickly going to Hell in a handbasket.

CHAPTER ONE
ARIA

"If I got rid of my demons, I'd lose my angels." -Tennessee Williams

Consciousness slams into me, and my eyes snap open to the city buildings and streets in minuscule size all the way down, down, down below. My heart plummets and terror seizes me.

"Fuuuucckk!" I scream and fling my arms about. Wind whips into me, throwing my hair into my face as it whistles past my ears. For a moment, I believe I'm falling, but that's quickly proven to be wrong by the talons digging into my sides, the massive shadow overhead, and the loud whooshing sound from each swing of leathery wings above me.

Craning my neck up, I have to do a double-take. The beast holding me hundreds of feet above the ground and soaring through the air is a freaking dragon! The dark scales covering its enormous body glint with a silvery hue, and when its long neck tilts down, the reptilian-looking head pivots to look at me with eyes sparking orange and gold, like fire.

I shudder as fear unlike any I've ever known grips me. Terrified of being dropped from this high and the horrible death that would follow, I curl in on myself and clutch onto the clawed legs I'm trapped between. The creature lifts its head and roars, the sound blaring against my eardrums.

It unleashes an inferno of flames into the sky. Heat backlashes over me, and a scream bursts past my lips, my heart thundering. I make the mistake of looking down again at the world rushing beneath me at a blurring speed. The city's given way to thick woods and sloping hills.

How the hell did this happen? My groggy brain struggles to recall the moments before waking up in a dragon's clutches. I was kidnapped by the Full Mooner wolves and brought to Sir Surchion's warehouse, I remember that. The fucking old bat had tracked me down because of the Orb of Chaos. Cain, Elias, and Dorian were outside. I remember hearing the pandemonium as they clashed with more werewolves who'd planned to ambush them. Something must have happened. God, I hope they're okay.

Then there's the whole 'Sayah becoming alive and feeding off my energy' thing. Sir Surchion had called her a demon, and I'll admit, with her stretched limbs and red eyes, she definitely seemed to fit the bill. But when I reach inside myself, I can't even sense her there.

It's like she's hiding from me, but maybe that's for the best.

Now, I'm flying through the air with a dragon. Another one of those ultra-rare supernatural types that only a few have laid eyes on.

Sickness churns in my gut. This isn't how I expected my life to turn out. For so long, I dreamed of moving out of my foster home and starting fresh, but instead, my world has turned into a sinking pit.

Sold to demons.

Kidnapped by a dragon.

Yep, I'm doing magnificently in the 'How to Get Killed Quickly' department.

Suddenly, we lurch forward, the dragon spearing directly for a mountain.

Wind assaults me, tearing at my hair and clothes. As the ground begins to rush closer, nausea rolls, and another scream rips from my throat. I hold onto the beast's claws for dear life and wonder what it plans for me next. Does it want to make me a meal for its children? Or is it going to add me as a token to its treasure collection?

I search the landscape, desperate to find a path I can use later if I manage to escape. Rivers snake amid the wild overgrowth of woodland. Sharp rock faces, hills everywhere. It's going to be a dangerous trek, but I'll take my chances.

The wind comes so fast now, I can't drag air into my lungs. We swoop sideways, and I hold on tighter. We're rushing toward the top of the towering mountain. Fear tears at my chest that we're going to crash-land with me underneath this creature.

The talons around me suddenly loosen and pull away.

I'm falling. My stomach lurches, and I see my own death. I flail about, screaming, and crash into a tangle of overgrown grass with a hard *thump*.

My momentum sends me tumbling forward, rolling and spinning through the brush and mud. My vision twirls, pain jabbing me from all directions.

When I finally come to a stop, I lay there, gasping and sputtering, my heart banging against my rib cage.

I could have died... That's all I can think. *I could have died.*

But, surprisingly, I'm not dead. Not yet, anyway.

I need to stay low, to vanish amid the greenery. Use the forest to my advantage.

An ache flares over my hip from the rough landing, and my muscles strain. Now that the initial fear of falling to my death is over, I'm hit with all the excruciating pain from the fight in the warehouse. Specifically, my shoulder, which hurts beyond words. With a shaky hand, I touch the jagged wound and wince as a burning, stabbing pain flares.

That's right. Freaking werewolf had bit me.

A thunderous roar booms from behind me, and the ground beneath me shudders. I whip around to find the dragon just yards away, smoke leaking out of its nostrils. Its fiery gaze pins on me, and it begins to stomp my way.

My wounds are going to slow me down, but there's no way I'm going to lay down and be eaten.

I'm up and running in the next second. Every step the beast takes has the Earth shaking and me tripping over my own feet as I run uphill. Ahead of me, the ground levels out, and the opening to a cave comes into view. Here, the vegetation is non-existent, charred black by fire. This must be the dragon's den. Its nest.

Shit.

Not good.

But turning back isn't an option. Not when the dragon is closing the distance, and beyond the cave, the ground drops off suddenly. Both options lead to an agonizing death.

My only hope is that there's another exit at the rear.

Knowing the odds aren't really in my favor, I hightail it toward the cave. Another quick glance over my shoulder, and I see the dragon's skin twitching. Slowing, it swings its head as if it's in a great deal of pain, and I pause. It starts to shrink before my eyes. Scales morph and take on a human skin tone. Bones pop as they readjust, and the thing groans as it turns to face away from me. The neck shortens, and the tail recedes until it's gone.

It's… shifting.

I didn't know dragons were actually a kind of shifter. As excruciating as the change seems to be, it happens in almost the blink of an eye. One second, it's a great creature, next, a man stands in its place with his back to me, stark naked. Complete with saggy ass. Eww.

Now *that* is a surprise. Who would have thought

such a powerful dragon would have the butt of a wrinkly old man?

He crouches down and picks up clothes from the ground, ones I didn't notice in my frantic running. Bright red tights, oversized cheetah print coat, and circular glasses. When he turns toward me, I gasp.

Sir Surchion! The collector from the antique store.

White hair, thick sideburns, a pale goatee, and beady eyes that find me in an instant. Ice fills my veins, and for a few moments, I'm numb. It's like there's nothing inside me, no need to run, no need for anything but to be in utter shock.

He's a dragon shifter? Since when?

My mouth hangs open as he struts forward, readjusting his coat on his body. Right then, a bird swoops down and lands perfectly on his shoulder. A big black crow. Mordecai.

In his beak are the three relics he stole from me, all still magically attached to one another. Sir Surchion reaches up, takes them from his pet, and grins.

A faint hum of music flares over my mind as the relics call to me. Their combined voices rise in a siren song. *"Danger. Danger. Danger."*

The hairs on the nape of my neck stand up automatically. The voices and melody might be smoother now, but it doesn't make it any less creepy.

Panic restarting my heart, I spin and rush for the cave again, my only chance at escape. All this time, I'd thought Sir Surchion was just a dirty old man who liked to hit on younger girls and had a severe hoarding problem. Turns out he's all that *and* a fucking fire-breathing dragon. And I'd say that's much, much worse.

The moment I pass through the entrance, I'm cloaked in shadows, and the temperature drops about ten degrees. I rush behind a group of big rocks further inside, nearly tripping over my own feet in the dark. Clamping a hand over my mouth, I try to quiet my rapid breathing, but it still sounds too loud to me. That and my frantic heart, which pounds like thunder in my ears.

"No use hiding, Aria," Sir Surchion says. "You're not going anywhere, and you have much to tell me."

I crouch low and peer deeper into the cavern. A black void stares back at me. I debate calling to Sayah and asking for her help to search it, but she's still out of reach. I'm on my own here.

Frantically, I pat the ground for a weapon as Sir Surchion draws closer. My hand closes around a rod-shaped rock that's broken on one end, giving it a sharp edge. I snatch it and tuck it into the pocket of my jeans.

This is crazy, I repeat to myself. *Absolutely fucking crazy...*

But if there really is no way out of here, and no Sayah to help, then I'm backed into a corner. I'll have to fight.

Drawing in a deep breath, I rise and step out of my hiding spot to stand before the monster.

"Why, Miss Cross, you looked a bit surprised to find out what I really am. Is it really that astonishing?" he asks.

"If you mean a saggy old windbag, then no," I say

past the thickness of my throat. "Just add wings and you're a saggy old windbag who can fly. Not that spectacular."

He snorts, smoke wisping out from the corners of his flaring nostrils. "You speak with such disrespect. In ancient times, they would have thrown virgins like you to me, and—" He stops and taps the side of his face as if he's remembering something important. "Oh wait. That's right. You're the demons' property now, so not a virgin anymore, I'm sure."

I grit my teeth. I don't know why the comment irritates me so much, but it does.

He moves with lightning speed toward me. I can't even register what's happened until his hand is around my throat, squeezing hard. I struggle to suck in another breath.

"I am the devil, the darkness, everything you fear," he sneers at me, and the damn crow squawks on his shoulder, wings spread wide.

I slap his arm to try and get him to let go, but it does nothing. "Technically..." I gasp, "Cain is the real devil, not you."

He snarls, his breath stinking like rotten eggs, and tosses me aside like I'm nothing but a rag doll. I hit the ground hard and moan, because as luck would have it, I hit my sore hip.

Fear tightens around my chest at how easily he threw me. Even as old as he is, he's still much stronger than me. And faster.

He's next to me in seconds, his hand snatching me

by my ripped top and wrenching me to my feet. I shove against his chest. "Leave me the fuck alone."

"Let's make a deal. You're good at those, aren't you?" he growls in my face, holding me close. "I won't burn you to a crisp for stealing my orb *if* you tell me more about your three little demon boyfriends."

His words take me off guard. Why would he want to know about Cain, Dorian, and Elias?

"I-I d-don't know anything about them," I reply. "They're asses, just like you."

His expression twists into a scowl, and he shakes me like I'm a milkshake. Everything gets stirred inside me, and the earlier sickness comes back up, fast this time.

"You will tell me everything. Where they found their relics and what they intend to do with them, or you will end up like the warlock."

He ceases the shaking, and bile hits the back of my throat.

"I don't feel too well," I murmur.

But he isn't listening and talks over me. "That pathetic excuse for a spellcaster begged for his life, you know. Saying he knew nothing about the orb you took. But you know what he *did* say before I strangled him and Mordecai pecked out his eyes? That you have abilities, and he'd tell me all about them if I let him go." He laughs like a hyena. "He tried selling you out in a heartbeat."

It only takes seconds for his confession to sink into me. It sits at the bottom of my stomach like a brick. "You're the one who killed my foster father? For information? You sick bastard!"

I throw my fists at him, nailing him in the face and chest, but he laughs at me like I'm nothing more than a pestering gnat. I loathe this man with every fiber of my being. I should've burned his whole warehouse down when I broke in that first time.

"Although..." he begins, his eyes glinting with interest, "what you did back there with your demon shadow was peculiar. Could come in handy at some point down the road..."

Oh no. I know where this is going.

He continues, "I could add you to my collection. Store you away for a rainy day."

Fuck no. Absolutely not. I'm not going to be set on some mantel like someone's trophy.

He shakes me again, so hard this time that my teeth rattle. It's impossible to keep the sickness down anymore, and the contents of my stomach decide to make a show. I gag and throw up all over Sir Surchion's coat.

"You bitch!" he squeals and recoils. He lets me drop, and my knees are the first to hit the dirt, but it's not long before the back of his knuckles slam into the side of my face. My stomach still roils, but this is my chance.

While he bats at the vomit on his ridiculous fur coat, I lunge toward him, lashing out with my stone weapon. The sharp edge bites into his side, and using all my strength, I drag it across his abdomen, tearing flesh. Mordecai squawks and launches into the air.

Sir Surchion leaps backward, growling ferociously and clutching the wound. Blood covers his hands in seconds.

I throw myself toward the front of the cave, running for the exit, but the crow is suddenly there, wings spread wide and claws reaching for me, so I whirl around and sprint back into the darkness.

Please, please, please let there be another way out!

"Go! Go! Goooo!" The relics sing, but the distance grows between us, and the music fades into eerie silence. Blindly, I run, stumbling over rocks and sticks and who knows what else.

My heart pounds as my feet shove against the ground, but I don't dare stop. Another monstrous roar fills the cave, the thunderous sound reverberating off the stone and hitting me from all directions. There's nothing I can do but plunge further into the unknown.

CHAPTER TWO

ELIAS

The hardwood creaks beneath my rushed steps as I burst into the library.

"Sonofabitch, I'm going to murder that dragon!" I snarl, my breaths racing, fists clenching. "He's not at his store, home, or even the damn pigeon fancier's club he hangs out at. I've been searching all day."

Cain stands over a map laid out on the table, staring at it. He doesn't even look up as I stalk closer, but I can see the shadows under his eyes and that his muscles are tense. The last time I saw him so closed off and focused was just before we tried to usurp his father, Lucifer, from his throne in Hell.

Dorian is pacing in front of the fireplace. "I've made calls all over town. Even in our contacts in Storm. Nothing."

"He's in the mountains," Cain says suddenly, lifting his head. His sudden break from silence startles us both, and we hurry over to his side.

"Of course he is," Dorian huffs, running a hand over

his mouth. "Where else would a fucking dragon go to hide?"

"The entire town is surrounded by woodlands and mountains. Miles upon miles of it." I know because I've run through most of it during our time here on Earth. "What do you expect us to do? Searching on foot will take days. Weeks."

Dorian shakes his head. "We can hire a plane and fly over it to cover more ground. At least until we find anything remotely resembling a dragon's hiding spot." The corded muscles in his neck flex as he speaks through his rapid thoughts. "We must do whatever it takes to get back the harp's pieces and Aria."

That sounded more like a plan to me. It was certainly the faster option, but still might not be fast enough. "One thing we can bet on is that he isn't going to be in plain sight. He'll need lots of coverage to hide what he is, otherwise we would've heard there was a damn dragon flying through our territory."

"That still doesn't narrow it down to any specific area," Dorian replies. "With Vermont's thick forests and mountains, it's prime real estate for a dragon."

"Dorian, bring the car to the front." Again, Cain's voice surprises us.

"Oh?" he asks.

Cain lifts his chin, glancing between the two of us, and his gaze darkens. He's got an idea. "We're taking a trip to Storm's markets."

Without questioning it, Dorian strides out of the room. His booming command echoes down the hall. "Sadie! We're going for a drive!"

The sound of the young maid's hurried footsteps follows.

As Cain walks past me, I snatch his arm to draw him to a stop.

I expect him to fight or scold me for touching him, but instead, he looks at me and says, "I know. We'll get her back." Like he can read my mind.

"And the collector?" Just the thought of him makes a growl vibrate up my throat.

Cain's jaw tightens. "We'll wear his scales as armor through Hell's gates."

The hellhound inside me likes the sound of that.

I let him go and follow as he walks out of the library. The front foyer is still damaged from our earlier cross with the werewolves. The bodies have been removed by our staff, but the signs of battle remain. Broken vases. Holes in the walls. Blood stains on the staircase and banister.

It feels like days since Aria was taken from us, not just a matter of hours. But she's never left my thoughts. Her being here was supposed to just be another business transaction for us. Another soul to use or feed from. It shouldn't bother me that she's in danger as much as it does, but in the short time the girl's been with us, she's managed to imprint on me.

I grind my teeth as anger lashes at my insides. I can't believe that scaly creep took her from us.

More specifically, I can't believe we failed at saving her. *And* getting the harp's pieces back. We never lose.

I storm after Cain into the front yard, where the day is steadily giving way to night. A black Ferrari pulls up in our driveway, the tinted window rolling down to reveal Dorian.

"You want a personal invitation, or are you getting in?" he calls with a playful smile.

"Why did you bring this car?" I snap as Cain opens the passenger door and pushes the seat back, then looks over to me to get into the back. I already know the answer to the question—he wants to torture me. I hate sports cars. They aren't built for real men like me.

"Get in," Cain says, while Dorian smirks at me.

I want to drive my fist through his face, but I go ahead and step inside. Squeezing into the back seat is like trying to fit a grizzly bear into a cage. Too tight in all directions and feels like the walls are pressing in. Trapped. Twisting and turning, I try everything to get comfortable, but it's impossible.

"All comfy in the back?" Dorian teases.

"Fuck you." Growling, I punch the back of his seat. I knew he'd pick it just to piss me off.

He twists around and glares. "Destroy this beautiful car and you're replacing it."

"Oh, I'll replace it," I retort. "With a real car. Not this small-penis car."

Dorian bursts out laughing. "If you're going to insult me, at least do it properly. Guys with small penises are known to get big cars. Like suped-up trucks."

I throw another fist into the back of his headrest just as Cain shoves his seat back, whacking it into my shins. I cry out.

"Enough," he barks before turning back to Dorian. "Drive."

15

We're off in seconds, the wheels spinning in the gravel and kicking up rocks. The bumps are tortuous while in the cramped back seat. At least the drive is fast, and once we reach paved road, it's smoother sailing. I'll give Dorian that about this shitbox—it moves low to the ground and whips through the streets like wildfire.

When we get to the painted black umbrella, that marks the stone of the underpass in the heart of the city, Dorian stops the car. A man dressed in rags and sitting in a lawn chair near a tent and shopping cart full of trash bags, glances at us. He may appear to be another homeless fellow using the underpass as a safe place to make camp, but when it comes to Storm, not everything is what it seems.

To stay hidden from human view, Storm's entrance is cloaked heavily by magic. It's located in the underbelly of Glenside, allowing supernaturals to gather freely, even thrive. Here, supes can be themselves. It's why most prefer to visit this side of the city. Or Purgatory. There's no need to pretend to be somebody else. But keeping it a secret from the human world is a challenge. You never know who is really watching, after all.

Dorian revs his engine three times, and the homeless man—really, the gatekeeper to Storm—stands up. His gaze searches the area for any prying eyes, and when he deems it safe, he turns and knocks on the painted umbrella. The stone face shimmers as the magical barrier gives way, and the ramp leading down into the subterranean level appears on the other side.

Saluting the hobo to show his thanks, Dorian steps on the gas, and we pass through without issue.

Another fascinating detail about Storm is that although it's located underground, it doesn't look to be. A false sky that mimics the one above is painted above us, again touched by magic. Now it looks like twilight, striped with shades of rose and gold as the fabricated sun sets.

Dorian guides the Ferrari through the tight streets, wandering aimlessly with no real direction in mind. Cain and I stare out the windows to search for more of the painted umbrellas. Following them is the only way to find the market's location, since it's never in the same place twice.

"There," Cain says, pointing to a building on our right. Partially hidden behind a dumpster is the familiar black umbrella painted on the brick. Dorian turns down the small alleyway.

Cain points ahead of us again, to another umbrella on a closed storefront window. Dorian whips the car left, onto another main street. We follow the umbrella breadcrumbs until they lead us into a dark lot with only one other car parked under a flickering streetlight.

This is it.

My skin crawls with anxiousness. I'm ready to get this over with. Better yet, I'm more than ready to get out of this fucking car. The second the car stops, I reach past Cain, rip the handle back, and fling open the door. He takes his time getting out, but once I can, I force myself through the small space so I can stand on my own two feet again.

Outside, I draw in a deep breath and lift my arms

17

high to stretch out my tight muscles. Bones crack, but I'm instantly flooded with relief.

Cain's already walking toward a dilapidated old office building that's attached to the parking lot, Dorian on his heels. I slap the car door behind me shut with my foot and catch up. The market isn't like your typical mall or swap-meet. It offers everything from human bones for spells to rare berries only grown in Botswana. Forbidden things. Rare things. Extremely powerful things. And if it's not goods you seek, the place is also packed with services. Witches, healers, apothecaries, even whores… all at your service, one way or another.

So, as any intelligent person may have guessed, Dorian comes here more than the rest of us.

As we reach the building's door, he takes the lead and shoulders the crooked thing open. The rusted hinges whine loudly, but as we step through, we're instantly hit with the sights, sounds, and smells of the ocean. We've been transported to another place entirely. And by the sounds of seagulls cawing, the feel of salt and sand on the breeze, and the ceiling of wooden boards above our heads, it looks like we're now under a boardwalk by the sea.

It's been a while since I came here last, but besides the location hocus pocus, not much has changed. The place is bustling with activity. Tables are set up at stalls in half a dozen long rows. Merchants of all shapes, sizes, and supernatural flavors sell wares and food with just as much diversity. It's a mish-mash of unique sights and smells. Something delicious tickles my nose, and I turn to see shish-kebabed lizards on rotisserie at a nearby stand. My stomach clenches with hunger.

My gaze sweeps the market, and I take notice of the guards posted throughout the place. Mostly shifters, from the looks of it. As one myself, it makes it easier to spot my own kind, even if I'm not exactly from this world. They must've caught our scent or spotted us coming in, because their yellow eyes land on us. I snarl and look away, an animal's way of telling them we want no trouble. If they're smart, they'll understand the cues and leave us alone. Although, I'm not opposed to releasing some anger for the hell of it.

When Dorian walks down a row of vendors, Cain and I follow. Bodies cram into every space, bumping into us. People shout their sales, and I'm quickly reminded of why I don't come here often. I loathe crowds.

The quicker we get this done, the better.

As we walk, some supes notice us. I catch their sideways glances, the glares, the terror... Demons are not popular with the locals, for obvious reasons. We barter for and eat souls. We're feared.

I'm not sure what I'm supposed to be looking for, exactly, but I keep an eye out for any witches or warlocks selling anything that could be helpful in tracking a person. Maybe some kind of location spell or totem or... hell if I know. *Something*.

As we stroll through the crowd, Cain and Dorian split, eventually going their own way and leaving me on my own. People press in around me, some treading on my feet, nudging me to get past. Fuck, I hate this.

"Magic amulet," a man with a strong Mediterranean accent calls out.

I turn instantly to my right where a small horde of customers has gathered around a merchant. Standing on top of a crate to be seen, he holds a leather cord with a bronze piece of jewelry dangling from it. It reminds me of a coin by its circular shape and size, but I'm too far away to see the markings on its face.

"This is the last one of its kind," the man calls out. "The Amulet of Truth will answer yes or no when asked a question by the wearer. This rare piece will never be offered again. Who wants it?"

I pause, my interest piquing. An Amulet of Truth... We could use that to help track down the dragon.

I shove forward, forcing my way through the throng of people, and call out, "I'll take it!"

At the same time, a bulky orc pushes his way to the front and snatches the amulet from the man's hand.

"Mine! It's mine," he snarls. His upper lip curls back over yellow teeth, his tusks dripping in saliva.

Fury rises in me. That green monkey pushed in!

"Don't waste your time." Dorian's beside me suddenly, his whisper like a bee's buzz in my ear. "It's a hoax."

"But what if it can help us?" I step closer, my gaze pinned on the orc palming what is rightfully mine.

"Everyone knows that vendor is a charlatan. The amulet's no different than a magic 8-ball. Or scrap metal."

The orc's lips split in a grin that makes fury burn through my veins.

"I claimed it first," I growl at him, drawing the crowd's attention. "Give it up."

The orc's nose wrinkles with disgust. "Not a fucking chance, demon scum." Spit splatters all over my face as he talks.

I lurch forward, rage blurring my vision, but Dorian's hand is quick on my chest to stop me. My mouth runs free, though. "You say something, asshat?"

The vendor looks more than pleased by the exchange. Especially by how much attention we're getting now. "Now, now gentlemen," he says gently, "we can settle this with a good old-fashioned bidding war. Do I hear five hundred dollars?"

Dorian huffs. "For a piece of junk? You're out of your fucking mind."

The orc presses closer, spreads his legs, and squares his shoulders. In both the animal world and the human one, there's only one way to interpret his stance—he's challenging me. It'll be the last mistake he ever makes.

"No one wants your fucking kind here," he shouts at me and Dorian. Behind him, two of his buddies emerge from the crowd, all green, bumpy skin and bald heads. I'm tall, but these ugly bastards have a few inches on me, their domes almost hitting the boards above us.

I crack my neck and raise my fists. I've never taken on three orcs at once before, but I do enjoy a challenge. This is going to be fun.

Smiling, the orc swings the amulet by the leather cord just to taunt me. I lean forward again, ready to knock his teeth in.

"Elias." Dorian's hand is still a firm pressure on my

chest. His tone is tinged with warning. "I know it's usually Cain's job to be the voice of reason, but we're here for a specific reason, and there's limited time."

"That's it. Listen to your boyfriend," the orc taunts.

My hellhound growls in my chest, the sound reverberating through me.

At the comment, Dorian turns and feigns repulsion at the sight of the creatures, covering his mouth with his hand. To really sell it, he swallows pretend vomit and grimaces. "Holy shit. You're so ugly, I almost lost my lunch. Phew, and that smell! Vile!"

One of the orcs, the shortest one of the three, bares his rotting teeth in a snarl. "Filthy demons. Crawl back to Hell where you belong."

"I'm sorry." Dorian puffs out his cheeks again and lurches forward as if he's about to hurl. "I just… I can't even hear what you're saying. I can't get past how hideous you all are. It's absolutely nauseating."

The orc with the amulet roars, beating his chest. Somewhere behind us, I hear Cain calling us, but I can't make out his words behind the pounding of my heart. All I can focus on is the sick satisfaction I'm going to get out of tearing these bastards apart.

"Six hundred! I'll even throw in an elf-made woven scarf," the merchant shouts but continues to be ignored.

My anger prickles across my skin, and my animal pushes for release. It doesn't like to stand down or show weakness when challenged. I never walk away. I have the scars on my body to prove it.

When the orc takes another threatening step forward, I do too.

"Practice some self-control, man. Just this once," Dorian snarls sharply and puts more strength behind his hold. "As much as I would love to pick my teeth with their bones, they aren't worth our time. *Aria*. Remember."

I hear his words—know they're true—but the fact that I lost Aria to those werewolves to begin with has left a bad taste in my mouth. The fact that I, a hellhound, can't even hunt her is the cherry on top of this shit sundae. My pride can't take another blow. And now, with these orcs taunting me, it's the third strike. There's no way I'll be able to take the higher road, tuck my tail between my legs and take a walk.

Like I said before, not my thing.

I am going to pry that amulet out of his dirty, sausage-like fingers, one way or another.

CHAPTER THREE
CAIN

I am yards away from the commotion, but through the throng of customers, I can see everything unfurl. For once, Dorian has done the smart thing and is trying to keep Elias from starting a fight instead of joining him like he typically would, but Elias is having none of it. He shoves past him and leaps at the closest orc's throat, growling like a wild animal. Being a top-heavy creature, the orc stumbles and falls, landing on its back with enough force to shake the ground. In an instant, Elias is punching it repeatedly in the face, blood spurting and bones mashing.

I sigh and place the black flame candle I'd been looking at back on the vendor's table. Dorian and I love the thrill of the fight as much as the next demon, but Elias is a different animal entirely. The scars marking his skin from all the fights he's started and subsequently finished proves it.

The circle of onlookers has already started to grow. Some even cheer. As the other two creatures lunge for

Elias, Dorian half-changes, his hair lightening in color and his nails sharpening. A collective gasp rises from the crowd.

Dorian uppercuts one orc hard enough that it staggers back, then he slashes his talons across the other's neck, slicing it clean across. Blood rushes from the wound and the creature grasps at his throat, making a loud gurgling sound.

This has gone on long enough.

Huffing, I slide through the masses until I get to the heart of the chaos. Dorian's about to attack the only remaining orc, but I seize him by the back of his shirt and haul him backward. His head whips around, seeing me, and the manic lust in his eyes that I know so well dies instantly. The orc takes his chance to flee and barrels through the rowdy spectators, knocking most of them down in his haste. Only when Dorian's demon begins to fade away do I let him go.

"So much for not causing a scene," I mutter at him.

He offers me an apologetic smile before glancing at Elias, who is still hammering the one's skull into oblivion. The bastard's been dead for a while now, but he doesn't let up. Like he's trying to make a point. To whom, exactly, I don't know.

"Elias," I hiss his way, but he's deaf in this carnal state. I turn to Dorian again. "We need to stop this before the guards throw us out or someone else decides to take their chance on us. We don't need a bloodbath now." We have too many enemies here, people who would love the opportunity to take their shot at dispatching us. And there isn't time. Not when Aria and the harp's relics are still missing.

He nods in agreement, and together, we seize Elias by the shoulders and rip him off the corpse. His hair, chest, and face are streaked in crimson, but between his fingers is the leather cord and bronze coin necklace he fought so wildly for.

I snatch it from him, my anger coiling around me like a serpent. "*This* is what you went off the rails for?"

Elias jerks out my grip with an aggressive roll of his shoulders. Lips curling, he snarls at me. "I thought it could help us find Aria."

I peer at the inscription across the center, seeing nothing spectacular to it at all. It's as useless as costume jewelry.

"It's a fake," Dorian says. "I told him that."

Clutching the thing in my fist, I squeeze. It doesn't take much for it to crunch in my palm. It's not even real bronze. More like tin foil. I understand Elias's desperation, given our circumstances, but he should have known better.

Annoyance growing, I chuck the remains onto the ground and look up. There have to be at least fifty pairs of eyes on us now, watching.

Bringing my darkness to the surface, just enough for effect, I set my gaze on the crowd. Anyone too close steps back in fear. My voice comes out deeper whenever my demon is unleashed, and it adds to the effect I need. "What are you all staring at?"

They scramble, shoving each other out of the way or pretending to be busy perusing the goods for sale.

Within seconds, it's as if nothing has happened. No one even glances at the two dead orcs on the ground again.

Spinning to face Dorian and Elias, I say, "Need I remind you *both* that we came here for a reason? The idea was to stay under the radar so we could get what we need and get out quickly."

Elias angrily wipes the blood from his mouth with the back of his hand. "Yeah, well, shit happens."

I narrow my eyes on him. "I'll muzzle you if I have to."

When Dorian's laughter erupts behind me, I throw him a warning glare. He clamps his mouth shut immediately.

I swear, sometimes the two of them are no better than children. I clench my jaw tightly. "Get in, get what we need, and get out," I repeat. "No more detours. No more mess."

"Fine," Elias snaps.

"We'll find something," Dorian begins, gesturing to the many vendor tables and the less than legal wares for sale. "And it'll be something better than some rusty old amulet to help us track her down… Wait—" He stops suddenly, eyes growing wide as if an idea has just struck him.

"What?" I ask. "What are you gawking at?"

His lips twist into a sly grin, and his green eyes become alight with mischief. "I know exactly what we need. Follow me."

He spins around and slips his way through the crowd again. One look at Elias and we're both hurrying to follow.

Dorian leads us to the very last row of tables, near the edge of the pier. Against one of the large pilings, a tent of multiple colored fabrics is hung. Christmas lights drape across them, and the overbearing scent of incense wafting from inside is strong enough to choke a bear.

As Elias comes to my side, he coughs and hacks. *Bear, hellhound... either way, my point is made.*

"What... the... fuck?" he sputters to Dorian, gasping to breathe. He rubs his nose frantically as if he's trying to erase the colliding smells of jasmine, vanilla, amber, lavender, and who knows what else from assaulting him any further. Even *my* eyes begin to water.

"Quit your whining. It's not that bad," Dorian says.

"It's worse," Elias wheezes and continues to rub his nose raw. "Is he trying to cover up the smell of dead bodies in there?"

Laughing, Dorian shrugs, but the glimmer of excitement is still twinkling in his eyes. "*She*," he corrects. "And maybe."

Who is this person he's bringing us to see, and how did he know she was here? I know he visits the market the most out of the three of us, but he's never mentioned a woman vendor in a tent before.

Pulling the makeshift tent's flap open, he disappears inside.

I turn to Elias. "Maybe it's best if you stay out here," I say. "Keep an eye out for the orcs."

He's squeezing his nose now, his eyes bloodshot and irritated. His words come out in short spurts as he struggles to breathe. "Works for... me. There was no way... I was going in there... anyway."

Nodding, I pull the curtain door open and step inside.

What I'm faced with next draws me to a stop. I'm in a vast circular room with high, peaked ceilings, large columns, and everything is decorated in expensive silks and floating lanterns that appear to be manipulated by magic. Is this mysterious person Dorian knows a powerful spellcaster?

The overwhelming perfume-like smells are even stronger in here, and I don't know what's worse at this point—the overwhelming stink of the markets outside or this. My throat feels scratchy and tight just standing here.

Dorian, though, strolls across the room, admiring the space. Humming, he kicks one of the many pillows on the floor. "Miranda," he sings-songs as he walks. "Miranda, darling, where are you?"

Across the room, another curtain pulls aside and a woman enters. Dressed in a long purple dress that ties around her neck and has billowing sleeves, her hair is decorated with stripes of vibrant colors, braids, and beads, reminding me of the motif humans cast most psychics in. All she's missing is the scarf wrapped around her head, some tarot cards, and a crystal ball.

When she spots Dorian, her arms cross and she cocks a hip, not looking pleased to see him at all. "You," is all she says.

Despite her chilly demeanor, Dorian is all smiles as he strides over to her, holds her firmly by the arms, and places a kiss on each of her cheeks. Her lip curls in disgust.

"I told you never to come here again," she spits, shrugging off his grasp.

"Oh, Miranda. Don't be like that," he charms in typical Dorian fashion. "We had fun, didn't we? You and me... in the sand... at sunset..."

Her eyes narrow. "And you never calling after..."

Dorian winces and rubs the back of his neck nervously. He's backed himself into a corner with this one. I should help him, but part of me is enjoying watching him squirm too much. I've warned him that his reckless behavior on Earth, especially with powerful supernaturals, would get him in trouble one day. We have a lot of enemies, but most of his are scorned women.

"Now you only come when you need something," she says.

"Yes, well... You know how it is—"

She waves his attempt at an excuse away. "You know what? I don't want to hear it. It's not worth my time. Just get out."

"Miranda, I need your talents—"

She cuts him off again. "Get. Out."

Dorian glances at me, hoping for backup, but I don't know what kind I can offer. I don't know this woman; I'm still unsure why he's even brought us here.

For the first time since she walked in, Miranda's gaze swings my way, finally seeing me. That's when the anger drains from her face and her eyes widen.

"Who is this?" she asks as she slowly makes her way

around the circular room toward me. Her movements are graceful but calculated, and her voice is suddenly silky smooth. She smiles as she draws closer until she stands before me. Eyes shining with mystery and extreme interest, she peers up at me.

Dorian's acquaintance or not, there's something about this woman that reminds me of a viper. Lethal. Deadly.

"Lord, Almighty. Who would've thought today was the day a prince of Hell would come strolling into my tent," she begins and continues to study me. "Cain, am I right? First son of Lucifer and Pride himself."

Although I am baffled how this strange woman knows me and my lineage, I keep the surprise off my face.

"Yes," I say. "You are correct." I've made it a priority not to discuss my father or direct connection to Hell with anyone on this plane. Well, besides Aria, but that was in a moment of weakness. Most know I am a demon, one that's not to be messed with, and that is good enough for me. There is no need for specifics.

So then, how does Miranda know? The only way is if Dorian told her, which makes my anger stir. It'll be something we'll have to discuss later.

"Of course I am," she replies, a grin splitting her ruby-painted lips. "I'm *always* right."

She leans in, chin tilted up, honeyed brown eyes dancing between my eyes and my mouth. Straightening my spine, I look at Dorian as he walks over. I don't know what this woman's game is, but I don't trust her. I certainly don't like how she's watching me, like she's been waiting for this very moment for decades. For *me*.

I clear my throat—a warning at her closeness—and she steps back. The slippery smile remains in place. "Dorian, dear, you never told me you knew a prince of Hell," she chastises.

"Didn't see the need," he replies with a nonchalant shrug.

So Dorian *hadn't* revealed me.

I start to put the small pieces of what I've learned so far together. Miranda and Dorian clearly had some kind of fling before this, which isn't too surprising given he's an incubus. But he did mention her having a specific skill that could be useful to us. One I was assuming isn't sex-related. And if she knew who I was and had foreseen meeting me, what could she be? The tent, the floating lanterns, the peculiar clothing choice…

Then it hits me.

"Ah, there it is. He's got it now," she says.

"You're a seer."

She lifts a bony shoulder. "Seer. Clairvoyant. Psychic. Doesn't matter how you label it really, but yes, I can *see* what others cannot. Whether that be the future, the past, or the present."

Now our reason for coming here made more sense. Seers are an extremely rare supernatural type. From what I've read during my studies of this plane, they're found mostly among Roma travellers. Or gypsies, which is the derogatory term for them. But the gift of seeing isn't guaranteed to pass to offspring like with other supes, so finding one at all is a rarity in itself.

If we can convince Miranda to help us, depending on how powerful she is, she could tell us where Aria is. Or, even better, where we can find the other relics so we can finish building the harp.

The moment I open my mouth to speak, she holds up a finger to silence me. Her nails are filed into sharp points. "Before you ask, no. I cannot find any of the remaining pieces of Azrael's harp that you seek."

I clench my jaw, my irritation growing. "And why not?"

"My sight does not extend to anything Hell or Heaven made. Anything from those realms I do not have access to. It comes in too blurry for me to understand."

"Then how did you know about me?" I push, not entirely believing her. "I am most certainly Hell made."

Amusement dances in her gaze. "You are very clever. But I was able to see you—well, most of you—because you were interacting with my future. I saw you through me. Does that make sense?"

Personally, it sounds like technicalities and a whole lot of bullshit. Excuses.

Old obsessions are rearing up. I step toward her, my darkness rising and darkening my sight. "Why don't you give it a try?"

At seeing a hint of my demon, she flinches back, but only slightly. Her fear is quickly replaced by curiosity and interest.

"It's not worth my life," she says. "Just trying alone could kill me."

My patience is wearing thin. "And what if I kill you if you don't?"

Her hand reaches out to stroke the lapel of my jacket, but before she can make contact, I snatch her hand and wrench it back to a painful angle. She cries out and buckles, pain contorting her face.

"Let go! Let go!" she screams.

When I do, she rubs her wrist tenderly and mutters, "Unlike Dorian, you don't like to be touched. Got it."

"Cain," Dorian cuts in. "Miranda can help us find Aria."

Aria. Yes, that's right.

Rolling her wrist to make sure it still works, Miranda grimaces. "You boys sure have a way with the ladies."

"Please forgive Cain here. He's still learning manners," Dorian says with an uncomfortable laugh. Trying to make light of the situation, like usual. "We need you to find someone for us. A girl."

Miranda's gaze slides to him. "A… *girl?*"

"A young woman," I correct. "Her name is Aria."

"Do you know her last name?" she asks.

"Unfortunately, no," Dorian replies. "But she was taken from us, and we need to know where she is."

"I'm starting to believe she's better off."

My anger flares. "Will you be able to help us or not?"

Her coy smile is back as she turns to me again. "Of course I can. But, as demons, you must know very well that nothing is given for free."

"We can pay any price," Dorian says.

"Not money," she says, looking back and forth between us.

"Oh, I get it." Dorian begins to undo his belt and then his pants.

She waves her hands frantically to stop him. "Not that." She huffs, and he begrudgingly redoes his clothes. "I do business in *favors*."

Favors. I don't like the sound of that. And from the hesitance in Dorian, he doesn't either.

But do we have any other choice?

"I prefer the sex," Dorian says.

"Of course you do." Miranda turns to me again. "But I'm looking for something… better."

"Better than sex? With me?" He appears offended by that comment. Apparently, she's bruised his ego.

She ignores him, still intensely focused on me.

"What is it you want, then?" The second the question leaves my mouth, I regret it. Something sparks alive in her gaze, something I know all too well. A secret obsession she holds, and I've just offered her the key to everything she's ever wanted.

A long moment passes. Then, she says, "I'll have to get back to you on that."

Dorian's brow furrows. "What do you mean?"

"Exactly what I said. I'll let you know my favor when the time comes."

"Like an IOU?" he asks.

"No. Absolutely not," I snap immediately. I'm not going to be in debt to anyone.

She spins and flips her long hair over her shoulder. "Those are my terms. Take it or leave it."

Dorian and I exchange looks. He's unsure but thinks we should take the deal, given our desperate circumstances—I can see it on his face. I, on the other hand, know that there is no way this doesn't come back to bite us in the ass later.

But again, what other choice do we have?

"If it makes you feel better, you can put it in the form of a demon deal," she offers. "Write it all out and I'll sign. Make it legal."

A demon deal would solidify our agreement, meaning she wouldn't be able to lie without risk of losing her soul.

Still… We don't know what she wants, and we'll be bound to that.

Miranda begins to walk away. "I'm sorry, but I'm very busy, and it sounds like you have a lot of searching to do. Though I suggest you work fast because your little Aria may not have much time left."

My chest clenches with worry and rage that she's playing us this way. We've been doing nothing but wasting time though. What could a seer want, anyway?

I draw in a deep breath and call to my power. There's a small sucking sound as the new contract pops through the veil and into my suit, and the distinct smells of smoke and sulfur linger. I reach into my inner jacket pocket, pull out the scroll, and hand it to her.

She unrolls it. The edges are burnt and still smoldering.

"You have exactly three hundred and sixty-five days to call in your favor," I tell her. "If you don't or if you die beforehand, you forfeit your claim to it and we take your soul."

She doesn't even bother reading it, but I note the slight hitch of her breath. "Then you, Dorian, or the other demon currently waiting outside and sneezing like a loon cannot cause my death. Or force me to call in my favor in any way within that year," she adds.

Damn, she's good. Caught the loophole I'd been hoping to take advantage of if I needed to.

"Go on," she says. "Write it down."

I snap my fingers and the new clause is burned into the contract.

Miranda grins. Then, using her pointed thumbnail, she pricks her finger until blood bubbles up and signs her name on the bottom. The paper shimmers, the deal sealed.

Placing the scroll back into my jacket, I pull my shoulders back. "There. It's done. Now tell us where Aria is."

She steps forward until she is dangerously close to me again. Every muscle in my body seizes from aggravation. Hasn't she learned her lesson already? Or is she testing her limits now that we're bound to not lay a hand on her?

I grit my teeth.

"You may sign contracts in blood to seal your deals, but I do things a little differently," she whispers. Then she grabs both sides of my face, lifts herself onto her toes, and crushes her mouth against mine.

My fury is instantaneous, but so is the snap of power zipping past her lips and into my head. My vision whites out, and I gasp. A shooting pain stabs at my temples, and I lose all sense of my own body except for the warm, tingling feeling of the kiss, the drumming against my skull, and the images slowly coming into focus behind my eyes.

The fog begins to clear, and as if I'm a bird in the sky, I see a massive, black-scaled beast soaring over the trees, wings outstretched and beating against the wind. A blast of fire spews from its mouth, singeing the tops of trees.

Rage pushes to the surface. Sir Surchion.

But where is Aria?

My spectral gaze shifts down, and I see a tiny shadow darting through the woodland below, moving fast, but not fast enough to outrun a dragon. My heart pounds fiercely. There she is. My Aria.

Watching Aria run for her life makes panic crawl over my skin. She skitters down the hill, half-tripping through the thick foliage and slippery mountainside. But besides a bunch of rocks and forest, there is nothing distinct that can help me pinpoint her location.

Fuck, if only I could get a closer look. Why am I so high up, flying with the dragon? I need to be on the ground.

Miranda's power is limited, it seems. It doesn't expand beyond what the dragon can see.

My gaze stretches out over the trees to the sparkling lights of a city's edge. It has to be Glenside. There is only one main highway that leads into it, weaving around the mountains and lakes. We're about thirty miles east, if I were to guess by the position of the lowering sun. It isn't much to go on, but it is something.

My vision clears again, and that strange electric charge surges across my lips. When I open my eyes, Miranda is pulling away, a predatory smile on her face.

My hand whips out and snatches her around the throat. My darkness rises, and I squeeze hard. Part of me wants to strangle the life out of her for kissing me like that, but the other part wants her to do it again so I can see more of Aria's location.

Her eyes bulge and her nails claw at my arm. I lift her onto her tiptoes, and she gasps for breath.

"Did you see something?" Dorian asks me. "Aria? Did you see her?"

Ignoring Miranda's sputtering, I glare at her, seething. "I saw the collector, but only got a quick glimpse of Aria. Barely anything helpful at all."

"That wasn't part of the deal, Miranda," Dorian snaps.

She sucks in a shallow breath. "I cannot see her clearly," she barely gets out. "She must not be part of this plane."

Dorian's gaze shifts to me. He's thinking the same thing. "She's like us?"

"Or..." She points up to indicate Heaven. Her sentence is cut up from the lack of oxygen entering into her lungs. "But... I brought you... as close as... I could... get."

I shove her back, releasing her. She drops onto the ground and rubs her throat, gulping down air.

Knowing that we've gotten the most we can out of

her—which isn't much at all—I nod for Dorian to follow me out. We head for the tent's opening where Elias is waiting, and I hold the curtain open for Dorian to step through before me.

"Remember our deal, Prince of Hell. You owe me," Miranda's wheezy voice calls to my turned back. It's enough to pause me midstep with the curtain in hand. "I'll be seeing you again very soon."

I don't look at her. There's no need to. The seer's ominous words do their job by sinking into me and following me out.

CHAPTER FOUR
ARIA

*D*arkness suffocates me.
I plunge through it, my feet slapping stone with each rushed step. Up ahead, a faint light appears, a beacon of safety, and I run for my life toward it. Anything to give me a sense of direction and security. A way out instead of running into more danger.

Darting forward, I glance behind me to the gaping mouth of the cave, the sunlight beaming outside.

Sir Surchion is a dark blot in the distance, his crow flying overhead.

A shiver zips down my spine. If he catches me, he'll kill me. I saw it in his eyes earlier, and I don't doubt his intentions for a moment.

I sprint faster towards the dim light. It brings me to an open area with a torch sitting in a metal bracket on the wall and four tunnels spiking outward in different directions. There's nothing else but shadows flicking across the stone walls and a heavy, stuffy stench.

For fuck's sake. Can't anything be simple?

Each passage is as dark as the next, without a hint of what lies inside.

With no time, I follow my gut instinct and dive into the one dead ahead for one reason—it takes me as far from the monster chasing me as possible.

Patting the walls, I race through the darkness, convinced I'm going to break my neck. Either that or be eaten by a dragon. I am fine with choosing the lesser of the two evils right now.

The walls are rough under my guiding hand, the stones loose and falling away like the whole mountain might come down on top of me at any moment. I glance back, and only the faint glow of the torch flickers across the tunnel, creating disfigured shadows.

Fear wedges in my throat that any second now, that bastard will step into view.

On my next step, my foot drops straight down through the floor. My heart lurches, as does my stomach. I'm falling, my arms flinging outward to find purchase, but I come up short. The cry in my throat is a strangled sound all the way down.

My fall ends abruptly. My ass smacks the floor, an ache lancing up my spine. I groan, my eyes watering at the pain, but there's no time to regroup. I'm already sliding down what feels like a shaft.

Suddenly, I'm thrown to the right, slamming into the wall. My head hits the squishy soil surrounding me. Soft feathery things scrape over my face.

Spiders?

Panic swallows me. I bat my face, yelling, squirming, when light abruptly rushes up toward me. Next thing I know, I'm flying out from the tunnel and slamming into a collection of unruly shrubs. Sharp branches dig into my neck and arms, twisting in my hair.

My head spins, but I don't wait another second. I scramble to my feet, tearing away from the branches attached to me. My heart bangs in my chest as every inch of my body aches from being shoved and knocked about.

Half expecting Sir Surchion to be on my tail, I glance at the tunnel I just escaped from, dreading he'll show up any second. But he never comes. Maybe someone is looking after me up in Heaven after all.

I snort a laugh at the absurdity of such a thought.

Taking a second to gather myself, I study the forest of where I've ended up. Woods are in every direction, firs and oaks, twisted branches and evergreens. I turn back, and behind me rises the enormous mountain made of sharp slopes and flat rock.

If I keep following the downward slope of this mountain and stay within the shadow of the trees, maybe I can escape. Really escape, too—from Sir Surchion *and* from the demons. I can be free.

Whipping around, I jolt down the hill, calculating every step around shrubs, broken dead branches, bent trees low enough to whack into my face. The place is a jungle.

Birds squawk in the distance. Mordecai, the crow?

I throw myself against a trunk, the bark prickly against my skin. Gasping heavily for breath, I plaster myself and glance up between the gaps of the canopy of trees. A black bird flies overhead, and I curse under my breath. Who would have thought I could hate a bird so much?

I stay pinned like that, against the tree, for five more tense minutes, my gaze never leaving the sky. If I can get out of these woods in one piece, this can be my chance to run from everyone. I know a few shelters that help out the homeless in Glenside. I can lay low for a couple of weeks, then decide my next steps. It sucks I don't have the Orb of Chaos, but better I have my life and soul.

My stomach flips at the thought of the demons, and not in the way a sane person would expect. But as much as I hate to admit it, a part of me—my libido, specifically—has grown attached to them. But that's not going to work long-term.

Demons eat souls.

I have a soul.

Demons live in Hell.

Definitely not my idea of prime real estate.

I've had sex with an incubus, for fuck's sake. I've even sucked a hellhound shifter's huge dick.

Sweet Jesus, something is broken inside me.

I need to get my priorities straight. No matter how much my insides tingle at the thought of the three demons, I need to get away from them before it's too late.

Breaking back into a run, I climb over a dead log. My pulse is racing. Sweat drips down my spine, and my breathing is ragged. The trees are less dense in this area, and my hope spikes that it means I'm reaching the base of the mountain.

HELL IN A HANDBASKET

A sudden, spine-tingling wailing noise pierces through the forest.

I freeze, looking around. There have to be wolves in these woods. Cougars. Bears. Lots of different wild animals that would love to eat me. I crouch and pick up a sturdy branch just in case.

The noise comes again from my right, and I duck behind a tree. Slowly, I peer out. There's nothing there. Only the trees swaying in the wind, branches grating together, leaves shaking. My heart pounds in my ears. Is Sir Surchion stalking me, too? My skin crawls, and I keep looking over my shoulder.

Another wailing sound, half sounding like a cat screeching in battle or in pain. My stomach flips with worry. Maybe it's just an animal that's hurt or trapped nearby?

There's only one way to be sure.

Holding my breath, I move toward the noise to investigate, branch held high and at the ready.

Farther ahead, amid the trees and shadows, a figure stands with his back to me. I can tell it's a man by his broad shoulders, round midsection, the dark cargo pants and jacket he wears, and short-cropped chestnut hair. With a shotgun sitting over his shoulder, it's clear he's a hunter in these woods, and my anger flares. Vermont is known for its vast forests, mountain ranges, lakes, and such, so hunting isn't an uncommon sport around here. Most follow the strict rules, having the necessary permits and licenses, and hunting within the right season. But then there are those backwoods creeps who think they can play God because they own a gun and kill anything that moves. This guy seems to be swaying on his feet, his movements jerky and unbalanced. Drunk, more than likely. So that tells me he's probably not one of the law-abiding types. It boils my blood.

He leans over and grabs for something on the ground. That crying sound comes again, a frantic whine for help. I see a small puff of gray and white fur, and coldness runs through me. Not a deer. Not a wild turkey or waterfowl.

Instinct kicks in, and I creep forward for a better look. My steps are noisier than they should be because of the dead leaves crunching underfoot, but the hunter is so drunk and the animal's cries are so loud, he doesn't seem to hear me approach. I see pointed ears, and my heartbeat falters. A cat? He's trapped a *cat?* Bastard!

Gripping the solid branch until my knuckles turn white, I shuffle closer and raise it in the air. My pulse thuds so hard in my ear, I'm sure the whole forest can hear it.

A tremendous roar booms across the heavens, shaking the ground. The horrific sound could only have been made only by a dragon.

There's no ignoring a sound like that. The man spins, suddenly seeing me right behind him. Shock startles him back a step, his eyes huge like orbs.

I go with pure, primal impulse, and a whole lot of panic, then I swing the branch sideways at him before he can react. It smacks into his head with a dull thump. His eyes roll into the back of his head, and he falls over onto the ground like a sack.

Oh, shit! Did I kill him?

Worry pinches that I did more damage than I intended to. I lunge forward and touch the side of his neck. A strong pulse beats against my fingertips. Okay, alive. Just knocked out.

I swipe a hand across my sweaty forehead and scramble back to my feet. One more look at the sky, and I'm relieved to see no signs of a dragon flying overhead

Something nudges into my leg and cries out.

I jump and drop my gaze to see a small animal. A tiny little bundle of dark gray with spots, long ears with tufts of hair jutting out from the tips. The fur under the chin and stomach is pure white. It's a gorgeous baby lynx with a chain around its neck. It peers up at me with gorgeous bright green eyes and cries out. My heart melts. I fall to my knees, quickly unleashing the little thing. It licks my hand.

I pat its soft fur. "You're free now. Go back to your mommy."

Another thunderous roar sounds just as a massive shadow swoops overhead, sending all the trees into a frantic shaking, swaying in every direction.

Damn, he's flying lower to the ground, searching for me. It's not safe to stay here. I have to move.

Giving the lynx one last wave to encourage it to go, I dart out of there, remaining in the shadows. I move with speed down the hill. The decline quickly steepens, and I'm forced to use low hanging branches to keep myself from slipping on the moist, slippery ground. It's a death trap in the making.

The uneven ground coupled with my panicked footsteps has me mostly staggering down the slope, barely able to stay upright. Then, as I fear, I slip on a patch of dead leaves and lose my footing altogether. I'm suddenly tumbling down on my ass and into a fast roll down, down, down. My world spins for those few death-defying moments, then comes to an abrupt halt when I slam into a log. All the air is knocked out of my lungs, and I groan as the pain catches up with me. Everything hurts. God, I hate these woods.

A bundle of fur rolls and crashes right into my stomach, making crying sounds. I shudder at first, until I realize it's the lynx.

"What are you doing here?" I whisper.

It's on its feet, twirling on the spot as if getting ready to settle down for a snooze next to me. That's when I also catch a quick glimpse of its backside to see I'm dealing with a little boy. A determined and reckless little boy.

The dragon swoops overhead once more, its wings swiping across the top layer of the canopy. Branches snap and rain down, and I immediately snatch the lynx kitten and press my back against the log. A second later, a branch crashes just a foot away, narrowly missing us.

Another thunderous roar, this time accompanied by an explosion of fire. Heat envelopes us. I hold the little babe tighter against my chest and curl up beneath the inferno.

When it dissipates, I raise my head. The lynx looks up too, making more little screeching sounds to tell me it's scared.

It's going to draw attention to us. My stomach

churns at the thought. "Listen, little one, you need to stay here, okay? Better yet, go back to your momma."

He responds by rubbing himself against my leg like a domestic cat.

"Seriously?" With no time to waste, I bend down and scoop him into my arms, which silences him, and run like the dickens.

CHAPTER FIVE
DORIAN

The dragon circling in the sky is a dead giveaway. With Cain's guidance and the information he learned through Miranda's foresight, we arrived at this mountainside outside Glenside's more civilized parts to find Aria. In hindsight, I probably should have warned Cain about what Miranda was and how she "shares" her visions through intimate contact, but it was more fun to watch him squirm. I'll probably end up regretting the choice later, but oh well.

The moment we spotted Sir Surchion's dragon flying overhead, we knew we'd found our mountain. The way the dragon is swooping over the mountain tells me Aria has been able to evade his capture. Smart girl.

The rest is up to us now, which is why the three of us have split up to search for her. Elias took the left-hand side, Cain the right, and I took the middle in hopes we could cover enough ground to find her before reaching the summit. All while not drawing attention to ourselves and ending up as barbeque.

I march quicker up the tree-covered hill, dried leaves and twigs crunching under each step. Even though we've narrowed our search down to this mountain, it's still a fucking mountain. We each switch into our full demons.

Shit. I should have bet who'd find her first. Elias might be a hunter by birth, but I am faster in my demon form. I have that advantage over them both, and it would have been nice to win and be able to choose what souls we get to devour next.

I'm damn tired of Cain's selection of criminals, people who already are destined for Hell. It's his justification for interrupting their lives early. And Elias always picks females who've cheated on their partners or killed them. Yeah, a blind man could see the pattern there… I enjoy the sexually tormented, myself. Virgins are the sweetest, of course, but the wild ones are my favorite. Not only do their overcharged libidos stimulate the ravenous incubus in me, they taste crisp and smooth going down, leaving me buzzing with power.

At the thought, my adrenaline rushes and I bolt up the terrain. I listen for any sounds, scouring the land all around me. There's movement to my right, but it proves to only be a fox darting into a burrow.

I sigh and keep going, never letting my awareness falter. If we're lucky, we'll retrieve the harp's parts as well. And if lady luck wants to keep on giving today, she can let me be the one to rip the collector's head off. That'd be the cherry on top.

Time passes. I have no idea how long I've been walking, but I'm sweating and growing cranky. I push away the hair stuck to my brow. This is not looking good. *Come on, Aria, where are you?*

Searching left and right, I spot a dark form lying on the ground, unmoving amid the trees. The shrubs are fewer in this location, and I step toward it for a better look.

My thoughts fly to Aria. Could it be her? Is she hurt? Dead?

I'm running forward in an instant, my heart jammed in my throat. But a few steps away, I pause. The figure appears tall and broad in the shoulders, plus it has short hair. No, this isn't Aria. Relief washes over me.

When I nudge the man with a toe, he doesn't respond, so I kick with my foot to roll him onto his back. He collapses, completely out like a light. His chest rises and falls with faint breaths, but the blood across his temple tells me someone clocked him good.

I survey the surroundings. The trampled grass and crushed evergreens make it appear like whoever did this rushed downhill from this very spot.

I step over the man and approach a faint footprint in the soil and crouch. I run a finger over the indent. It's small. Aria is small. Lines across the tread are horizontal, clear it's from a sneaker. Something my little girl wears all the time.

When I look around me, I spot something else near the trees, and I stand to gain a better view of a dead lynx, a bullet wound in its neck. An empty chain lays beside it.

Glancing back at the man on the ground, I see a shotgun lying near him, and I am certain now that Aria was here and knocked out this trigger-happy asshole.

He starts groaning and lifts his head, glancing my way. Eyes squinting, he blinks and rubs his face.

"Where am I?" he groans.

Well, it might not be Sir Surchion, but it's still an asshole just the same.

"You're in Hell." I lunge at him.

The poor sucker doesn't know what's hit him.

Snatching his hair, fisting and wrenching his head back, I drop to my knees and inhale. "Don't move," I command, pushing my power into my voice. He stills instantly.

I open my mouth wide. Energy bites into my flesh like ants as I suck the soul right out of him. He tastes peppery and gritty, but it sates me. A newfound energy kicks in, and I take him in faster, filling myself with the stained tinge of his soul.

In seconds, he's drained, and I let him drop back to the ground, a shell of himself. His cheeks are gaunt, skin gray and wrinkly like he's aged in seconds. I crack my neck and exhale, feeling ready to ring circles around this mountain.

Shaking myself, I call back my demon beast, knowing that if Aria sees me this way, she might keep on running. After seeing how she reacted to Cain's demon, I certainly don't need that. My horns retract, the intricate tattoos across my torso vanish, and the stark silver falls from my hair.

I stand and turn in the direction the footprints

headed, then I sprint back down the hill, convinced Aria is near.

The woods are a blur, and I listen for any sound, watch for movement, shadows that don't belong in the woods.

A faint cry finds me, and I swing left in its direction, leaping down from a sharp ledge about ten feet off the ground down below. I land with ease and dart toward the sound that comes again. An animal, but there's something else. The downwind carries a whisper... a female voice. I smirk to myself.

There she is.

Dashing in that direction, I careen around lofty trees and jump over logs, my pulse on fire that I might find her.

When I swing around several trees tangled together, I see what I long for.

My Aria.

My human.

My addiction.

It surprises me how much of an impact she's had on me in such a short time.

She's rushing forward, head low, dodging branches, and crushing over shrubs. Her top is ripped across a shoulder, the back of her jeans covered in dirt. Moving fast, she surprisingly doesn't make that much sound. She's holding something in her arms, but I can't see what, and my first thought is that she took the harp's pieces.

I rush up behind her silently. "Are you lost?" I whisper.

She halts, making me do the same, and whips around to face me. Fear pales her expression, and when I look down, I see she's cradling a spotted cat against her chest. Not the relics.

"Dorian!" Her eyes are wild, and she sounds surprised and almost unsure if she's happy to see me. Smudges of dirt stain her cheeks and nose, a bruise beneath one eye, and she looks like she's been lost in the woods for days.

In flash, a dark shadow falls over the landscape, a bellowing roar following in its wake.

Aria ducks, cradling the animal. The forest trembles around us as I stare up at the dragon swooping over the woods. Then I drop my gaze to the cat, which I now notice is a baby lynx, and put two and two together.

Of course Aria would take the kitten from the hunter. I wouldn't expect anything less from her.

"Where are the relics?" I ask, standing again.

She huffs. "With the psycho dragon, I barely made it out alive, so he can have the damn things."

My gut clenches at her flippant remark. I remind myself she doesn't understand our predicament and the relics' importance, but damn, we were so close to having three of the seven! So fucking close. Now we're back at square one, only with a dragon standing in our way this time.

"Let's move. Our car is at the bottom of the mountain," I tell her, already starting to walk. She hurries to my side to keep up.

"Cain and Elias are here too?" She glances around the woods for them.

"Yes. But they are ugly and scary enough to look after themselves. My priority is getting you away from Firebreath."

"I didn't expect anyone to find me."

I tilt my head and cut her a narrowing gaze. "Didn't expect or didn't want?"

She scrunches up her face, looking like she's about to burst out laughing at my implication, but it's fake.

"Of course I'm happy to see you," she finally says, then keeps moving forward, cooing to her little pet.

Her intentions aren't lost to me. She had every resolve to run away from the dragon and from us.

The little girl hasn't changed her stripes.

"Why are you looking at me like that?" she asks as she ducks under a branch.

"Just surprised you still have plans to escape from us. I thought you were starting to enjoy living with us at the mansion."

She stills and looks at me. "Are you serious? I don't have a choice but to live there, so I make the best out of it. Don't mistake my acceptance for enjoyment."

Her brazen response impresses me. "So you're telling me there is nothing about staying with us that makes you want to stay of your own accord." I step closer, studying her. "Tell me, Aria, what do you really want?"

She blinks up at me, her eyes glazing over for a moment, and I wait for her response.

"Freedom," is all she says.

"That's all?"

"What else is there?" She shrugs as though all the

problems in her life could be fixed so easily, then begins to stride down the hill. I close the distance quickly.

Cain, Elias and I once had the same naive belief on freedom. We wanted to give it to those under Lucifer's tyranny. Fuck yeah, we're from the underworld, but we're not monsters. We wanted to free the masses from the devil's daily torture and dictatorship. We had support. Or, at least, we thought we did. It seemed like an easy goal, but we'd been foolish to think others would fight alongside us when standing at Lucifer's gates. Everyone ran like cowards, and the three of us were left to face the Lord of Darkness alone.

Some days I question why we bother chasing down the relics to return there. We could make a life for ourselves up here—we've had a cushy start already. We could snack on all the souls we want, enjoy all the pleasures this plane brings. But even I know the honeymoon stage won't last forever. Maverick's recent visits attest to Lucifer's interference. He won't leave us alone for much longer. I feel our so-called freedom up here on Earth sliding away quickly. So, like Cain says, we will fight to the end.

"What are you brooding about?" Aria tosses the words over her shoulder at me just as the dragon roars somewhere in the distance.

"Brooding?"

"You make these huffing sounds when you're thinking something dark and menacing." She wrinkles her nose as if trying to replicate the noises I make.

"I don't think so. And if you haven't noticed, I'm here to save you. You're welcome."

She pauses in a small clearing where the sun falls perfectly over her head and shoulders, illuminating her gorgeous long hair, her pouty expression, and her dark eyes. Fuck me, she's beautiful. Her lips are full and moving, but I haven't been listening. I only catch the tail end of it.

"...and you can go back to where you came from. I'm fine on my own."

I laugh. I love her all fired up. The way her shoulders bunch up, her mouth tightens, and her eyes spear daggers into my chest. That's how I like my girls… feisty.

She whips around, huffing, while her little cat makes crying sounds like it's agreeing with her.

"Remember the contract," I reply, suddenly sounding like Cain, and I mentally kick myself.

"Yes, I know, you own my soul, blah blah."

My mouth parts, but my response flatlines when I spot the dragon swooping toward us, wings spanned outward and mouth gaping open. Fire already flares from his nostrils, and the air suddenly smells like burning coals.

That's when I realize my mistake, my horrendous mistake. My stomach drops to the pits of Hell.

Aria stands in a clearing and has been spotted by the creature.

She doesn't even see the danger diving toward her from behind because she's too busy glaring at me.

"Out of the way!" I bellow, throwing myself toward her.

Panic-stricken, she clutches the lynx tighter to her

chest and twists her head toward the dragon barrelling at us from above. A small cry of panic falls from her lips. The cat screeches.

With razor-sharp teeth exposed, the dragon unleashes an inferno from his mouth.

My veins freeze over, and terror clings to my mind like cobwebs.

Everything happens so fast.

I collide into her as our world morphs into darkness from the great beast smothering the light. We hit the ground with a hard thud.

Flames erupt, licking across my back and the side of my face. Fiery agony envelops me, and for a moment, I'm paralyzed, unable to take another breath. Dragon fire is unlike any other. It rips through anything.

I have just enough strength to roll off Aria and flop onto my back in the grass. She scrambles onto her knees, crying out with dread.

"Shit, shit, shit! Are you okay?"

Through the canopy, the dragon's dark form flashes, and terror seizes me. Despite the pain, I push myself to my feet and snatch her arm. "We have to move!"

Holding onto her wrist, we run for our lives. Behind us, the dragon sears a straight line through the forest. The blaze roars almost as loud as the creature. Smoldering heat chases after us, the intensity overwhelming. Flames crackle and snap, swallowing the woodlands behind us.

I half-drag them both in my speed. Aria struggles to keep up with me, but she doesn't complain. We're both desperate to get out of range.

I haul Aria down a steep hill, my heart jackhammering just as fast. Quickly, we leap over a small creek and sprint into the woods. I can't let her get hurt, not under my care. Behind us, the woods burn, dark smoke curling upward.

When I look between the branches again, I watch the dragon swoop up and out of sight. Maybe he thinks he's gotten us? Or maybe he's given up? I don't know. But once I'm sure he's gone, I jerk Aria toward a large tree, and we use the few seconds to catch our breath again.

"Which way?" Aria rasps, her voice strained. She glances left and right. The woods spread in every direction.

"We need to keep going down. The car is at the bottom. Ready?"

Her face pales, but she nods anyway.

"Follow me." I take her by the hand again and wrench her to the left—not directly downhill, but still in the opposite direction of the blaze. My hope is that it'll be enough to throw Sir Surchion off our trail if he decides to come this way again.

Not wasting a second, we move fast, and I wrap my arm around her waist to help her keep up. She's gasping for air but never slows down.

I don't know how long we've been running, but when the smell of smoke is fainter, I slow and come to a stop. Pine trees crowd in around us, the sweet scent heavy in the air. Better still, the sky seems to be dragon-free.

Aria sucks gasps of air into her lungs. "That looks

like it really hurts," she murmurs, reaching for the side of my face. "Are you okay?"

I wince the moment she touches the raw flesh. Since we've stopped running and my adrenaline has calmed, the pain rises, the sharp kind that feels like my skin is boiling. I don't even want to know what the true damage looks like. I know I'll heal—demons have a faster ability to heal than humans, as long as we feed—but that doesn't make the pain any less excruciating.

"It's just a flesh wound," I assure her. "I've been through worse." Which is true.

Her warm, worried eyes meet mine, and I could swear she truly cares about me in those few moments.

"I'll survive," I say and blink to break the eye contact. I don't want her to be concerned about me, not when we're still trying to escape. "Are you alright?" I take her by her shoulders and turn her around to check her body for damage. She's all clean.

"Fine." She snuggles up to her little cat. "You saved us. But you could have burned to a crisp." Her voice shakes, and I bring her closer to me. Well, as near as the lynx in her arms allows.

"I'm not going anywhere. I'm a tough sonofabitch to kill. But you, I need to protect you with my life." As the words slip past my lips, all I can think of is the black outline of her shadow back in the warehouse when we found her. The thing stood upright like its own entity, ruby-red eyes shining toward us. So maybe I'm underestimating exactly how much protection she needs.

She doesn't turn away but tucks the lynx under her arm and leans in toward me. Unable to stop myself, I slide my hands up and cradle the sides of her face so our lips brush. A thrill buzzes through my gut, and soon, she's kissing me tenderly and without a care. I'm not used to the sweet stuff, but Aria does things to me I can't explain. For some reason, when it's coming from her, I adore it. She's warm and soft, and just from our connection, I can feel her compassion for me. Her gratitude. The chemistry between us is unquestionable.

When she breaks away, I groan in protest, and the lynx shoves its head up between us, physically pushing us apart.

Catching her lower lip between her teeth, her cheeks blush. "You don't need to risk your life for me. No one does. But thank you."

I smirk. "Little girl, if your 'thank-you's' always come with a kiss like that, you have yourself a personal guard."

She laughs. "Let's get out of here. I've had enough of these damn woods."

"Agreed." We make our way down the hill once again, and I can't stop sneaking glances her way. She is full of surprises. Absolutely mesmerizing. She stands shorter than me, long, almost black hair framing her face, her dark eyes glinting. Slim built, but curvy in her hips and perfect breasts. She never backs down, and I don't think she knows how to be anything else. She grew up with a hard life, fighting for everything. And in all honesty, I don't want a girl who's a pushover or fawns all over me. I can get that from any woman under my influence.

Except, I feel different around Aria.

Something in the back of my mind tells me not to get my hopes up, to remember she doesn't want to be with us. Though, she's not going anywhere while we own her soul. Still, doubts nudge forward about the time when we will face Lucifer and our past. I am under no illusion that the train wreck isn't waiting to happen. So how exactly will Aria fit into that?

The lynx's cry draws my attention to it, leaning its chin on her arm and staring at me. The little thing has taken to her. Already I see the protectiveness in its eyes when it comes to Aria.

There is so much mystery around her, isn't there? As we reach another creek, we step across rocks large enough for our steps to cross the water, and I ask, "Why did you steal the orb from Sir Surchion?"

"Does it matter?" She doesn't look at me as she responds, just keeps walking faster.

"Immensely, actually."

She shrugs and steps over a shrub as she scratches the cat's head. "I needed money and my friend told me about this new artifact in his antique store. All that shit has landed me here."

"Wait, so you were simply stealing it to what... sell it to make money?"

"You got it, Einstein."

I scratch my head. "So you steal a priceless relic from a dragon, and—"

"To be fair, I had no idea he was a dragon or I would never have stolen from him."

I continue, "Okay, I can accept that, but then how did you track down both of our relics in the mansion?"

She looks over to me, wearing a serious expression, then pauses before speaking. "I stumbled onto the string piece after I heard it singing. And the second was similar. Drums."

I remember Elias mentioning her saying something about hearing the cord sing, but I didn't believe it. How could I?

"Why are you three collecting relics anyway?" she asks, turning the tables on me.

"They are crucial for our future," is all I give her, hoping it's enough to satisfy her questions.

The crunch of twigs steals the conversation, and I lift my head just as Elias steps out from the shadowy woods to my right, Cain right on his heels.

Elias lowers his head, telling me he's been following our scent to track us down. But he didn't find Aria first, and when he meets my gaze, I can't help but grin.

He repays me with a glower.

Cain steps forward, scanning Aria. "What's that?" He nudges his chin toward the lynx who half-growls, half-screeches a sound in response.

"A lynx, I think. I found him in a hunter's trap. He's… He's kinda taken to me." Aria clutches the animal in her arms like a small baby.

Elias's nostrils flare as he draws in the kitten's scent, and he shakes his head frantically. "No. No way," he growls. "Leave it here."

"No!" I stiffen at Aria's protest. "Cassiel stays with me."

"You *named* it?" Cain says.

"After an angel, of all things?" I ask her with wide eyes. She hadn't told me that.

Her uninjured shoulder lifts in a half-shrug. "I thought it'd be funny."

Cain's expression remains stiff, as if carved from stone. "Hilarious."

"If I'm coming back with you, Cassiel comes too," Aria says.

Elias growls. "You don't have ground to negotiate here—"

I throw him a glare to cut him off. Hellhounds and their territory. We found Aria. She's in one piece. We've all been through a great deal. Can't we just pick our battles here and worry about the damn cat later?

"You're burned," Cain interjects suddenly, directing the statement to me. "Have you got the lost pieces?"

I shake my head. "I only found Aria. The dragon still has them."

He clenches his jaw, the muscles at his temples jumping. He doesn't need to say a word. We all know he's unhappy.

Hell, so am I.

"We're not getting it now," I reply before he commands us to return to the beast's lair. "He'll burn down the damn woods with us in it. This isn't the time to confront a dragon."

"We know he has the relics, so we'll return," Elias states, staring at the lynx, who hisses at him.

Suddenly, I'm loving the new addition to our home. Anything that aggravates the hellhound is a win to me.

"Can we get out of here already?" Aria pipes up.

Beside me, she trembles, and I'm not sure if it's from fear, exhaustion, the temperature dropping, or all of the above.

Cain turns to her, and I watch the war on his face, the things he wants to say to her. From lying to us, stealing, hiding her shadow ability. I expect Cain to charge into a rant, and I step forward to stop him. This isn't the place.

But instead of lashing out, his shoulders fall and a heavy sigh escapes. "Alright. Let's go home."

Just like that, the big sin demon surprises me. It's apparent I'm not the only one being influenced by this woman. Cain has always been in charge, his temper rampant. Elias is always lost in the wind, a wild beast trapped in a man's body. And now they are both struggling to make sense of what way is up… all because of a human.

Except, Aria's so much more than a human, isn't she?

CHAPTER SIX
ARIA

We make our way down the rest of the mountainside. When a black sports car comes into view among the weeds, I almost weep with joy. Everything hurts. Every inch of me throbs and stings, and all I want to do is rest my aching body, if only for a few minutes.

The fact that I feel safer with three just as deadly demons (maybe even more deadly) says something, but right now, I don't care. I'm just glad to be away from that fucker and his crazy crow.

At the car, Cain opens the passenger side door and folds down the seat. He waves for Dorian and Elias to get in.

"Oh no, you're not driving, are you?" Dorian asks, wincing from the pain that moving his mouth brings.

"Don't start," Cain warns and gestures for Elias to help him into the back. This must be something they've bickered about before.

"But it's my car…"

Elias growls in annoyance and pushes him into the back seat before squeezing in himself, and the entire car rocks from his sudden weight. I don't know how either of them fit, honestly. The ceiling is so low, and the space looks so cramped, it almost looks painful for them.

Cain shoves the passenger seat back, causing a grunt of pain from Elias, before he holds out his hand to help me in next. His touch is strangely warm compared to mine, but his eyes are icy cold. He tries to help me into the car, but I pause, looking up at him.

"Cain…" There's so much I want to tell him. My mind is chaotic with all the thoughts running through it. The last time I saw him, he was standing over a man and sucking out his soul. He'd been a complete monster, with wings and all, and I still wasn't sure how to feel about it. Terrified, for one. And… curious. Especially since he'd helped me get to safety before the Full Mooner werewolves attacked. He even worked to find me after I'd been taken by Sir Surchion—all three of them had. But why?

The relics. That's why. It was the only reason I could think of. But I didn't have any of them now, and they were still driving me home.

You're their property, remember?

That was true, too. But now that they knew for sure I'd taken the relics and lost them, was I going to be punished? Dorian didn't seem mad when he'd found me, but Cain… I could never get a true read on him.

He waits there for me to continue, my hand still in his, but I've lost my voice. The storm raging in my head has won out.

"Th-Thank you," is what comes out instead. I'm not sure why.

His head tilts as if my words have confused him as well. A bit embarrassed, I slide my hand out of his and climb into the passenger seat by myself. When the door slams shut, I release a held breath and try to settle into the stiff leather seat. Despite my discomfort, Cassiel curls in my lap, seeming to be right at home.

Taking his place beside me, Cain turns on the car and grips the wheel. His lips press into a tight line, almost as if he wants to say something to me but is struggling with it, too.

"Please tell me you remember how to start a car." Dorian's voice cuts through the tense silence. Cain's expression changes to the mask of controlled rage I know so well. He turns the key in the ignition to answer Dorian's question, and the engine roars to life.

"That's a relief," Dorian continues to tease from behind him. "Perhaps we can speed things up this time?"

"Dorian." Cain's lips barely move as he growls his name in warning.

But, like usual, he persists. "With Cain driving, by the time we actually get home I'm going to be dead."

"If you don't shut your fucking mouth, you'll be dead before I even step on the gas pedal," Cain snaps.

"Alright, *grandpa*."

Wow. Sounds like I'm not the only one who's had a rough day.

"Maybe you should knock him out, Elias," Cain says, glancing over his shoulder. "Put him and us out of our misery."

The car shifts again as Elias moves.

"Don't you fucking touch me," Dorian shoots at him and then heaves a sigh. "Fine. Let's just get home."

Cain eases forward, the Ferrari's tires struggling to find purchase through the dirt and leaves, but he's able to steer us out of the woods and eventually onto a paved road. Once we're on asphalt again, I expect him to punch the gas to race us home, but he keeps up his slow and careful pace. Confused, I glance over to the dashboard and read our speed. Only forty miles per hour.

I guess Dorian wasn't kidding about the grandpa comment. For a demon—one driving a sports car, no less—I expected him to drive like a bat out of Hell. Not a turtle.

Dorian smacks Cain's headrest impatiently. "This thing can go zero to sixty in two seconds, you know."

Cain grits his teeth in annoyance. "I'm not going to scare Aria."

"Me?" I quip in surprise. "You don't need to worry about me. I'm fine. I just want to get away from that mountain as fast as possible."

"See?" Dorian continues. "Hell forbid if you actually hit the speed limit."

Elias snickers, but Cain's grip tightens on the steering wheel.

This is one of the most absurd things I've ever witnessed. Demons arguing about who's the best driver? And I thought I'd seen it all.

Hysterical laughter bubbles up my throat, and despite how fucked-up everything is right now, I can't help myself. Maybe it's because everything that's

HELL IN A HANDBASKET

happened to me in the last twenty-four hours has finally caught up with me—I've been kidnapped, beaten, bitten by a fucking werewolf, my life drained by my own shadow, kidnapped *again*, this time by the same asshole in dragon form, and chased all over a mountain. I laugh because if I don't, I'll cry, so I just let it go.

I can feel the stares of the demons on me. Hell, Cassiel is even looking at me like I've lost my mind. And maybe I have.

When I start to wheeze and my chest feels like it's wound too tight, I sink in the seat. The car grows deathly quiet, but I don't look at anyone. My gaze drifts out the window at the passing scenery. Exhaustion washes over me, and in the silence, I let my eyes drift closed.

ELIAS

No one dared wake Aria up during the ride back to the mansion. Even when we reached the house, I carried her out of the car and upstairs to her room so she could keep sleeping. She snuggled into my chest, her head pressed against my naked torso, and all I could feel was sympathy and rage. She was covered in bruises, scratches, and dried blood. The chunk missing from her shoulder from the werewolf bite seemed to be her biggest injury, and if I had the power, I'd resurrect that Full Mooner asshole and kill him all over again for doing it to her.

She appears so fragile in my arms. So small. I hate

that I wasn't able to chase down the van and rescue her before things got out of hand.

When I place her in bed and pull the covers over her, she doesn't even stir. Heavy sleeper, which makes sense considering she doesn't wake up whenever I come into her room in the middle of the night. The little lynx kitten she found in the woods hops up and takes its place on the pillow near her head. It hisses at me, and I growl back.

Unintimidated, it circles on the pillow and curls up to sleep.

Freakin' furball. I'm going to have to talk to Cain again about letting her keep that thing. There's no way I am letting a feline stay here. There's already one wild animal living in this house, and that is *me*. We definitely don't need a pet, especially one that is snack-sized.

As I walk out of her room, I lock the door. With everything she's been through, I doubt it's even needed. She doesn't have the strength to try to pull some daring escape right now, but I don't need Cain yammering at me either.

Speaking of the Pride demon, I find him and Dorian in the parlor in their usual spots—Cain is brooding near the fireplace, staring distantly into the fire, while Dorian's stretched out on the couch, legs up on the armrest and a bag of ice pressed against the side of his face. He's lucky he fed before catching the dragon's fire, otherwise, who knows if he'd be talking right now. Our ability to heal is dampened on this side of the veil as it is. Feeding on souls helps recharge us. And since the flesh around the side of his face and along his neck is still raw and angry looking, the dragon must have really done a number on him.

"I hope this doesn't scar," Dorian mumbles, more to himself than anyone else. Lifting the ice pack away, he touches the side of his face and hisses. "Shit."

"I think scarring is the least of your worries," I say, holding out my own arms to show him the patchwork of marks lining my skin from the hundreds of fights I've been in. "Besides, it'll make you look tougher. Not so much of a pussy."

He swings his legs over as he sits up, then glares at me with his one good eye. His mouth opens to counter, but Cain interjects before he can.

"We have more important things to talk about right now," he says, still not looking our way. "Like what we're going to do with Aria."

"And the relics," I add, eyeing him skeptically. I'm surprised he didn't mention them first.

He twirls the crimson-stone ring his father gave him around his finger in thought. "Yes… right."

"Speaking of the dragon and his rat-bastard of a bird, how are we getting the relics back from them?" I direct the question to either of them, whoever can offer a good answer.

"We can't go back to the mountain," Dorian says and gestures to the side of his face. "He knows the landscape better than us. He has the advantage there."

"But we know this town." Cain says, still not looking up. "A dragon won't leave its treasures behind for too long, and his hoard is at the warehouse and shop."

I grin, an idea forming with his words. "We can catch him there."

"That's what I'm thinking as well."

"I'll go." A growl rumbles in my throat. I have some serious unfinished business anyway.

"I'm in too," Dorian adds.

"Not yet." Cain's response is clipped short. "We'll call on Ramos to see what souls are due to be collected. Then we feed. Regain our strength. Heal."

Dorian slumps lower on the couch with the ice pressed to his face, knowing he's talking about him, mostly. "And what of Aria?" he tacks on. "She's been through a great deal. I say we have the maid, Sadie, go to her room in the morning, clean and bind that nasty werewolf bite of hers, and then we let her rest. Maybe for another day or two—"

"And what about that ghostly figure with the red eyes we saw slip back into her body?" I ask. "What if she unleashes it again, this time on us?"

Dorian hesitates. I know he wants to defend Aria, but he's still unsure of her motives, like the rest of us. "I don't think she will," he settles with.

"You don't know that."

"To me, it appeared like she didn't know how to control it," he says. "She even lost consciousness—"

"That could have been from the blood loss, not the shadow creature," I retort with an annoyed huff. "You're thinking with your dick again, Dorian."

He rolls his eyes. "I'm just suggesting it's not as black and white as we may think. If she wanted to use the shadow on us, she would have done it weeks ago."

It's then that I realize Cain's remained silent during this entire exchange. Usually he's told us to knock it off by now.

Dorian must notice it too, because he swivels on the couch and asks, "What say you, Cain? Do we give her a bit to recoup? Maybe let her gain some trust in us, that way she can tell us willingly? Or do we bombard her with questions right out the gate, possibly causing her to lie and making us no better off?"

"Well, when you put it that way…" I grumble under my breath.

For a long moment, Cain still doesn't respond. Only stares into the dancing flames in the hearth and twists the ring on his finger.

"Cain?" Dorian asks again.

He blinks as if shaken from a dream and turns to us. "We give her the night. Then tomorrow we get the answers we need."

Worry passes over Dorian's expression at that. "You're not talking about our usual methods of questioning, are you?"

Torture, he means. Even I have to admit thinking about using those forceful tactics doesn't sit well with me either. Not on her.

"Hopefully it doesn't come to that," Cain replies.

"I don't think it's necessary," Dorian adds. "I spoke to her before, and she confessed to me that she stole the harp's eye from Sir Surchion for money. She truly believed it was her way to get out of poverty."

"And you believe her?" he asks.

Dorian hesitates, glancing at me for help, but I have

none to offer him. I'm just as confused and conflicted. This woman and all the mystery she carries is new territory for us. Is there any real way to tell if she's ever being honest with us? Without Dorian's powers of compulsion, I don't know.

This scenario is starting to remind me a little too much of Serena, and I'm sure Cain and Dorian are seeing the parallels there as well. I swore I'd never make that mistake again, that I'd never put that much trust in someone, because this time, it could end with us losing more than just our homes. We could lose our lives.

"I want to," Dorian answers finally. He shakes his head, sighing. "I truly want to."

Don't we all.

"Tomorrow then," Cain says, pulling his shoulders back. He may not be completely happy with the decision, but he's made up his mind. "She rests for now. She will be bandaged and cared for in the morning, and then…" His gaze flicks to me again.

I nod. "We pounce."

CHAPTER SEVEN
ARIA

I flip open my eyes at the same moment a guttural snore erupts from beside me. Any hope I had of sleeping in this morning is vanquished immediately. Rolling onto my side, I find Elias on his back, one arm up on the pillow, the other across his stomach, and most of my blanket wrapped around him.

Cassiel, my little lynx, is curled by my feet, sleeping like a round ball of fluff. He's taken to me quickly, and I have every intention of keeping him by my side. But Elias... he's neither a pet nor my boyfriend, so he has no business sleeping here with me.

Another snore draws my attention back to him. How many times are we going to go through this? It's getting ridiculous.

Bed stealer. I shove a hand into his arm. "Hey buddy, get out of my bed."

He groans and turns his back to me, wrenching all the blankets with him, so I'm left completely uncovered. A small whimper comes from the bottom of the bed where Cassiel is on his side, eyes half awake, fur a mess, looking utterly confused by being so rudely awakened. He curls back up in his spot and is sleeping again in seconds.

Maybe the trick is to start sleeping in Elias's room and see what he does. Who's heard of a sleepwalking hellhound anyway? It's the only rational explanation for his behavior, but why he chooses my bed remains a mystery.

I flop back onto my bed for a few moments, staring up. The morning sunlight streams across the ceiling, igniting the crystals in the chandelier and throwing twinkling lights all over the bedspread. The severity of everything I've been through sits like a weight on my chest.

I tremble at the memory of how close I came to death. Part of me wants to laugh again because everything is too insane. I was kidnapped by a dragon! A dragon that's alive and might still be gunning for me. Hopefully now that Sir Surchion has his orb back, he'll leave me alone. Wishful thinking…

Cain's expression when he realized I didn't have his precious relics confirmed his business with Sir Surchion wasn't finished. The demons would be going back into the fire—so to speak—to get them back. My stomach turns with worry, but I tell myself they can take care of themselves.

I just don't want to be involved in any of it.

I recall Dorian talking about the relics in the woods. *They are crucial for our future*, he'd said.

Even though I want to push all of this behind me, I

want to know why they call to me directly. Is it the darkness inside me sensing them, or is it something more? Whatever these items mean to the demons, it's clear they're hiding secrets they're willing to kill for. And I'm sure that after finding the relics on my own, the three demons are going to want answers. It's going to be near impossible to lie my way out of this one.

I can't help but wonder how different things would be if I just hadn't stolen the Orb of Chaos from Sir Surchion. I'd still be sold to the demons, but there wouldn't be this chaotic mess involving a psychotic dragon. One less thing to worry about.

Rolling onto my side to get up, a familiar icy prickle slides across my skin, reminding me of walking right into a cobweb. And even before I see her emerging, panic strangles my lungs, and I jump out of bed, breathing frantically.

Sayah slides out of me, her shadowy form skittering over the bed and across the lump that is Elias.

I shudder. I want to leap out and grab hold of her, but that's not how it works. Memory after memory slams into me of her escaping in the warehouse, freezing me on the spot.

Those bright red eyes.

Freaky, long, opaque arms.

Reddish-orange wisps of power spiral around my body and through the tether binding Sayah to me.

My dark little secret is on display. Except she's never looked like that before.

I'd lost control of her in the warehouse. But worst of all, she took her strength from me... draining me.

She used me, and I can't help but wonder if this whole time she's been some kind of parasite living inside me, feeding off my energy. Terror tightens around my chest as I focus on the present reality of her sliding out of me so freely.

I can't breathe as I watch her lifting her head over Elias like a cobra about to strike.

A hiss streams from Cassiel, and I flinch out of my frozen state. The little lynx is crouched low at the end of the bed, the fur on the back of his neck fuzzed up, teeth bared, ready to pounce. Even he identifies danger when he sees it.

Sayah snaps around toward the cat, those ruby eyes meeting mine. I tremble, but this isn't who I am. I'm not a scared girl. Sayah has been part of me for so long… even if she's a monster, she's linked to me.

And I won't let her overpower me.

Come back! I growl in my mind. *Sayah, you listen to me.*

The outline of my shadow shimmers, like she's struggling to hold onto form.

Steeling myself, I clench my hands, standing up to her. *Return now.*

In a flash, she retracts like a yoyo, and she's gone just as quickly as she arrived.

I stumble on my feet and suck in shaky breaths. What the hell just happened? Is this how it's going to be? Living with an unstable creature inside me, one not even demons know about? For the first time in my life, knowing what she is and how she got attached to me when I was a child are crucial pieces of information I desperately need.

Reaching down, I scratch Cassiel and pat down his fluffed-up fur, and instantly he pushes his head against my hand. In moments, he spins on the spot two times, then settles back on the bed to sleep like he hadn't just confronted a terrifying specter.

I stumble over to the window, and lean against it. The iciness of the glass helps settle my nerves. Slightly. Peering out toward the woods, I catch a glimpse of something white standing at the tree line.

I still, the hairs on my nape rising. Squinting, I try to make out distinct features, but they're at a far distance, and all I can make out is a white aura around them. I can't even tell if they're male or female… or if they're here to hurt us.

They move slightly, their head tilting back to look up at my window, and panic punches me in the gut. I duck out of pure instinct, suddenly feeling stupid, and stay crouched there for a few heart-hammering moments. More Full Mooner werewolves? Or maybe Sir Surchion's hired someone else to bring me back to the mountain? He does know where the mansion is, after all.

My breathing picks up as my anxiety spikes. As long as I stay in this house with Cain, Dorian, and Elias, I'm safe. Right? Yeah. I'm definitely *safer* here with them. I just need to keep telling myself that. It'll make the 'them owning my soul' thing a lot easier.

Cautiously, I peer back over the windowsill and gaze

onto the grounds below. It's empty. The mysterious person in white is gone.

The hell?

Getting back up, I press my face against the window for a better look, scanning the whole yard and woods. Nothing. Just greenery, the wind rustling the naked branches and swirling the fallen autumn leaves.

Okay, now isn't the time to go crazy and start imagining things. Or start seeing ghosts. I have enough on my plate already—I don't need to add apparitions to my list of weirdo talents.

"What are you doing?" Elias mutters behind me, the springs of my bed groaning from his movement.

I turn to face him, still a bit spooked by the whole Sayah incident and the mysterious phantom person outside.

"You look like you've seen a ghost." He chuckles as he wrestles to free himself from the tangle of blankets around him.

I glance over my shoulder to the window to find the property still clear of anyone in white. "I just may have…" I mutter to myself, but I hesitate to tell him about my morning happenings. Last thing I need is to have them think I have no control over Sayah and then have them lock me up. And the same goes with whatever I spotted outside in the woods.

"What?" he asks sharply, and I curse myself for forgetting about his super-sonic shifter hearing.

"Uh, don't worry about it. I'm still waking up." I rub a hand over my face and force myself to shake the heebie-jeebies off. "It's hard to get sleep around here when I keep getting an unwelcomed visitor in my bed every night."

He walks around the bed but stops when he passes the busted-in door.

I cock a brow at him. "Hm? So, why are you always in my bed, again? This isn't a hotel room, you know."

"I regret nothing," he murmurs and stretches his arms upward, causing an array of bones in his back to crack. My gaze slithers down his back, at the myriad of muscles shifting beneath his skin… and then at the way his sweatpants sit dangerously low on his hips.

Is it hot in here? Because I'm suddenly flushed with prickling heat all over.

I swallow hard, telling myself to avert my eyes, but I can't. I know all too well what lies under those sweatpants.

Healed cuts cover his torso, along with intricate black tattoos. Some aren't the best, artistic-wise, and it makes me wonder if he'd gotten them done professionally or in a dark basement somewhere.

This demon has probably faced legions of nightmarish creatures, yet he suffers from a small sleepwalking problem. It's kind of cute… or it would be, if it didn't involve my bed.

"Seriously, though, Elias. If you're having a problem—"

He cuts me off with a sharp, sideways look. "No problem," he growls viciously, and I flinch. Well, shit. You'd think I was accusing him of having erectile dysfunction or something. His messy hair covers half his face, making him look even more wild and unpredictable, but damn him and those sexy bedroom eyes. The sprinkling of hair on his chest that tapers down into a funnel over his abs and vanishes under the elastic of his pants… it's drool-worthy. Did I mention he has that deep V of sculpted muscle that guides the eye right to the family jewels? I don't have a clue what that part of a guy's body is called, but they might as well be named 'fuck-me-muscles' because they make me go lust-crazy. On cue, a tingle flares in my lower belly.

"I'll take my pants off. All you have to do is ask."

I blink rapidly and snap my gaze up. Having caught me clearly eye-fucking him, he smirks.

Embarrassment crawls up my neck, but I attempt to play it off. "Why are you still here?"

He laughs, the sound deep and sensual, bringing another flutter of desire down below. Man, he drives me insane.

"I never thought I'd ever say this, but my eyes are up here," he teases.

"Get out of my room!"

He doesn't leave. Instead, he turns toward Cassiel at the foot of the bed and lifts his lip in a snarl. Cassiel peeks an eye open but shows no sign of being intimidated. That only seems to annoy Elias more.

"Fucking furball," he grumbles.

Looks like two animals are sleeping with me. Soon I could open a zoo in here.

"So, you sleepwalk?" I ask, wanting to bring the question back to the table. "It's nothing to be ashamed of. Plenty of kids in my foster homes used to do it, or at least talk in their sleep. I even read somewhere that

Jennifer Aniston sleepwalks around her house, so it's not as uncommon as you think."

One thick brow arches, and he snaps back, "Who says I'm ashamed of it?"

"Woah. I'm just trying to say it's normal." Touchy, much?

He crosses the room and flops down on the bed, sending Cassiel flying. He hisses at him before making himself comfortable again.

With his back to me, he pushes his hair out of his face with a shake of his head and sighs heavily. "I've never sleepwalked in my life. Well, until recently."

Taking a seat on the bed next to him, I tuck a leg under myself. "It's probably stress related," I suggest. "Being forced out of your home into a new world… Anxiety does things to your brain."

Lips tight, his gaze falls to the floor. "Recently, as in never until *you* came into this house."

"M-Me?"

He nods.

"But why?"

He hesitates. "I'm… not sure."

I'm pretty sure that's a lie. I can see the distress and unease in his stiff posture, but I don't press. This is the first time he's talking to me without making everything a joke. Maybe I'll get lucky and he'll actually open up a bit.

"You know what's funny?" he goes on, and I don't stop him. "That I miss so many things about Hell, like my pack of hellhounds, my own place on a mountain, far from others, plus the hunting grounds were incredible."

"But…"

He snorts. "We've been trying to get back there for a century, but I'm not sure if it's worth going back anymore."

"What do you mean?" I ease, hoping I'm not pushing the boundaries here with my questions. You know what they say about curiosity and the cat, but I want to know more about the demons I live with. They're so secretive.

He eyes me for a long moment, debating how much to tell me. Then, his tense shoulders ease and he replies, "It's in ruin. It's chaotic."

"It's Hell."

"This is true, but with Lucifer in charge, things are quickly sinking. And he's going to take all his people down with him."

That surprises me. The way he talks about Hell, it sounds like a tyrant king or dictator kind of situation. Like Lucifer is making his people suffer or sacrificing them or something. I didn't expect the underworld to be that way.

"But," he begins quickly to redirect the subject, "nothing compares to the monsters I'd hunt there, the fights they put up. I crave the chase, and these woods out here give me nothing worthwhile to track. Nothing bigger and scarier than me to sink my teeth into. Earth could do with a predator in these woods."

"Speak for yourself," I say, which draws a chuckle from him. "Oh, I know. How about a dragon? You've got one of those now."

His expression hardens, and his voice drops to an ominous rumble. "You're right. I do."

Is it something I said? I was trying to be funny.

He gets to his feet suddenly and strides to the door. "I'll see you downstairs."

When Elias leaves, I'm left confused and a bit dumbfounded. I'm not sure why he took that wrong, but maybe he's going through some demon version of PMS.

Telling myself not to dwell on it, I march into the bathroom and start to get ready for a fun day. Minutes later, a knock sounds on my door, and Sadie's sweet voice drifts into the bedroom.

She's come to help dress my wounds.

After I shower, she thoroughly cleans and bandages all my bites, cuts, and scrapes. My muscles are still sore from everything the day before, so she also helps me get dressed.

She pulls out a rusty-colored dress covered in white polka dots. I'm about to object—it's far from my style—but when she looks me up and down, smiling broadly, I find I don't have the strength or energy to tell her no.

After slipping into my shoes and running a brush through my wet hair, Sadie and I head out of my room. I can't help but notice that the guard is no longer at my door.

Huh. Guess the demons aren't worried about me trying to escape again. And they're probably right, at least until things with Sir Surchion calm down. Then I may just use their trust to my advantage and find a way to get the H-E-double-hockey-sticks out of here.

At the bottom of the grand staircase, I try to swing left to the dining room, but Sadie shakes her head and points right, where the parlor is. My stomach sinks instantly. I know exactly what that means.

"The masters are waiting for you," she says.

So this is what Elias meant about seeing me downstairs. Not about breakfast.

Looks like the interrogation is about to begin.

I pause and glance back up the steps, debating if there's any way I could make a dash for it. But even I know that'll only make things worse for me, ending up with me thrown over Elias's shoulder as he carries me back downstairs.

At that thought, naughty images flash in my mind, ones that make me flush with heat. Clearly, I can't be trusted around the demons. Maybe I ought to wear a chastity belt instead. It'd be safer.

"Aria," Cain's rich but stern voice snaps from the parlor, and my pulse kicks up a notch.

Well, there goes that idea.

With one last glance at Sadie, I suck in a deep breath and walk inside. I find Cain standing by the roaring fireplace and Dorian lounging on the couch. With a welcoming smile, he pops his head up and glances my way, calling me over with a flick of his chin.

His friendly demeanor helps my rising nerves. A little. He may not want to eat or kill me yet, but I can't say the same about the other two. Especially Cain, who is watching me with such intensity as I shift further into the room, that goosebumps creep along my arms.

The tension in here is suffocating; the air is thick

with the heat of the fireplace and my mounting worry. I expected them to demand answers from me—after all, I *had* stolen from them, lied to them, and kept secrets from them—but telling them the truth could make me their next meal.

Elias enters the room then. When I glance up to meet his gaze, he quickly looks away and leans against the bookshelf along the wall, hands deep in the pockets of his sweats.

"What's going on?" I play dumb at first and flop down on the opposite end of the couch by Dorian. "An intervention?" I half-laugh, but no one responds. "Tough crowd."

"You know why we need to talk to you," Dorian starts, his expression soft as he turns to face me. "We need to know everything. It's time you tell us."

I sigh and sink into the cushions of the sofa, a sliver of unease curling in my gut. Maybe there's a way I can keep Sayah a secret. Just tell them about my ability to track magic, how it led me to the relics, and leave it at that. Sayah has always been the one constant thing in my hectic life, but after her going rogue in the warehouse and seeing what she was really capable of, even she isn't reliable. Even now, when I try to get a feel for her, she's keeping low, out of reach instead of pushing to come out like before.

I need to be smart about this. Tread carefully through their questions and not make things worse for myself... whatever the fuck that means.

"What do you want to know?" I ask, glancing at the three of them.

"Tell us what you are," Cain demands from behind me, and the harshness of his tone makes me wince. He's going straight for the jugular, of course. Should have seen that coming.

"I told you already. I don't know." That isn't a lie. I truly have no idea.

But my answer only seems to fuel Cain's annoyance. "Then how did you track down our relics in the mansion? In the basement and in my room?"

I blink up at him. Ah, so the overly stuffy, vintage inspired bedroom had been his. Saw that one coming a mile away. It fit him to a T.

Three sets of eyes are on me, and I'm battling in my head how much to tell them. Exactly how much did they see in the warehouse?

They did risk their lives to save me when they didn't need to. Maybe they did it for their stupid relics… or the contract or whatever… but they knew I didn't have them when they found me, and I'm still alive. That has to count for something, right?

Elias clears his throat. "We saw your shadow side in the warehouse, so just out with it."

Well, that answers that then. So much for keeping Sayah to myself like I wanted. "Okay, fine. As I told you before, I don't know what I am. Murray told me nothing, and well, I didn't have parents to answer my questions. But when I was young, after some traumatic shit, my shadow seemed to come to life and move on her own. Usually she listens to my instructions, but what happened in the warehouse…" My throat parches as the memories spark fear, especially those from this morning, and I shiver. "She's... She's never done that before. I lost control of her. But it was a one-off thing."

Dorian exchanges a dark glance with Cain, but they don't say a word, and that worries me. Do they know something about my shadow that I don't?

I lick my dry lips and grab one of the small cushions to hug against my chest.

Cain watches me intently, while Elias scratches his head and Dorian presses an ice pack to his shoulder. The skin along his face and neck are still an angry pink color, but it looks much better than it was. He's healing pretty quick, considering.

"Is that how you tracked down the relics?" he asks me. "With your shadow?"

"Hmm." I shrug. "Not really. That's..." I pause, wondering how much to reveal. "That's something else." I glance down at my lap. Maybe it is time to just spit it all out. *All* of it. What do I really have to lose if they know the real me? They own my soul, and I'm not going anywhere. Would it really be so bad?

"Aria," Cain starts. "The secrets and the lies need to stop. How can we protect you if we don't know what dangers are coming for you?"

The mention of wanting to protect me catches me off guard. Sure, Cain had said something similar while washing my hair in the bath, but I didn't think much of it beyond the need for them to keep control of their property, which includes me. There were these brief moments, though, like now, where he almost sounded... sincere.

"Stealing the orb was a dangerous move," Elias adds in.

"Yeah, but like I told Dorian before, I did it for money," I tell them. "I had no idea what the Orb of Chaos was. Hell, I still don't know."

To my surprise, Dorian bursts out laughing, his head thrown back and his shoulders bouncing. "Orb of what, now?"

I hesitate. "The Orb… of Chaos? At least that's what Sir Surchion called it. Something about it containing the waters of the River Styx?"

"Well, part of that is right. The eye does contain the waters of the Styx," Cain explains.

The eye? Eye of what? I cringe at the thought that I've possibly been carrying around a real eye all this time. It definitely wasn't as detailed-looking as the heart relic was, appearing more like a Christmas ornament filled with liquid than an eyeball.

"Wait," Dorian cuts in and leans forward slightly, his eyebrows pulling together. "How did you find the heart and the hair?"

Hair? This was getting weirder by the second. Did he mean the cord? "For some reason, I've always been drawn to magical objects. The darker the stuff, the more pull it has to me. It might sound flashy, but really, it's stupid. It feels like I was given these gifts with no instructions on how to use them. I had to figure it out by myself."

Like everything else in my life, pretty much.

"Elaborate," Cain says.

I exhale loudly. "I don't really know… When I'm

close to something that's been touched by dark magic, my toe starts to buzz." I hug the pillow tighter, waiting for them to howl with laughter. But it doesn't come, only confused expressions.

"Your toe?" Elias repeats. "Why your toe?"

"How should I know? Does it matter if it's my toe, my ear, or even my hand? It directs me toward magic. Cursed objects. Protective runes. All kinds of things. I found out on a school trip to a museum of all places, so you can imagine my shock when my pinky toe went berserk on me."

Only Dorian smirks at my attempt to lighten the mood, while the other two seem stuck on the idea.

"You wanted the truth, so that's it. Yes, I can sense relics with my toe. Yes, my shadow has a life of her own. And I found your string-thingy and heart piece by accident. They sang and played music to me. The orb seems to warn me when danger approaches. When they're all together, they produce music. It's freaky."

Wow, that was a lot. But it feels incredible to finally get that off my chest. The demons' silence is a bit unnerving, but at least I don't need to dance around the subject anymore.

When a few more tense moments pass by without a word, my worry doubles. If my ability shocks demons, then it has to be bad…

"That's a powerful ability." Elias is the first to break the wall of silence. "Do you think your shadow and toe thing are related? Feels like they might be."

"If you know anything about what I am, feel free to share. I'm opening up here because I want answers just as bad as you do." I turn in my seat and look at Cain. If any of these three will know, it'll be him. "What's up with those relics anyway? I've never come across anything as powerful as them before. And I've never seen a relic influence anyone other than me, but it was clear you were affected, too."

His eyes widen, as if my words surprise him.

"Wait… Didn't you know?" I glance at Dorian, who's looking just as anxious, then back at Cain. Okay, I guess they didn't. "I wasn't around when you found the hair or cord piece, but the heart definitely changed you. You…"

I pause. How do I say *'You couldn't keep your hands to yourself'* nicely?

"You weren't exactly yourself," I settle with instead.

A shudder runs through me at the memory of what happened when I first touched the heart. The images in my head of all three demons having their way with me at the same time… They had been so vivid, too, like a quick flash into the future.

More like my wet dreams.

"She's right," Dorian speaks up. "After we collected it from the ice, you started acting off."

Cain's expression morphs into a scowl.

"You were pretty jittery yourself," Elias says to Dorian. "I noticed it right away. So I wouldn't be so quick to point a finger at him."

Dorian's mouth flops open to argue, but then clamps shut, knowing he can't.

Hopefully I don't get shit for saying this, but… "I think it brought out your true thoughts and desires."

Cain's gaze drops back to the fire, and I know he's thinking the same thing I am. About our close encounter on top of the dining room table. He'd been influenced by the heart's magic then. It had been forcing him to show his true feelings for me.

My throat suddenly feels tight, so I decide it might be better to change the subject. "So, since the heart's effects clearly have worn off by now, can any of you tell me what I really am?"

Another wave of silence stretches over the room, and anxiety crawls up my spine.

"Anyone? I'll settle for a hunch..."

Rubbing his jaw in deep thought, Cain's gaze remains glued to the fire. "You truly don't know." It's a statement. Not a question.

"Not the foggiest idea."

More uneasy quiet, and my legs begin to bounce with apprehension.

Finally, Cain looks up again and replies carefully, "We have never come across anyone with your... *skills* before. They're new to us."

Oh, that doesn't sound good.

"But now that we know what you can do, we can try to find out your heritage."

The idea of them tracking down my past sounds fantastic, seeing as I've had zero luck. So I ask more questions. "Why are you collecting the relics anyway? Dorian mentioned that they're crucial for your future. What does that mean?" I shuffle on the couch, turning to face all three of them and tucking a bent leg under me.

Cain shoots Dorian a glare.

"You said no more secrets," I remind Cain.

Dorian reclines, watching Cain with amusement. "She's got you there," he says.

Leaning against the bookshelf wall, Elias has his legs crossed at the ankles, arms folded over his chest, ready to roll his eyes.

"The short answer," Cain starts, "is that, as you already know, the three of us were banished from Hell. The relics are our only chance of returning home."

I push my feet to the floor and inch to the edge of the couch. "You told me you were banished but not why."

Cain stands tall, but the torture that flashes in his eyes tells me this topic is painful for him. I can't imagine what it would be like to be kicked out of your home… Hmmm, actually, maybe I can, seeing Murray did something similar to me. But still.

"We tried to usurp my father."

"You planned a coup?" I don't know jack about the underworld, but, I mean, hello, he's Lucifer. The evilest bastard around. That seems like an unwise move.

"He's a fucking monster," Elias adds.

Dorian snorts. "Understatement of the century."

Cain stiffens, his shoulders squaring. The fight in his expression paints the image of someone scorned. It's clear whatever they had planned failed disastrously. And suddenly, the way I look at these three demons changes completely.

Here I assumed they were untouchable, able to do

whatever the heck they wanted. Except, that's not it at all... They are just as messed up as me.

We have no true home.

Our families don't want us.

We're trying to find our way through this shit-hole of a place.

"But if you're banished, why are you trying so hard to get back there?" Just as the words leave my mouth, I feel stupid. Family, right? Always family. Why am I always trying to find out about my past and holding onto the hospital receipt I found in Murray's house?

Because I'm desperate to belong somewhere.

I glance up at Cain, and for the first time see a vulnerable side to him. My chest clenches.

"We have unfinished business," he finally answers.

"And what will happen to me?" The question spills free before I can rein it in.

"We're not going to leave you behind," Dorian says, reaching across the couch and pushing a loose strand of hair behind my ear.

"That's what worries me. What if I don't want to go to Hell? Don't I have to be dead to go there? Will you kill me so I can join you? I mean, you're going there to fight the actual devil, and that's not the war I signed up for." Suddenly, I'm hyperventilating, sweat dampening the back of my neck. I hadn't intended to blurt all that out, but my panic took over.

Elias laughs, and I glare at him. "It's not funny," I say.

"If we are going to Hell, we're not going to leave you here all alone."

"So, what, you get the relics back from Sir Surchion

and then you plan on heading back home?" My breath catches in my throat.

"Not quite that simple. We've been searching for them for a long time and have never been as close as we are now." Finally, Cain meets my gaze, and I know immediately what he's implying. They've never been close until *I* came along. Because of my gift to sniff dark magic out.

That means they're planning on using me as their personal relic-finder. But tracking down all of them will send me straight to Hell with them.

Shit.

Dorian eyes me, and sensing my dismay, he mutters Cain's way, "Maybe we're done with the questions for today? Hm?"

Cain nods, agreeing. "Your breakfast is waiting for you in the dining room." Then he gestures toward the parlor's doorway.

It takes me a second to realize he's telling me to go. I jolt to my feet, unsure what to say. Right now I want alone-time more than anything, anyway. Without a moment's hesitation, I head out of the room.

Panic bubbles in my gut. Somehow, I feel like I've just been handed my death sentence.

CHAPTER EIGHT
ELIAS

*T*he only shred of *normalcy* is every morning, when I open my eyes, Aria is there either shaking me awake, threatening me, or whacking me in the head with a pillow. After learning about her strange sixth sense to detect magical objects and her parasitic shadow creature, waking up in her bed isn't the smartest idea.

Of course, if I could stop myself, I would, but as soon as she re-entered the house, the dreams about Serena started again. As did the sleepwalking.

Looks like Cain was right all along not to trust her fully. I'm still not sure if I'm buying her truly not knowing what she is or how to control that shadow entity of hers, but having a way to track down the rest of Azrael's harp is beneficial to us. And, as Cain put it after Aria left our interrogation, worth the risk of keeping her alive and with us. It just means keeping an extra close eye on her from now on and looking out for any shadows that move when they aren't supposed to.

In the meantime, Dorian and I make our way to the antique shop where we know Sir Surchion will return eventually, if he hasn't already. I don't know much about dragons, but I'm sure now that he knows we've found his stash of treasures, he'll want to relocate them. Dragons are notoriously possessive. Hoarders.

Dorian's driving his Ferrari again. The skin on his face, shoulder, and back has healed, but even with all the feeding we've been doing, there's still traces of scarring along the side of his face and down his neck. He's obsessed with it, wearing turtleneck shirts or lifting the collar of his jacket to hide them. They're barely noticeable, but he's always been such a pretty boy. It drives him crazy, so naturally, I enjoy torturing him about it.

"I don't know why you're so hung up on that scar. It's not even that noticeable..." I flick his ear, and he jerks the car as he waves me away.

"Don't fucking touch me," he snaps and lifts his turtleneck higher. "It's bad enough Cain's making us both go on this little adventure. I could've done it perfectly fine alone."

"Believe me, there are a million other things I'd rather be doing right now than being stuck in this metal death trap with you."

His hands clench on the steering wheel. "Then get out. You can run behind the car instead."

"Behind? I could beat you there." It was an idea. One I might need to seriously consider. In my hellhound form, I could probably keep up.

He snorts a laugh. "You poor, deluded creature. Not this car." As if to prove his point, he steps on the gas and rears us up to a higher speed. It's the dead of night, so of course, the roar of the engine echoes throughout the quiet city streets. But since there isn't much straight road to use here, he quickly has to slam on the brakes to whip us around a corner.

My stomach lurches, and I suddenly feel sick. I hate the city and I hate being confined in small places, like cars, where I have no control over myself or the space around me. It's unnerving.

Dorian takes another corner fast, and I grip the door's handle tight enough to crush the plastic. "Fuck, man. Who the fuck are you racing here?"

"You're the last person who should be commenting on my driving," he replies. "You refuse to even try it."

Between Dorian going too fast and Cain driving slower than a hundred-year-old tortoise, nah, I'm good.

As we come to a stoplight, bright red, white, and blue lights flash from the next street over. The one we have to go down.

Dorian and I exchange knowing looks. That's where the collector's store and warehouse are.

Something's up.

The sharp smell of smoke and fire invades my nostrils immediately. Even with the windows rolled tightly shut, it still fills my lungs.

Instead of waiting for the stoplight to turn green, Dorian glances at the opposing streets and drives us right through the red. Then he pulls the car over and throws it into park.

We both get out and stride into the adjoining street, which has been blocked off by barriers and cones. The smell of fire and smoke is harsher outside, making my eyes water. Sometimes having a super sniffer sucks.

"Oh shit..." Dorian says.

I look up. Three firetrucks fill the lane. Men in full protective garb hold hoses to the crumbling remains of a building with flames licking up the sides. It's obvious they're struggling to keep the fire under control, despite the three trucks and all the manpower at their disposal.

It's clear what's happened here, but I say it out loud just for the hell of it. "The bastard torched his place."

As expected, Dorian isn't impressed and rolls his eyes. "Clearly. But *why?*"

"How the fuck should I know? The old guy was crazy."

Dorian pauses, thinking. "Couldn't be to deter us or scare us..."

"What do we care if he burns his stuff?"

"Exactly my point." He lets out an exasperated sigh. "He could've been destroying some kind of evidence? Or trying to get us off his tail before he moves to another nest location."

I don't like the sound of that. The flying range of a full-grown dragon? He could cross continents in days. We could lose track of him and the harp's pieces forever.

Dorian must be thinking the same thing because he slaps my arm and nods toward the Ferrari. We hop back inside, and he speeds dangerously fast through Glenside's city streets, straight toward home. This time, I don't complain.

Oh man. Cain isn't going to like this.

ARIA

I lie in bed with nothing to do but stare at the ceiling. There's no clock in my room, but I know it's late by the full moon's light spilling through the window and the way my eyes burn from keeping them open for so long. But sleep isn't coming easily tonight, especially knowing the demons are thinking of using me and Sayah to find more of those relics.

The idea of releasing Sayah scares the shit out of me right now. After what happened in Sir Surchion's warehouse—seeing her with those evil, glowing red eyes and how she almost killed me to become more solid—I don't want to risk it.

Until I figure out a way to protect myself, she's staying put.

That just means that for once in my life, I am truly, truly alone. Well, besides Cassiel, but I'm not sure how much he counts as an actual friend, being an animal and all.

You'd think I'd be used to it by now, but whenever things got hairy, I at least had Sayah there. She's saved my ass so many times. Now I couldn't even trust *her*. I don't understand.

"What are you really?" I ask her for the thousandth time since getting back to the mansion. And like the thousands of times before, she doesn't answer, making sure to stay far in the dark recesses of my mind, only a faint flutter against my consciousness instead of the

strong presence she used to be. Maybe she's afraid to come out, too. Or ashamed…

Or maybe she's just waiting for the right moment to try to kill me.

A tremor of fear skitters through me. Yep, I'm definitely not sleeping tonight.

Sitting up, I swing my legs over the edge of the bed and hop down. Cassiel only rolls and stretches out on my pillow, enjoying the leftover warmth from my body. At least someone's getting rest tonight, because it's certainly not me.

My pjs for the day consist of leggings and a long button-up thermal shirt. I head to my hiding place—also known as my wardrobe—and ruffle underneath the clothes, extra sheets, and blankets. Once my fingers brush against paper, I know I've found the hospital receipt I've hidden in there and pull it out.

Might as well take this time to find some answers. There's a good chance Cain's already at Purgatory tonight, and I saw Dorian and Elias get into the Ferrari and drive off not too long ago. If I'm truly alone besides some outside guards, I could use this time to get answers. About my birth, my parents, and well, *me*.

I'm about to walk toward the door, but instead, I hurry to the large stained glass window and peer toward the front of the house, just to double check no one's returned home during my musings. Like before, the driveway is empty, and there are no signs of anyone coming around the dirt road, as far as I can see. It appears safe enough, and since I learned earlier that the guard is no longer at my door…

Before I push away from the window, something catches my eye outside, and my heart freezes in my chest. A figure stands in the middle of the grounds, the same one I'd seen at the edge of the forest this morning, lined in white, with an eerie glow surrounding him. He's closer now, standing in the middle of the fog, and I say "he" because I can see now it's a man. Tall with sharp features and wispy blond, almost silvery hair. Wearing a white sleeveless tunic and fitted jeans, he appears almost ethereal standing there with his hands clasped behind his back, like a beam of light against the stark darkness.

Right then, his chin lifts to meet my gaze.

Shit!

Stomach flipping, I jump away from the glass and press my back against the wall, breathing hard.

Who the fuck is that? And why is he here?

He's still pretty far away to make out specific details, but he definitely doesn't look like the other burly biker gang members I've seen. That could just mean Sir Surchion hired someone else. Maybe a fae? The blond hair checks out there.

I could be wrong, but it's possible he's another guard the demons have stationed outside in case I try to escape again. That could be it, too.

I need to get another look at him to be sure.

Carefully, I slide along the wall to peek out the window again, but just like before, when I look onto the grounds below, the spot where the stranger once stood is now empty. Goosebumps crawl up and down my arms. The dense fog that floats along the ground swirls as if recently disturbed, but the man in white is nowhere to be found.

He's just... vanished. Again.

Thoroughly creeped out, I rush out the bedroom door and hurry down the hall.

CHAPTER NINE

ARIA

My frantic running somehow brings me to the mansion's library. And since I need to find more information about Saint Charity General Hospital, a place stocked floor to ceiling with centuries worth of knowledge might be a good place to start.

I circle the colossal room, my gaze scanning the book bindings for any titles that could be helpful. *The Art of Dark Magic*, *Untold Stories of the Underworld*, *The Mystical and Extinct: Magical Creatures*, and the all too famous Dante's *Inferno*. Although interesting, none of these would help me look up hospitals. Maybe I could find a map somewhere in this place?

I spin, staring up at the full shelves all jammed with books, scrolls, and God-knows-what. The library is massive, taking up two of the three floors. There must be at least a million books in here alone. It's going to take forever to find what I need.

If only I had access to the internet. A phone or a computer.

My gaze lands on a room at the opposite end, tucked in the back, almost hidden, but I can see the glass French doors and the glow of a screen.

Bingo.

Just what I need.

After a quick glance over my shoulder, I hurry to it and discover that it's an office. Inside is a large desk covered in papers and open books, as if someone has been frantically searching through them for answers. A modern and fairly new-looking laptop sits on top of it all. Excitement bubbles up inside me, and I reach for the door's handle to find it permanently twisted down, broken.

Huh. Well, at least I don't have to worry about breaking in. I push the door open easily and walk inside.

There's one window in here, and it throws streams of light across the room. But besides those touches of light, everything else is dark. Mahogany furniture, a rich wine color on the walls, and gothic paintings of men locked in battle with demonic figures.

I know instantly that the office is Cain's. It matches his room and overall style too perfectly to be anyone else's.

That fact only heightens my anxiety. Also, unlike the other two demons, he's more… complicated. I never know which way is up with him, and without Sayah's help as lookout, I'm on my own. I have to make this quick.

On quick feet, I pad over to the computer. When I see the familiar wing emblem, just like the one on my necklace, as the background, I know my assumption was right. It's Cain's.

I pull out the chair and sit. A few quick clicks later, and I've found the internet search feature. Another nervous glance at the doors to make sure I'm still alone —I am—and I type in 'Saint Charity General Hospital, Centreville, Illinois' and hit the button.

The first thing to come up is the address, which I already know since it's on the receipt I found. What I need to know is more about *me*. But how I'm going to get that information, I have no idea. Maybe there's a patient portal or something... A phone number I could call?

I find the hospital's website and click the link. What pops on screen next shocks me: *Page Not Found.*

My heart sinks, and I refresh the page just to make sure what I'm seeing is true. It is.

What? No. How is that possible?

Are they having technical difficulties?

I back out of the errored website, returning to the main search page, and see a phone number listed. At the corner of the desk, covered in papers, is a black phone, much more modern than that antique thing in the parlor that Elias made me use before.

I quickly type in the number, hold the receiver to my ear, and hold my breath. A second later, the *dun dun dun dun* sound of a dead line blares.

I slam the phone down. *Dammit!*

Of course it couldn't be easy.

I reach into my pocket and pull out the paper I found in Murray's secret compartment. Unfolding it, I read over the words again, like I have so many times before. My name, date and time of birth, sex as female, and the price of over eighteen thousand dollars. No other names. Not even a signature. No clues as to who I am.

No. There's no way this could be just a dead end.

Looking back to the screen, I scroll further, eyes skimming the headlines. Mostly about awards the hospital has won for outstanding service or notable doctors joining their research team. Nothing that could actually help me.

The laptop snaps close, and I jump in surprise. My gaze flicks up to see Cain standing on the other side of the desk, blue eyes shining dangerously and lips twisted in an angry scowl. My heart leaps into my throat. I've been caught.

"What are you doing in here?" he growls through clenched teeth and leans forward.

"I-I-I—" The words won't come. They're stuck on my tongue.

When he spots the paper still in my hand, his hand whips out and snatches it faster than a blink. Panicked, I leap out of the chair and lunge for it, but he holds it out of reach as he reads it over.

"Hey, that's mine!" I croak, swiping for it.

"And this is my office," he replies coolly. "And that was my laptop you decided to use. Without my permission, I might add."

As he continues to look at the receipt, I hurry

around the desk, but before I can grab for it again, he quickly folds it and sticks it in the inner pocket of his suit jacket, saying nothing.

"Can I have it back at least?" I ask.

"Maybe another day."

"Bastard." The word slips past my lips without permission, and in the next second he's over me, pushing my ass against his desk, face mere inches from mine. I crawl backward, over the scattered papers and books, just to create more distance between us, but he only comes closer, those piercing eyes never leaving mine. They burn into me.

All I can imagine is the creature I found in the parlor the other day. The thing with marble gray skin lined in black veins and huge leathery wings that was consuming the soul of a werewolf. And that terrible sucking sound... It's haunted my dreams since.

He's going to do that to me. I just know it.

As I scramble backward, my palm touches something cold and smooth. I don't care what it is. I grip it and lash out, slashing it wildly between us.

Cain recoils, fingers pressing against a three-inch slice across his neck. It's not deep, just a flesh wound, but blood drips past his fingers.

I look at the object in my grasp and discover that it's a silver letter opener. Both sharp and pointed at the end. The tip gleams red.

Oh shit. If he wasn't going to kill me before, he sure is now. I instantly regret this decision.

Breathing heavily, I glance up at Cain. "I-I'm sorry," I gasp. "I didn't mean... I didn't—" But I did. I had meant to hurt him. I don't even know why I'm apologizing at all. My hand trembles, but I keep the letter opener pointed at him.

His surprise is quickly replaced with anger, the icy cobalt color of his eyes swallowed by the ominous black. He takes a threatening step toward me.

"Are you trying to kill me, Aria?" His voice is deeper, his accent richer. He drops his fingers, no longer caring about the wound I made.

My mouth opens, but again, I can't speak. My fear paralyzes me.

As the dark lines snake down his face and neck, I notice the blood oozing from the gash has turned black, too.

This is it. He's going to do it. Devour my soul.

Another step and the tip of the letter opener presses against the middle of his chest, right where his heart *should* be. "Do it," he says, challenging me. "And it's one less demon holding your contract. Kill me, Aria. *Kill* me."

All I can do is shake my head frantically. Everything he says is true. Killing him would mean I'd be one step closer to freedom, and really, he's making it easy for me. The letter opener is so sharp that one hard push could… No, there's no way it'll be that simple. If demons even have hearts, could stabbing one kill them? I don't know. And that isn't something I want to find out through trial and error.

Even if I managed to do it without dying myself, I still had Elias and Dorian to worry about. The odds aren't really in my favor here.

Cain pushes closer, and the letter opener pierces his flesh. Not a hint of pain flickers across his face, and that's terrifying in itself. It's like he doesn't feel it. More tar-like blood bubbles up, staining his white dress shirt. Still, he leans in even more, sinking the blade deeper, until his mouth hovers over mine.

Holding my breath, I don't move. I'm too scared to.

"Kill me," he whispers, but this time, there's a hint of something else in his tone. Something sensual. My heart thunders against my ribs.

His steps have brought him to stand in between my legs, and since I'm on the desk, our bodies press against each other in all the right places. I can feel his rock-hard erection through his pants, and now my stomach flips for another reason. The intense fear running through my veins turns into an even fiercer desire.

"Well?" he asks softly. "I'm waiting."

"Maybe another day." The words are barely out when his mouth crashes onto mine in a kiss that has my head spinning. Just like the kiss in the dining room, he is demanding and relentless, clinging to me. His fingers rake through my hair, tangling, and I drop the letter opener between us to grasp the lapels of his jacket instead. I can feel him shaking against me as all his control, all his reserve and resistance, finally comes undone. The dam has broken within him.

In one swift move, he swipes an arm across the desk, sending papers, books, and even his laptop flying across the room. It makes a terrible cracking noise when it hits the ground, but he doesn't seem to care. He's already grabbing me by the shirt and tearing it off me. The buttons pop, the material shredded, and excitement flares to life inside me at what I know is coming next.

This time, I hope he doesn't pull away. I've told him my secrets, after all—well, for the most part. We're beyond the games by now, aren't we? God, I hope so.

After chucking the torn scraps of my shirt to the side, he continues to kiss me and moves to my bra next. It takes only seconds before that, too, is snapped off me and thrown to the wayside. At the same time, I pull off his jacket and start undoing his blood-soaked shirt, both our movements rushed in our urgency. He doesn't want to wait another second longer, it seems, because he scoops me up by the back of my legs and quickly yanks them up, forcing me to lay on my back across the desk. One yank and my leggings are off. He's still pretty much fully clothed, but I'm only in my underwear.

"Cain…" I whisper, my hands covering my breasts. He ignores that and kneels before me, resting my legs on his shoulders. My breathing hitches at the sight of him between my thighs, his black-eyed gaze pinned on my sex. How many times have I dreamed of him exactly like this? Using his mouth and tongue to bring me to orgasm over and over? I've lost count.

When he peeks up at me, those black abysses give way to crystal blue irises again. They sear into me.

"Oh, my sweet, sweet Aria," he murmurs. His finger glides along my lace panties, tracing the place where I burn most for him. "What am I ever going to do with you?"

He's full of hunger like I've never seen before, and the sweet tingle of anticipation races down my spine.

Knowing he's been thinking similar things turns me on like nothing else.

"I have a few ideas…" I breathe, and he chuckles at that.

"Good. Because so do I." He tugs the fabric separating us aside, and in a blink, he's on me, his tongue swirling around my clit in the most expert fashion. My moan is instantaneous, pleasure rocketing through me. Gripping my thighs, he growls too, and the vibrations from his mouth only heighten the intense sensations rushing throughout my body.

He continues to lick and flick and ravish me, holding onto my legs for dear life, and as that delicious pressure begins to build in my lower stomach, my back arches and I fist a handful of papers on the desk. Hopefully none of them are important.

My orgasm crashes into me like a freight train, and I cry out from the sheer power of it. I don't think I've ever come so fast in my life. As it rips through me, it leaves me gasping for air, unable to suck enough into my empty lungs and bring my body back to equilibrium.

My muscles twitch, and tingles spread all over my skin. But it doesn't matter. Cain is showing no signs of stopping. Instead, two fingers slide into me, sinking deep inside. I suck in a sharp breath as he stretches and fills me while his tongue continues its relentless torture.

"Oh my G—"

His guttural growl of warning cuts me off, and I clamp my mouth shut. Not smart to use the Lord's name here, even if it could be considered in vain.

He pumps his fingers in and out, and every muscle turns to jelly. At the same time, his tongue circles my already ultra-sensitive nub, and I'm forced to grip his hair to keep myself from rolling off the desk. Already, I feel myself start to tremble again as another sweet climax builds.

"Holy fuck. Cain."

"Yes, Aria. Say my name when you come for me," he says against me between licks. "I want to hear it."

This time, when my climax peaks, I have no choice but to scream. I don't know if it sounds like his name or not. I have no control over myself in the moment, because pleasure unlike anything I've ever known spirals through me. My vision blurs, and all other sensations become lost.

As the residual tremors from my orgasm make their way through my body, my muscles clenching and unclenching in the best kind of way, Cain moves. Stands. He makes quick work of shrugging off his shirt and undoing his belt, and I push myself onto my elbows to get a better look at him. My gaze finds the gash in the center of his chest right away. Blood still drips from it, running down his front, but I'm quickly distracted by how muscular he is. The business clothes don't do him justice. He's wide at the shoulders, his body slender but solid and sculpted everywhere. His waist tapers in, and when he steps out of his pants before me, I'm left gaping like a deer in headlights. My heartbeat's a thundering boom in my ears. I've seen Elias and Dorian naked before, but not Cain. And he's… wickedly sexy. Dark. Drool-worthy. Dangerous.

And right now, all mine.

The outline of his erection is visible through his tight boxer briefs, and I bite my lip at the idea of what's coming next. I scoot closer to the edge of the desk, reach out, and hook my finger into the waistband.

His hand snatches my wrist, holding me there, preventing me from going any further. I see the flash of hesitation in his eyes that's making him pause. He's trying to resist again, but there's no way I'm going to let this end before we reach the good part, like in the club. I can't let him sink back into his own head.

He wants me. And, as fucked up as it may be, I want him, too.

Sitting up fully, my other hand comes up and seizes his boxers, wrenching him closer to me. Right in between my legs. When I meet his gaze again, I smile, letting him know there's no turning back now. And from the look of deep-seated lust hovering in his gaze, I have a sneaking suspicion his anger with me before was nothing more than a ruse. A front. It's his safety net; it's all he knows.

It's about time I fix that.

Holding his gaze, meeting his challenge, I pull his boxers down and release him. His cock springs free, and it takes everything in me not to look down at what he's packing, but from the times he's grinded up against me, I know I'm in for a rough—but fun—road ahead.

Then, slowly, I wrap my fingers around his hardness and watch his lips part in surprise and satisfaction. He doesn't stop me this time. Instead, his hand slides behind my neck and he kisses me hard. I kiss him back just as ardently, stroking his cock at the same time.

Our breathing picks up as the urgency rekindles between us. His fingers gather a fistful of hair and wrench my head back, making me gasp as pain spikes through my head. He kisses my exposed neck, and I feel the tip of him pressing against my sex, ready to enter.

Fuck, he's big. And I'm so tight and wet from the two orgasms before...

He tugs my hair again, and I cry out. He uses that moment of surprise to thrust into me, and a delicious mixture of pain and pleasure clashes. It's indescribable.

Suddenly, he leans forward, forcing me onto my back again. With his body hovering over me, he seizes my right leg and lifts it to sit on his shoulder. I know I'm flexible, but this is really testing the waters. He pushes closer even more, his face inches from mine, my muscles stretching to their limits. The position tilts my hips up, and when he moves in and out of me again, I whimper as another wave of pain and pleasure washes over me.

"Shit," he hisses through gritted teeth. "Aria..."

I won't lie. Hearing him say my name in his accent like that sends shivers through my body.

He begins to pick up the pace. The thrusts turn more forceful, brutish, and soon he's slamming into me so hard, the desk underneath us trembles and creaks from the force of it.

For the first time since the incident at the warehouse, I feel Sayah stir inside me. She's still hiding in the background, hoping not to be noticed, but I sense her there. Curious but cautious. But I can't think about her right now. Not when I'm finally with Cain the way I've craved to be for so long. I won't let her ruin this.

When I meet Cain's gaze again, I notice something about him has changed. His eyes flash from blue to black and back again. Dark lines slither down his face, and his skin appears to shimmer before my eyes. His jaw is tight, the muscles in his shoulders and arms bulge, and his entire body is vibrating. It's clear something's wrong. Or he's still holding something back. Whatever it is, he's struggling.

That's when I realize what's happening here. He's trying to keep his demon at bay.

For me.

Sayah must have sensed it before me.

Cain must think his demon will scare me. Maybe he's afraid what'll happen if he lets go fully and releases that side of himself. Honestly, I am too, but it's clear that the restraint is hurting him. He needs to stop holding back.

I cup the side of his face, and the soft gesture makes him hesitate. It's one he's not used to, that's obvious.

He searches my face, confused. "Aria, what—" His voice is a deep rumble, another sign that the demon is close to the surface.

"Do it," I tell him. "Unleash the demon, Cain. It's okay. Really."

He blinks at me, the color of his eyes still changing rapidly. Then he squeezes them shut and shakes his head. "No. No, I can't. I won't."

"I told you before, I'm not scared of it. Or you." It's a

lie, of course. I am afraid of what he's capable of, but I'm holding onto the sliver of hope that if he really wanted to kill me, he would've done it by now.

"You ran."

Two words, but I know what he's talking about—when I found him draining the soul of the werewolf in the parlor. I had run, it's true. But if Cain was ever going to open up to me, trust me, even just a little, then he was going to have to let me see him for what he really is. A sin demon and the Crown Prince of Hell.

I run my thumb along his bottom lip. The urge to kiss him again and show him I'm willing to take the chance is overwhelming. I want him to know I'm not afraid. I want to prove it to myself, too. "We all have a little darkness inside us, right?"

He dips his chin in a subtle nod.

"Well, I'll show you mine if you show me yours." Then I hook my hand around his neck and pull his mouth down to mine.

CAIN

She kisses like a storm. Electrifying, fiery, and unforgettable. Holding onto me, Aria never relents. She takes what she craves. Here I assumed the girl was innocent to begin with, except I'd been so wrong. A blaze burns inside her, a darkness swirls around her very soul, making her irresistible.

My tongue glides into her mouth, and I explore her, taste her, own her, unable to get enough. She is mine.

Her body quivers beneath me, and my cock twitches with building need. Her scent and taste fog my head. My mind usually races, but now, still buried inside her, it calms. My pulse beats through my veins, my demon wanting to unleash itself on her, too. But despite her coaxing, I'm unsure if revealing that side of myself to her again is wise. She may say she's not frightened, but...

She moans against my mouth, and my hesitation fades away. It's so easy to get lost in the feel of her.

I whisper, "You smell incredible." I inhale deeply against her neck, drowning in her scent of sex and sweat. Her hand splays wide, settled against the hard plane of my chest. My muscles clench, and I lean in and press our foreheads together.

"Cain," she breathes my name like it gives her oxygen, her eyes swimming in desire. "Show me the real you."

Every inch of her is so perfect. From the curve of her lips, to her sweet taste lingering on my tongue, to the burning fire between those gorgeous legs. I could have stayed down there and pleased her until the sun burned out, but there's so much more of her I crave. So much more I *need.* Even her persistence is growing on me.

She is burning up against me, and I lean in, kissing her neck, licking my way along her collarbone. Her nails dig into my arms, and her moans drive my pulse.

"Please, Cain," she begs, sounding unbearably sexy.

When I draw back, I can't keep the smile from my mouth. The morsel I desire sits on my desk, her dark hair wild and loose, hanging over her shoulders. I lower my hand to her thigh, and that fully gorgeous mouth parts in response with a gasp. Her perky breasts, each tipped with a deep cherry nipple, are beautiful and tight. Her legs remain spread, her small mount of hair glistening with her arousal. I still taste her honey on my tongue.

Just the sight of her drives me crazy, and I curse myself for ever resisting.

She's waiting for me to take her in my real form, and I never disappoint. Stepping back, I call the change forward, power pricking down my arms and spine. Heat rolls over my skin, surging through me like an inferno, the world gleaming with a pale reddish hue through my vision.

Aria's gasp is her only reaction to my black-veined skin and the leathery wings jutting outward from my back, casting a shadow over her. In my real form, I'm stronger. Prouder. And after walking around this plane for so long in a human skin, it's refreshing to not have to hide my true self.

Her mouth parts and she reaches over. "May I... touch them?"

"Yes." I curl a wing forward, and she runs her fingers over the thin membrane stretched between two bones, each tipped with a sharp talon.

Her touch is feathery soft, sending a buzz right through me.

"They're magnificent," she says.

"Are you still sure about this?" I step close and take her chin in my hand, forcing her to face me. She doesn't flinch at my appearance, but rather pulls her lower lip between her teeth, tugging at the flesh, staring at me like temptation itself. In demon form, the call of whatever darkness hides inside her is stronger. I can feel it buzzing through our touch. "There'll be no going back."

She nods, but a sliver of trepidation swims deep in her eyes. She gets turned on by playing with danger, I see that now. If that is what she wants, I will indulge her curiosity and satisfy my craving at the same time.

I lower my hand and wrap my fingers around her wrist. "On your feet."

She responds with wide eyes, and it doesn't take her long to slide off my desk. I draw her to me, our chests pressed together, my arms around her waist, my wings curling forward. Her gaze takes them in as a corner of her mouth quirks into a grin. The way she admires me in this form... it only adds fuel to my already raging fire.

I slide a hand down her back, over her sweet ass and under, then lift her off her feet as she quickly grabs my shoulders. Her legs instantly coil around my waist.

A blush of pink sweeps over her cheeks, and my arousal spikes, so I let it take the lead. I walk her over to the window of my office, pressing her back to the cold glass, grasping her ass. She arches from the chilled touch of the window, glancing over her shoulder at the woods behind her. She is exposed to anyone out there, but when she glances back, her confidence returns.

"No going back?" she says with a smile.

I half laugh, admiring her passion, her forwardness. Her hands grip my shoulders harder, and I claim her lips, taking her as the devil she desires.

Holding her close, her tight little body presses against me, her tongue twirling with mine. She's so small, and my damn dick aches for release. Heat burns at the core between her legs, and she adjusts to tilt her pelvis to accept me again. We groan together.

Without ceremony, I drive into her, take what is mine, and her small gasp of surprise has her pussy walls clenching around me. I hiss through my lips, the ache devious and intoxicating.

"You wanted the monster," I whisper against her mouth, unable to deny the irresistible urge to fuck her senseless. I want to draw every kind of reaction out of her. "Here I am."

The talons on my wings embed into the wall above us, allowing me more leverage to increase the speed and power behind my thrusts. Crying out, she clings to me, her breaths quickening. The window at her back rattles in the frame, the wood creaking and groaning, and I wonder if we'll break it. Part of me hopes we do.

Her fingers wrap around my wrist suddenly and guide my hand up toward her face. It takes me a moment to realize what she wants, but when she lifts her chin, I grasp her by the throat and squeeze. Her eyes roll back in ecstasy.

Looks like someone likes being handled roughly. Something I have no problem obliging.

A growl rumbles through my chest. She is perfect in every single way, from the desire clouding her gaze, to the small moans rolling through her throat, right down to her fingers digging into my arms. Mesmerizing, stunning. I'm caught in the web of her addictive smell, her luscious body, and all the things I intend to do to her.

One hand holds onto her ass as I drive myself deeper, stretching her, and she purrs, her head thrown back. I doubt I could hold back if I tried, so I thrust into her, pushing in and pulling out, so that nothing is separating us. Ever since her first visit to Purgatory, she's been a drug on my mind, distracting my every thought. What we have is primal and raw, and at this moment, I'd die before letting her go.

My power flares over me in waves, shaking me. This right here, her moaning for more, me plunging into her tightness, is what I've been looking for. I've been missing it for years. I can't explain it, this effect she has on me. It's unlike anything I've ever experienced before.

Electricity flows from her body to mine and back again, tangling us together. There's so much more to Aria than I think any of us realize.

"You'll be the end of me," I growl, sinking into her over and over. Gently, I lean closer and kiss her lips, unable to get enough of her taste.

Her whole body shudders with each thrust. Her cries are a siren of song to my ears, but that's when movement beyond the window catches my attention.

It's Elias. I see him standing near the edge of the woods. Shadows gather under his eyes as he glares at us, his mouth twisted in a snarl. Seeing him there watching us makes something primal surge through me. A hunger, a possessiveness. After I mistakenly allowed Dorian to get to Aria first, I want Elias to know where we stand. She's my claim.

Locking eyes with him, I ram into Aria harder and faster, my intentions clear. Hissing my exhale, I can't stop. Fury flashes in his eyes, and seconds later, he drops to all fours, shifting into his hellhound form, and rushes into the forest. Gone.

It's better this way.

Aria squirms, screaming, and suddenly pulses against me with the most incredible climax. Her fingers grip the wrist of the hand that's still wrapped around her throat, and her nails bite in. Her gaze meets mine, a silent challenge hovering there. She wants more.

Astounding.

Our energy clashes suddenly, fast and powerful, and I groan as my cock jerks inside her, pulsing into her.

Power nips across my nape, and in that heightened moment when we both come, a shadow emerges from the window, growing and stretching from a thin black cord. As if it's alive, it crawls along the wall to where my shadow is cast. Aria's skin glows in a reddish orangey hue, almost sparkling.

The shadow creature!

I'm curious and fascinated, but mostly concerned after what happened in the warehouse. Aria's eyes shoot open in horror at the sight before us.

The instant the shadow mingles with mine, an exhilarating shudder collides into me. Pleasure consumes me, as if every sensation has been amplified tenfold. As if striking her too, Aria cries out, drowning in the same magic of desire that's engulfing me.

I don't know what's happened, but our dark essences whirl around each other in some kind of erotic dance, and we're both left trembling against each other and struggling for breath. It's the most intense feeling I've ever experienced.

We both ride the waves of pleasure until my vision blurs. Aria moans, and we rock together. I'm still buried in her, and the way she squeezes me has me groaning. I don't care about the shadows, not when I'm lost to this woman in my arms. We are one.

I don't know how long we are caught in this perfect moment, but when we finally float down from the high and recover, Aria is panting, sweat dotting her brow. At the same time, we look over to the wall and find her shadow is gone. Only mine remains.

Her breaths are heavy and raspy. Her smile, when she glances back at me, is bewitching. "I didn't expect that," she murmurs.

"The earth-shattering orgasm or your shadow joining in on the act?" I ask, still holding her close, not entirely ready for this to end.

Something dark sweeps over her gaze then, and her thoughts seem miles away. Finally, she answers, "She shouldn't be able to do that."

Carefully, I lift her off me and place her on her feet. I tangle my hands in her hair and bring her attention back to me. I hate to see her worried and afraid like this. "We're going to figure all this out," I tell her. "I swear it."

CHAPTER TEN
ARIA

With so much chaos going on in my life, I've been eager to get back to work and retain some shred of normalcy. Who would have thought that working in a supernatural club with half-naked dancers on the stage would be my sense of *normal*? Ha!

Even stranger than that, these last three days I've woken up without Elias in my bed. I shouldn't complain really, but a small part of me misses him. Not so much his bearish snores, but our morning routine of bickering back and forth is something I've gotten quite used to. Talk about messed up. I would never admit to missing him out loud, though. It'd go straight to his head.

Cain insists that Elias has gone hunting in the woods and it's normal for him to vanish for days at a time, so I shouldn't be bothered by it or expect him back any time soon. But I'm not sure what to make of his sudden disappearance. It seems odd to me.

Besides that, I have been attempting to train Cassiel to use the new litter box I convinced Dorian to buy. The box is located in my bathroom, and surprisingly, so far there haven't been any mishaps. I guess all cats, no matter how wild or domestic, have the same core instincts. Not to mention, it's nice to have little snuggle breaks with so much shit going on.

"Aria!" Antonio bellows, and I flinch in surprise, glancing to the top of the stairs, where he's looking down at me. "Are you growing the pineapples down there, sweetheart? Pronto!" He clicks his fingers at me, and I jump instantly toward the shelf of canned goods, bottles of various drinks, and stacks of glasses.

I guess my break is over. I snatch a can of sliced pineapples and dart upstairs, the upbeat tune in the bar picking up in volume as I go. As usual, Purgatory is bustling with customers. Every seat and standing spot is taken. There never seems to be a down moment here.

I hand over the goods to Antonio, whose lips are pinched with distress.

"Sweetheart, I need the big can. With the group of Hawaiian fire dancers who've just ordered ten Pineapple Whiskey Sours, there'll be more." He waves at me with an impatient flick of his hand while turning to the fox shifter working in the bar with him. "Sting, don't you dare use that room-temperature mixer for the chilled cocktail."

Antonio presses the can back into my hand and darts toward Sting.

I groan under my breath but am also curious about who the fire dancers are because my first thought goes to dragons. And I've had enough encounters with those to last an eternity.

I rush back downstairs, silently thanking Charlotte for her tip of wearing flats on breaks and in between rushes. Once I dump the small can, I wrap my arms around the oversized one. The fucker is heavy! I struggle to lug it up to the bar and slide it on the counter near the sink.

"You're a godsend," Antonio says. His usual slicked-back hair lays in disarray around his face, and even his eye patch is slightly twisted. "Now go and collect orders, sweetheart." I grab my small notebook and pen from the pocket of my skin-tight leather pants as he barks orders at Sting to open the can.

Poor guy. Antonio's clearly in a mood today.

Not wanting to be his next victim, I hurry into the crowd, my gaze sweeping around for Dorian. He brought me here tonight, and I have no doubt he's been ordered to watch over me.

Instead, my attention settles on five tall, gorgeous men dressed in traditional Hawaiian grass skirts and nothing else, all clinking their whiskey sours together. It feels like I'm looking at five versions of Jason Momoa—all broad chests, rippling muscles, tan skin, and long curly hair. Am I drooling? I might be drooling.

From looking at them, I can't for the life of me work out what they are. Well, except for ungodly handsome.

"Captivating, aren't they?" a familiar voice comes from over my shoulder, and I look at Charlotte as she steps alongside me with her notebook in hand to take orders.

"Are they dragon shifters?" I ask, unable to look away from them. "Maybe mermen. That would make sense."

"Dolphins," Charlotte whispers in my ear. "The randiest shifters on the planet. Are you telling me you haven't heard of Man Swell?"

I blink at her, still trying to process what she just told me about them being dolphin shifters. "The male stripper group that tours around the country?"

She smirks wickedly and nods.

"Wow. So they're doing a show here tonight? It explains why three-quarters of the clientele here are female."

Charlotte laughs at me, her hand on my shoulder, and presses in closer. "Purgatory is a place where people experience desires and fantasies. And whenever Man Swell is in town, they offer special one-on-one sessions with the ladies. They've been booked out for months."

My mouth drops open, and I stare at her, stunned. "'One-on-one' like a private dance? Or…"

"All the way, baby." She chuckles and looks at me like I'm the most naive person in the world. "One thing you should know about dolphin shifters is that they can go all night. It's like they have natural Viagra in their system."

I glance back at the five of them. No wonder they're so happy—they're man whores!

"Excuse me, can we place an order?" a girl calls from my right.

"Back to the grind." Charlotte winks and swats my behind. "Off you go."

I paste on my brightest customer-service smile and turn to greet the girl. "Of course, what would you like?"

After that, the next several hours fly by. I work nonstop until my legs feel like jelly and threaten to give out at any second. During my shift, I couldn't resist keeping watch of the Man Swell guys as they came and went from the Red Rooms with different women. I lost count of how many passed me.

Don't ask me why, but it fascinates me. I don't blame the women, but part of me wonders how many of them are in relationships and have partners waiting for them at home.

I like to think that I'm an open-minded kind of person, but cheating of any kind is where I draw the line.

Collecting three Screwdriver cocktails from the bar, along with a cheeky grin from Antonio, I saunter across the room to the back corner where several young women sit around a small table. "Ladies, your drinks."

By their flushed cheeks and the bed-hair on the one brunette, I'm going to say this is an after-sex drink where they exchange notes. I place the cocktails in front of them and turn away, smirking. Why the hell not have fun if hot men are offering themselves?

Strong hands latch around my waist, and suddenly I'm flying backward into the dark corner of the club. My stomach lurches into my throat, remembering the handsy werewolf who pushed his luck with me last time. Whipping around, I shove against my assailant, my pen raised as a weapon, ready to stab. Until my gaze lands on Dorian's handsome face.

"What the hell?" I gasp. "I almost made you a shish kebab."

His gaze narrows, studying me with a look of indulgence. Shadows darken half of his face and make his green eyes shine with mischief and danger as they roam over me. It reminds me that Dorian may be the most civil of the three demons, but he's just as deadly. I shouldn't take his kindness as weakness.

Despite knowing all that, I can't help the tingles fluttering at the base of my stomach. They burst into full-blown butterflies, beating their wings. A single look and I'm putty in his presence. What has become of me?

I clear my throat. "I'm trying to work, you know."

"I see the way you look at those men," he replies, glancing toward the Red Rooms. His lip curls. "Dolphins."

I relax into a huge smile. "Oh, wait... You're jealous of Man Swell?"

"Of fish dancers?" He's laughing hysterically, placing one hand on his stomach. "Absolutely not."

"You know what they say about jealousy," I murmur, studying the way he looks me up and down like he's unsure if he should drag me into a back room this very moment.

"And what's that?" he finally answers, mocking me with his tone.

"You most envy those who have what you desire." I shrug and offer him a wide grin.

He lashes out and grabs my wrist, hauling me closer to him. I stumble into his chest, my hand snapping to press against the hard plane of his body, while my pen slips from my grasp and tumbles onto the floor.

"Little girl, you have no idea what you're talking about, but I can show you what's really happening in those rooms if you've got a marine fetish."

My hackles bristle, and I rip my arm out of his grip. "Eww, why do you have to say it like that? Now it'll be creepy when I think of them."

"Good. But tell me—as you fantasize about them, are they dancing just for you? Maybe waving a flipper at you?" He can't stop laughing. My irritation grows.

"Well, all these women can't be wrong," I snap. "They must be doing something right in there."

"I can guarantee you, if I offered myself to these females, I'd make a million dollars in a week."

"Well then, what's stopping you?"

He smiles broadly, showing off perfectly white, straight teeth. "You."

I hesitate. I don't know what that's supposed to mean, but I brush it off. "Sure, you keep telling yourself that. Now, I have a job to get back to."

Turning away from him, I crouch down, collect my pen, and march away, just as his large palm lands with a loud clap across my ass.

I flinch and throw him an evil glare from over my shoulder.

"Go, have a flipping good time," he says, still chuckling to himself.

What a dick. He can try to hide it all he wants, but it's obvious he's jealous of all the attention Man Swell is getting tonight. It's bruising that precious incubus ego of his.

At the bar, Antonio is rushing around and barking orders at poor Sting. When I approach, Charlotte hops up on a stool next to me. She pushes her blonde, soft curls over her shoulders and breathes heavily. It's definitely a busy night, and she's been working her tail off.

She watches Sting glare at Antonio every time he turns his back.

"What's the deal between those two?" I ask Charlotte as Antonio focuses on the violet cocktail he's creating in a hurricane glass. He places his hand over the top of the drink, and in seconds, a small trail of air bubbles rises to the surface. There's something hypnotic about watching him put spells on his cocktails. They all have various short-term effects on people, he once told me.

She glances over, her blue eyes framed by heavy eyeliner. "They're lovers. You didn't know?"

I shake my head. But now that she's mentioned it, I guess I can see it. They do bicker like a couple more than anything else.

She leans in closer to me. "They are always like this. Fiery at work but even hotter in bed."

"You've seen them?" I gasp, picturing them in the Red Room. Then my thoughts fly to Cain catching me spying on Charlotte having sex with her vampire master. My cheeks instantly heat up, and I thank the dim lights in this place.

"No, no. Antonio brags all the time about it." She lifts her head as he approaches and places two long glasses with something orange inside in front of us.

"What is it?" I ask.

"Relax, Ms. I-Don't-Drink-Alcohol-at-Work. It's just juice."

With that, I gulp the sweet drink down, sating my growing thirst.

"So how did you meet Viktor?" I ask and then immediately regret my words, as I'm not sure if this is a normal thing to ask someone of her master, so I quickly add, "But you don't have to answer if you don't want to. I mean, I didn't really get a choice in meeting the three demons in my life."

"Take a deep breath," she assures me, placing a hand on mine. "Ask me anything. I have no secrets. I met Viktor at a BDSM club I used to work at. It was his first time visiting the place, and he didn't even make it beyond reception before he swept me off my feet. He then left, saying he no longer needed to enter the establishment, which made me swoon. The man is everything I've ever dreamed of. Tall, dark hair, and so fucking handsome I still pinch myself that he chose me. And in the sack, he is a god. Well, I mean… you kinda saw that." Her smile is infectious, and I'm burning up with embarrassment, suddenly feeling feverish and sweaty.

"Do you mind if I ask... I mean, do you want him to turn you?"

She shakes her head. "We've both talked about it extensively, and I'm not ready. He accepts my decision, but I can tell he intends to eventually."

There's a slight waver in her voice, and I don't push the matter further. Don't want to touch on a sour topic.

"How did you know he was the one for you?" I ask, not sure if that's a loaded question considering she is dating a master vampire. For all I know, he forced her into the union using his glamor.

She chuckles to herself before turning in her chair to face me. "Don't laugh, but I knew he was mine when he bought me the most incredible gift." Her voice softens, her mouth breaking into a wide grin.

"What was it?" I ask curiously and fiddle with Cain's wing necklace around my neck.

"A unicorn goat."

I stiffen. "Come again?"

She laughs at me, setting a hand on my crossed knee. "Not a real unicorn, silly. He only has one horn, and it's curled toward the center of his head, so to me he looks like a unicorn. But he's adorable."

"Sounds cute." I blink at her, trying to decipher why exactly a goat is the perfect gift.

"I know what you're thinking. But I grew up on a farm and had a pet goat that I loved. When I lost him, I was devastated, and well, Viktor remembered my story." She shrugs.

"I completely get it. It's the small things that guys do, right?"

"Yes." She takes a sip from her juice, then whispers seductively, "What about you and your three demons?"

This time, I'm the one laughing. From the outside, I'm sure it looks like a woman's wet dream. Three gorgeous and wealthy demons? Sure, it sounds good on the surface. Yeah, I live with them and, as much as I hate to admit it, have kissed all of them—more than kissed—

but they're crazy. Deadly. And oh, so sexy. The thought has me blushing like mad.

Instead of speaking about the obvious, for some reason, I say, "I kind of owe them, I guess. They did save me from a dragon."

Her eyes bulge. "What?"

Checking over my shoulder, I note that the club is a lot quieter than earlier, and no one seems to be screaming out for a drink yet. Even Antonio and Sting are calm, chatting in the corner, so I turn back to Charlotte. Then I give her a summarized rendition of what went down with Sir Surchion, the escape, and even finding my own little pet.

Charlotte's mouth hangs open. "And you're okay? I have a fantastic psychiatrist you can talk to if you want... that kind of thing can really affect you." She's holding my hand, genuinely concerned, and it touches something deep inside me. She reminds me a lot of Joseline, who has the biggest heart, and that makes me miss her even more.

"Thank you," I say to Charlotte. "I think my biggest worry is that he'll come back for me."

She straightens in her seat. "He wouldn't dare. Not when you have three deadly demons protecting you."

"Charlotte, your baby boo is here!" Antonio calls out. Almost in unison, we swivel to follow in the direction he points, and my sights settle on Viktor.

Her master vampire.

The man is the epitome of tall, dark, and handsome, and he's wearing an actual cape like Dracula. Is that a thing vamp masters do? Despite him catching several women's attention, he only has eyes for Charlotte. She's on her feet and rushing over to him. I can't help but admire how much she loves him, how she runs to him, how he picks her up and off her feet before they kiss.

Like everyone else in the club, I watch as he carries her across the dark room and down the hall directly towards one of the Red Rooms. Well, someone is getting lucky tonight. I sure hope there's a free spot with all the Man Swell bookings.

I hop off my stool and do the rounds to collect empty glasses and take orders, seeing as I'm on the floor alone for a bit. It's only when I swing toward the back corner that I spot Cain, sitting alone, reclined in a seat in a black dress shirt gaping open at his throat.

My heart leaps in my chest, and I'm already rushing over to him, smiling. Images of us together in his study has heat flaring over my body. After seeing Charlotte with her charming prince, I'm eager to catch up with Cain.

When I get there, he doesn't get up to greet me. He just sits back, staring out across the room.

I blink at him, suddenly feeling foolish. "When did you get here? I didn't see you come in."

Finally, he glances up at me. There's no smile on his face. I burn on the inside. After what we shared, this is how he treats me?

"I have a business meeting," he says coldly. "Bring us two whiskeys, top shelf, neat."

My mouth drops open with words that never come. With hurt that stings like barbed wire. I somehow believed Cain, the original sin demon himself, might show me a sliver of what Viktor, Count Dracula, showed Charlotte.

Feeling stupid, I whip around just as an older man arrives and takes a seat across from Cain, both ignoring me.

Clenching my hands into balls, I march back to the bar, seething. My pulse bangs in my ears. This bullshit of claiming me and making me feel like he cares one minute only to then shove me aside the next is just downright cruel.

I give Cain's whiskey order to Sting. "And please, can you deliver it? I can't go back there," I murmur.

He glances over to Cain, who's sitting forward in his seat in deep conversation with whoever that old man is. "You sure you wouldn't prefer to do it?"

"One hundred percent certain." I slide onto a stool. Seeing there is no one else at the bar, I might just order a cocktail after all.

Strong hands slide around my waist, and the warmest breath washes over my shoulder and cheek.

"Don't pay Cain any attention," Dorian whispers. "He's in a pissy mood today."

I flinch and turn toward Dorian as he flops down onto the stool next to me, adjusting his tailored jacket. It sits open, framing broad shoulders. Everything about him captivates me, from the way his deep red button-up shirt curves over his strong chest to his spectacular eyes.

"You mean like every day," I say.

He chuckles and takes my hands in his. "Yes, that's right."

"What happened?" I ask, my mind spinning off in so many directions that all my thoughts knot into one massive tangle.

"Elias and I went to visit Sir Surchion's store and warehouse a few days ago to see where he had stashed our relics."

"And?" I sit on the edge of my seat.

"The whole place had been burned to ashes. He'd torched it. Nothing was salvageable. And even with all our resources, we've had no luck finding where he's disappeared to."

"Oh crap." That reaction seems extreme. I chew on my lower lip for a moment, then ask, "Does this mean he's gone for good?"

I hold my breath, hoping that's the case.

"We suspect he's looking for a new nest, hiding out before he flees."

"You think he's going to run for it?"

He nods solemnly. "And nothing will stop Cain from tearing down the whole living plane to find those relics."

CHAPTER ELEVEN
CAIN

*L*eaning against the bookshelf in my office, Dorian stares at the paper I'd taken off Aria the other night. I have no idea how it came to be in her possession, but one thing's for certain, we finally know her surname.

"Cross," Dorian says, mimicking my thoughts back to me. "Not a distinct last name, is it?"

I sit at my desk, staring at my closed laptop and the scattered papers before me. It's hard not to imagine Aria spread across it completely naked with me thrusting into her wildly. Ever since that night, it's been near impossible to be in here and get any work done. I thought that after indulging myself, I'd be able to clear my head and move on, but it's seemed to have the opposite effect. I only want her more.

"Cain," Dorian calls as he questions my silence.

I quickly try to recover. He'd mentioned her name, hadn't he? "'Cross' is old in origin," I say, hoping it's enough to follow the conversation where he'd left it. "Seventh century Old Norse, if I recall."

One of his brows arches, telling me he knows me too well to have missed my blunder. But lucky for me, he doesn't comment on it. "We can see if it leads to anything. Maybe a powerful supernatural ancestry?"

"I've already called contacts and searched records. Mother and father were both human. Father died eighteen years ago, and the mother has been deemed mentally unstable and put into a state facility."

"Human." Dorian rubs the scarred side of his face as he mulls over the new information. "Human… human and not an ordinary, even."

"Correct," I reply. "From what the investigators found, she comes from a long line of humans. Not an ounce of magic in their veins."

"How fascinating."

I glance out the window to the acres of woods surrounding our property and remember how Elias had been standing outside watching as Aria rode me to ecstasy. And how seeing him had only fueled my possessiveness of her. Elias hasn't been back to the mansion since, and I'm sure seeing us together is the reason. Did I care that he was off brooding in the woods again? No. Not only is this part of his pattern, it means I got my message across. Aria is mine if and whenever I want her.

"Anything about this Saint Charity General Hospital then? I'm assuming you called there as well." Dorian's voice forces me back into the room, back to the conversation. "This must be some kind of record from her birth. $18,590… Is that how much having a baby goes for on Earth? That's highway robbery."

"The hospital is closed. Permanently." Of course, after Aria had left my office, I'd checked my laptop to find she'd been searching for the place, too, only to come up empty-handed.

"Shit." He throws the paper onto my desk with an exasperated sigh. "It's nothing but a dead end."

Exactly. Now he understands my frustration. Then, to hear that Sir Surchion is also on the move with our relics… We're failing in all aspects.

My cell phone rings, and I quickly pull it out of my jacket. The number is unrecognizable, but that doesn't mean anything. Most people in our line of work use burner phones for tracking purposes. "Yes."

A man answers on the other line. "Mr. Cain. It's Freeman… With the search team Delta?"

I quickly rack my memory for what team Delta is and where they were assigned to look. With so many of my groups searching for relics scattered all over the world, it's hard to keep track of them. Especially by name.

"We're the west division," Freeman says to my hesitation, and it clicks at that. Ah, yes. He was one of the two teams assigned in the States.

"Do you have an update for me?" Usually, the teams check in periodically via email. It was easier to note progress—or in most cases, failures—in a simple note. Leaders rarely call. My pulse picks up at the thought of some kind of good news, like Alfonzo had given us with the heart. "Have you found something?" I ask in a rush.

"Yes, we think we struck a bit of luck here in Missouri," he says, a thread of pride in his voice.

Missouri? What a random place to have hidden a powerful relic, but I suppose that was the point, wasn't it? Put it in a place no one will think to look.

"What is it?"

"The spine," he replies, and my excitement surges immediately. I slide to the edge of my chair. "I believe we've tracked it to the Milo Swamps."

I glance up at Dorian, who's watching me intently. I'm sure he knows something's up just by my change in posture. "Send me the exact coordinates, and I'll be on the next flight over." Then I hang up the phone and set it down.

"What was that all about?' Dorian asks right away.

It takes me a while to respond. My brain is still processing the call and the possibility of having another relic in our possession. Once we retrieve the others from Sir Surchion, of course. Which is a hurdle we'll have to cross as well.

With both hands on my desk, he leans forward. "Well?" he presses. "What is it?"

"They've tracked the spine," I begin, but before I can continue, Dorian's excitement gets the better of him.

"No fucking way. Where? How far do we have to travel this time? Is it close?"

I hold up a hand to stop him. Running a hand over his face, he sucks in a breath to steady himself.

"It's in Missouri," I tell him when he's finally settled.

His eyes widen. "Missouri? What the hell's in Missouri?"

"Swamps, apparently."

Dorian's mouth twists in disgust. "Of course. It couldn't be hiding on the sunny beaches of California, or a five-star day spa in the mountains. Or better yet, in wine country."

Sure, marshes and wetlands aren't ideal, but this isn't exactly supposed to be a vacation, either. I am going for the relic, then coming straight back. There are too many important things here to attend to. Like retrieving the eye, heart, and hair strand from a dragon before he flees the country.

Which gives me an idea.

Slowly, I stand on my feet. "I have good news for you then. You're not going to be coming with me this time."

He looks at me in disbelief.

"We've exhausted all our normal outlets of investigation and have found no leads. I'm sure we don't have much time before the collector flees. It's time to narrow our focus. I need you and Elias to find Sir Surchion and take back what's rightfully ours. We need those other relics. With Elias's tracking and your speed, you should be able to do it."

"That's *if* I can pry Elias's ass out of the woods, and *if* we don't end up killing each other," he grumbles. "A lot of uncertainties there."

I narrow my gaze on him. "I'm counting on you to work together on this. You've done it before, you can do it again."

"Right. Fine." He seems less than thrilled to agree, but we both know it's something that has to be done.

"Alright then, it's settled. I'll see if I can charter a

private jet out to Missouri for the morning," I say and open my laptop. The screen is cracked in the bottom corner from when I threw it across the room, but it's still usable for now. I'll get a new one soon enough.

"And what of Aria?" Dorian asks.

His question takes me off guard. "What of her?"

"We can't just leave her here by herself. What if she escapes?"

"She won't escape," I reply. "We'll post guards to watch her again. Restrict her to her room only while you're gone. Bring meals to her—"

"That's cruel," Dorian says, shaking his head. "You can't just keep her locked away like a pet."

I don't see the harm in it. "It'll only be for a few days."

He sighs heavily. "Haven't you learned anything?"

I clench my jaw, my annoyance building. "What do you expect me to do? Bring her with me?"

Suddenly, his lips split in a grin, and I instantly realize my mistake.

"Oh no. Absolutely not," I say shortly. "No way in hell am I bringing her across the country—"

"And why not?" Dorian interjects. "I think it'll be good for you two."

"Good for us...?" I'm not sure what he's getting at here.

"You know... Since you've recently spent some time getting more acquainted." He wiggles his brows. When I don't take the bait and respond, he adds, "Since you fucked."

I stare at him, stiffening. I hadn't told Dorian about

my and Aria's encounter in my office, and I doubt Aria did, either. But, as an incubus, he can sense these things. It's part of his power; he absorbs the sexual energy in a room, and since Aria and I had sex in this very spot… let's just say I should have seen this coming.

"We'll discuss this later," I say to brush off the topic. It's not one I want to deal with right now.

"Oh, you can bet your ass we will."

A conversation I'm not looking forward to. I heave a sigh. "Fine, I'll bring Aria with me. Maybe she can prove to be useful."

Dorian crosses his arms and smirks my way.

"That's not what I meant, and you know it," I snap.

He shrugs.

"I meant with her ability to track down dark magic. It can be helpful when searching the swamplands. Maybe her power can pinpoint an exact location and save time."

"If you say so," Dorian says and laughs. "I'll admit, I'm a bit jealous. I get beast-boy and a dragon while you get Aria and a mini-vacation out west. If you'd rather, I'd be up for a trade."

My head is shaking 'no' before I even realize. When he puts it like that, I guess this could be a somewhat enjoyable trip. Gaining another relic and spending more time alone with Aria… Is there really a downside to this?

A zap of electricity races to my groin, and my cock jerks just at the thought of having her legs wrapped around me again, her shuddering and screaming as I make her come over and over. This woman does things to me I can't explain or control. And although her influence over me is unnerving at times and a bit dangerous, that's what makes it... dare I say, fun?

Now my head is spinning for another reason entirely, and I'm itching to leave even more than before.

ARIA

*A*fter eating lunch alone—like most days recently—I leave the dining room and make my way up the grand staircase toward my room. I'm supposed to work at Purgatory today, but with a few more hours until my shift, I figure I'll relax in my room. Maybe play with Cassiel before I have to leave him for the night.

As unexpected as our meeting was, I'm glad I found him. I've grown quite attached to the little lynx kitten, and now that Sayah is untrustworthy and unable to keep me company, it's nice to have someone around to talk to besides the demons.

Plus, it's given me more time to think through my next plans. There is no chance of me tracking down the orb, so that's out. I can always try taking something from the mansion—like one of the smaller sculptures or paintings—and selling that instead. Then I could use the money to get as far from this town as possible.

I don't know why, but the idea of stealing from the demons again feels... wrong. Especially since they rescued me from Sir Surchion and the werewolves.

Things have certainly changed in the past few weeks.

Sayah is uncontrollable.

I possess powers I shouldn't.

And I still have no lead on who my parents are.

The thing is, now I'm wondering if the smarter decision is to stay here and let these demons help find out about my past. They seem to be just as interested as I am, and they certainly have the money and influence to find things out. More than I do. I would never get a chance like this again.

Then there's the hard fact that these three men are starting to grow on me. I never thought I'd say this, but I enjoy their company. No matter how arrogant, dominant, and crazy they are.

What am I doing?

"Aria."

I turn in the middle of the steps to see Cain at the very bottom of the staircase, looking up at me with his business attire on. He looks so sexy dressed in a charcoal gray suit and black shirt underneath. Polished. Refined. Absolutely droolworthy. And with his hair combed back from his face and his blue eyes sparkling, it's like being in the presence of a model from magazines and billboards. But I know better. He's the devil in disguise, and all that sexiness and danger wrapped in a perfectly tailored suit only makes him even more irresistible to me.

His gaze scans me from head to toe and back again, lingering a little longer on my hips and legs. And it takes me a moment to realize why. I'm wearing a short-as-sin pleated skirt and knee-high stockings for work—part of my overly-sexualized uniform—along with a see-through white blouse that shows off my black lace bra underneath. The only comfortable thing I went for this time was the sneakers, which I was hoping Cain would let me keep and not complain about. And the way he's staring at me, with hooded eyes and the slightest curl to his lips, sends a delicious shiver down my spine. Looks like I might get away with not wearing high heels after all.

"Yeah?" I call back to him. "Do you need something?"

His body tenses as if he wants to say something, but after a moment, he decides against it. "I'm having the servants throw some of your things into a suitcase. Our plane leaves first thing in the morning," he says instead.

I blink. His words are the last ones I'd expected. "Wait, what? A plane?"

He nods. "You're coming with me to Missouri. For business."

Okay... Now I'm more confused. "But I have work tonight," I say. It's stupid, I know, since he's technically my boss, but I love my job. It's the little break I get from all this Hell craziness.

"No work for the next couple of days. You'll be with me instead."

It takes a minute, but his other words register with me late. "Did you say Missouri? What the heck is in Missouri?" What business could possibly be there?

"Like I said. Business."

I roll my eyes. "Okay then. But why do I need to come?"

"So you do *not* want to join me?" he asks, brows lifting in surprise. "I thought you'd like some time away... with me."

"Just-Just you... and me?" My pulse begins to race at the idea of us alone together again. Especially since the last time in his office had been so... intense.

"Would you like that?" he asks, eyeing me carefully and coming up a step.

Fuck yeah, my mind screams automatically, but my gut twists with uncertainty. Sure, I'd love to have some private time with Cain, but something feels off about his offer. It's just so out of the blue. He's not the romantic type. At least, as far as I've seen. That's more Dorian's scene. Unless Dorian encouraged him to do this... maybe gave him the idea? That would be the more innocent and desirable of the scenarios, but I can't help but feel like there's more to this trip than him wanting to spend more time with me.

When it comes to Cain, there's always something more behind what he does. Another motive.

"Why do you need me to go?" I ask him straight out.

He blinks in surprise. "What do you mean?"

I cross my arms over my chest and give him a deadpan look.

"Does there have to be a reason?" he counters.

"With you, there always seems to be."

He rubs his jaw in thought, seeming impressed I'd figured it out. "Very clever of you, Aria."

I try to think of what "business" Cain could possibly want me there for. He'd shooed me away yesterday when meeting with one of his business partners, so this has to be something he needs me specifically for. What could that be...

"The relics."

The answer pops into my head immediately. He would need me for the relics, to help track them down by using my gift. Why else drag me across the country with no warning? It's the only thing I can think of.

His smile is slow and deliberate, only confirming my suspicion. "Very good."

"You want me to help you track them down?" I ask him. "Is Sir Surchion in Missouri? Is that why?"

"No, it's a new relic. The spine."

Spine? Yuck. What's with these relics being modeled after body parts?

"It's been tracked down to the swamplands of Missouri, but it's a lot of ground to cover," he continues and climbs up another step closer to me. "That's where you come in."

But I'm already shaking my head frantically, my anger stirring. Stupidly, I thought he'd wanted some trip away with just the two of us. Or I'd hoped for it. But all he wants is to *use* me. What a complete and utter asshole.

"I'm not going," I snap. I turn sharply and trudge up the rest of the steps to the second-floor landing. I'm about to go up the next set of stairs to the third when there's a rush of air and Cain's suddenly in front of me, eyes black. He leans forward, pushing me back into the banister. I glance over at the foyer way below. If I fall, there's no doubt I'll break my neck. My heart hammers against my ribcage.

His hand snatches my chin and forces my attention back to him. That sly, devilish smile returns, the one that makes my stomach somersault with mixed emotions. He peers down at my mouth briefly, and I hold my breath, unsure what he'll do next.

"Oh, Aria," he says, mimicking sincerity, "I'm sorry if I misled you to believe otherwise, but you don't have a choice."

I glare at him. I hate myself for my own stupidity. For thinking he cared about me and our time together. He only wants me around so I can help him get what he truly wants. The relics. Is that my new role now?

His eyes swirling back to their normal blue, he releases me, and my jaw aches from his firm grip. Still smirking, he pulls his shoulders back and proceeds back down the steps. I watch him go, wishing looks could really kill. He'd be dead in a heartbeat.

"We leave at five a.m. sharp," he says without turning. His hand glides along the wooden banister as he descends. "Don't keep me waiting."

In that moment, I realize I hate him. Hate his arrogance, hate how he affects me, the way he can manipulate me so easily. I fall for it every time.

Furious, I grab the wing pendant around my neck and pull, snapping the chain. I'm done wearing the thing and being considered "his." D-O-N-E. Done.

I throw the necklace to the foyer, and it slides across the marble to his feet just as he hits the bottom step. He pauses, head tilting in curiosity before bending down to pick it up. With the gold chain in his hand, he looks up at me, and for a second, I swear

I see hurt hovering in his gaze. Another ruse, I'm sure.

"Aria," he tries, gentler this time, but I don't want to hear any more of his sugar-coated bullshit anymore.

Shaking my head, I push off the banister.

"Fuck you, Cain." As strong as I want to be, I can't help the pain lacing my voice, but I don't care. I hope he hears it. Then I turn sharply and hurry down the second-floor hallway, hoping to god he leaves me alone and doesn't follow me.

I get halfway down the corridor when I conclude he has. Good. It's bad enough I'll have to endure a few days alone with him for this trip. I may be under his stupid contract and forced to do what he says, but that doesn't mean I'm going to make it easy for him along the way.

With no true destination in mind, now that I'm off work tonight, I stroll along the second floor. My gaze swings from the many portraits and other art pieces hanging on the walls to the large windows on the opposite side. Movement below catches my eye from outside in the grounds, drawing me to a stop.

The mysterious white angel guy again?

I creep closer and realize quickly that it's not him. It's Elias, stalking across the property, back hunched and muscles stiff. Like someone's ticked him off.

Join the club.

I haven't seen him in days. I wonder what's up with him. He can't be that peeved because of Cassiel, can he? It's just a cat.

Knowing I have to be quick to catch up with Elias before he vanishes again, I race down the hall to the back staircase, past the library, and out the door. Since winter is fast approaching, the sun is already starting to slide down, some of the trees in the yard rustling in the breeze. I spot Elias's dark figure right away, heading for the woods again, as expected. I run over.

Nostrils flaring, he pauses when he catches my scent, but when his head swings my way and he sees me, he picks up his pace.

"Elias! Wait!" I call to him, waving like a loon. He definitely saw me, so that means he's avoiding me for whatever reason. I'm fast, but I'm not hellhound fast. Not to mention how long his human legs are. I'll never catch up. "Elias!"

Finally, and to my relief, he slows. I reach his side.

"Hey," I say. "Where have you been?"

He doesn't respond. Doesn't even look at me. Just keeps walking through the grass. The earth sinks under my sneakers, damp and cold, and the wind bristles past, making me shiver. Dammit. Skirts and late fall weather don't go well together. I should have brought a coat or changed into pants first.

Elias seems unfazed, of course, even though he's only wearing sweatpants and a tight-fitting tee. I hug myself in an attempt to keep in some warmth, and he glances at me.

"What are you doing out here?" he grumbles. Whenever the sunlight hits his face, his eyes shine amber, like a wild animal's.

"I wanted to make sure you're okay," I say, which is the truth.

He harrumphs at that. "I'm fine."

"A bit grumpy, if you ask me."

He stops, drawing me to a halt, too. "Go back inside," he says. "You shouldn't be out here. Especially alone."

"But I'm not alone, am I? You're here."

His jaw clenches, and the muscles pulse at his temples. Wow, something's really got him mad.

"Look, if this is about Cassiel…"

He blinks, seeming surprised by me bringing him up at all. "The lynx?"

"I thought maybe having him in my bed now may have upset you somehow? Encroaching on your territory or some animal thing like that."

Elias continues to stare at me, saying nothing, but I wait him out. After a few minutes, he lets out an exasperated sigh. "I don't feel threatened by anything I could eat for breakfast."

My stomach sours at the thought, and I swallow roughly. Okay, note to self: Don't leave Cassiel with Elias. Ever. He might become hellhound chow.

I try to shake it off. "I thought something might be wrong with you since I normally wake up with you there annoying me first thing in the morning, and the past few days, I've been alone. Have you figured out how to stop sleepwalking?"

Elias looks at me with an arched brow, appearing like he might growl any second at my comment. I don't understand why his sleepwalking is such a touchy subject. "I've been… busy."

"Busy, huh?" *Lie.* But I decide to indulge him anyway. "Doing what?"

"Aren't you needed somewhere else?" he snaps in annoyance.

"I was supposed to have work today, but that got tossed to the wayside."

He side-eyes me. "I'm sure Cain's wondering where you've run off to."

"Fuck him." I scoff. "He's the last person I want to see right now. Or last demon, I should say."

His expression softens, the anger he's been holding onto draining away. "Oh really? Well, that makes two of us, then."

CHAPTER TWELVE

ARIA

*S*o that's what this was all about? Cain?

Huh. I wonder what he did to Elias to piss him off. Had to be big.

"Where's the furball now?" Elias asks, clearly changing the topic. I'll have to see if I can pry more information on Cain out of him later.

"Last I saw, he was sneaking into your bedroom," I tease but keep a straight face and watch his mouth part with surprise.

"If I find claw marks in any of my clothes, I'll..." He doesn't finish but marches past me toward the house.

I lash out and snatch his arm, grinning. "Stop. I'm only kidding. Geez."

He pauses and twists at the waist to glance at me, but instead of an expression of disbelief, he smirks. "You were being funny."

"I was *trying*. But you take everything so seriously."

"No, I don't," he says, his tone confident, eyes

guarded and drifting down my body and back up, pausing on my lips. "I just… have a lot on my mind."

"Y-yeah?" The inferno in my gut melts through me and collects between my thighs, my chest heaving up and down with rapid breaths. "We all do, don't we?"

He sighs, head turning toward the house. "I suppose you're right."

I quickly take my hand back from his arm. "I think you just need to take a moment and chillax."

"Chillax?" His brows pinch.

"You know… Chill out and relax?" I say. "You should try it sometime."

He studies me for a long moment, then his gaze starts to wander. A phantom touch traces down the valley of my breasts, covering me in goosebumps.

Unexpectedly, his hand hooks around the back of my neck, forcing me toward him. Body to body, we press together, my breasts squashed against his strong chest, while he forces my head back so I'm staring up at him. "You want to know what relaxes me, Aria? A hunt."

My throat dries. "A… hunt?"

He smirks. "I'll give you to the count of ten. It's only fair."

I choke on my next breath. "W-what are you talking about? Count of ten?" My heart drums loudly in my chest with trepidation.

There's a hunger in his eyes from this deranged game he's playing, the animal within him waiting to pounce, catch, and devour. "And when I catch you, you are mine."

I shudder at the seductiveness and fear his words

bring. I shove my hand against him, but he doesn't release me.

"Are you crazy?"

His smile spreads into a full, toothy grin. "Maybe."

A tremor of anticipation runs through me. God, what is wrong with me? I don't even know what this mad man will do to me.

He throws back his head, laughing, the muscles in the arm that holds me flexing. "Okay, one rule only. You can't run into the house or you forfeit automatically."

I blink at him in disbelief. "Where am I supposed to go, then?"

"You'll have to figure it out."

"No way," I snap. "I'm not playing this ridiculous game with you."

He releases me, and I stumble away. "Ten."

Shit. I'm frozen on the spot, my pulse a raging river.

"I'm not doing this!"

He licks his lips, and my mind races. Where should I go? What do I do? I don't want to play this game of his. There's no way I'll win.

"Better start running, little rabbit." A slow, cruel smile twists his mouth. "Nine."

I turn and run. I don't even know where I'm going, but I'm careening around the massive mansion, my heart beating frantically and my feet shoving into the soft grass.

I glance over my shoulder. Elias isn't giving chase yet, but I can hear him counting in the distance.

"Six."

He was just on nine! Of course he'd cheat. I should've expected that.

Instead of swinging toward the house where he'll most likely expect me, I swing left and plunge into the thick woods that I know lead to the lake Dorian took me to. Water will conceal my scent, then I can keep going and he won't find me.

I may not have speed, but I can be smart about this. Show him that two can play this game.

The ground slides beneath me, but I don't dare slow down. Already between the trees, the sparkle of the lake catches my eye. A flash of excitement flares over me, and I rush faster.

What number is he down to now? Three?

Looking back, there's no thundering figure charging after me. I suck in each rapid breath before bursting out onto the bank of the lake. The water glistens, still as glass, and the whole area is tranquil.

For a split second, I reconsider going in. The water has to be bitter cold—it's nearly frozen in some spots. Do I really have to risk hypothermia to escape him?

The sound of thundering footsteps and the sight of trees snapping to the side has my adrenaline spiking to one hundred. Elias is driving down the hill like thunder, headed right this way. That notion alone has me dashing into the cold embrace of the lake, fully clothed. It's icy cold—the kind of cold that steals your breath away—but my racing panic wins over the chill right away. I push myself deeper into the middle of the lake, thankful I'm wearing sneakers and not those stiletto death shoes. There's no way my ankles would've survived this.

Just before he explodes from the brush, I take in a deep breath and submerge myself into the water. I'm not sure how long I can hold my breath, but it looks like I'm about to find out.

ELIAS

I shouldn't tease myself, shouldn't pursue something that will only come back and bite me later.

The thought circles my mind as I race down the embankment toward the river. Except the animal inside me leads the charge, snarling in my chest, and any logical thoughts fade into oblivion.

The chase consumes me. It's been so long since I pursued such a worthy target, something I yearn to hunt down and take.

Her sweet honey and sex smell mingles on the air like a dangled carrot, and I find it with ease and pursue it with frantic desperation.

My chase brings me to the lake where the sliver of the setting sun heats my shoulders. The surface of the lake ripples outward from a strange spot not too far from the shore. I smile with certainty and kick off my shoes, then wrench off my shirt and pants. Naked, I lunge into the crisp, cold water, the heat from my body cooling.

Swimming underwater, I rush forward until the

movement of water flows against me. Murky water makes it hard to see her right away. She comes into view in a blur at first, remaining underwater, holding her breath.

Dark hair sways back and forth around her, and for those few seconds, I could easily mistake this beauty for a siren. Pushing through the water to curl behind her, I dig my toes into the muddy ground and push myself directly toward her.

My arms hook tightly around her middle, and with my momentum, I drive us both up and to the surface. The little thing struggles in my arms, gasping for air, hair sticking to the sides of her face. I love seeing her so surprised—she truly didn't think I'd catch her in her hiding spot.

"Found you," I whisper in her ear, keeping my chest flush to her back and holding her off her feet.

She twists her head to look at me, her glare dark, and I can't stop laughing because she knows I'm right.

"This is a stupid game. Of course you were always going to win." She shuffles about in my arms and turns to face me. Her hair sits flat against her head, droplets running down her face, over her tempting, full lips. She is stunning in every possible way. She jerks herself out of my grasp and propels herself away from me. "It was hardly fair."

"Life is rarely ever fair," I tease.

She pauses and stands where the water reaches her neck, eyeing me, then glances over to the shore. "Why are you naked?"

"Why aren't you?"

She narrows her eyes like the very notion is absurd, like what I'm proposing is never going to happen. It shouldn't excite me, but it does. When I look at her, all I remember is her pressed up against the window in Cain's clutches, and my heart ignites into a fireball. I can't get the image of them out of my head. It's haunting me.

Gradually, she swims away from me, moving backward to put more distance between us. "Why are you doing this?" she asks, breathing heavily, water sloshing around her jawline with each movement she makes.

"Because you are not *only* Cain's." It surprises me that I admitted that out loud, but it's not the first time I've said crazy shit. And I have nothing to hide. I'm attracted to Aria. That I can't deny, even if my head tells me I'm a fool to let myself ever get close to anyone again.

And now this girl who has secrets of her own puts more distance between us. I recognize the shock on her face from my words. Her features sharpen, and a new confidence slides over those beautiful dark eyes.

"New game," she declares. "If I can reach the house before you, I win. I get until the count of ten before you start running."

I run her words over and over in my head. I already know there's no way she can outrun me, but how do I make this game more… interesting?

Gaze glued to mine, she continues to make jerky movements toward the shore. My muscles tense at a promise of another hunt, and with it, desire stirs.

What am I going to do when I catch her this time?

My mind races with possibilities.

"Okay," I say. "I'll play."

Not a second passes before she whips around and swims out of the water. Frantically, she gets out, her skirt and shirt clinging to that stunning little body of hers.

"Ten, nine... one," I whisper under my breath and throw myself out of the water after her. She forgot the biggest rule when it comes to making deals with demons—check for loopholes. There were no rules about how fast or slow I could count to ten, after all.

I charge onto the shore just as she bursts into the woodland.

What my little rabbit doesn't know is that I gave her extra time on the first round, but now, all bets are off. She's mine, and nothing will get in my way.

I run up the hill, over the grass that covers the land between lofty firs, and catch up to her in no time.

She glances at me over her shoulder, her breaths racing, eyes flooded with terror. Her gaze scans my naked body, which seems to scare her more. That look alone drives me to want to take her over and over.

Behind her, she leaves a sweet scent of arousal on the air, along with the freshness of lake water and the earthiness of the soil she kicks up in her race to escape me. My cock twitches, the image of what I'll do to her already imprinting on my mind. Rip her clothes off, spread her wide.

No one has ever made me feel such an overwhelming need before.

I push forward and snatch her by the waist, tugging her to me.

She cries out and drives an elbow into my gut. "You aren't winning this time."

I groan from the sharpness shooting through my side, but my hold on her tightens. In one swift move, I kick her legs out from under her with a nudge of mine. She falls, and I sweep her into my arms just as she turns to shove me aside. I lose my footing on a dip in the land, and suddenly we're both falling to the ground, her in my arms, her fury taking over her gaze.

I take most of the brunt of the fall, cradling her against me as we fall on our sides.

"Hey gorgeous." I grip her hip with one hand, finding skin where her skirt has ridden up to her waist. Finding the thin fabric of her underwear, I curl my fingers under it and rip them off her in a savage move.

Her mouth drops open as I toss her panties somewhere behind me. "Only fair, seeing as I'm naked."

"You monster." She scrunches her nose, then makes a sound not too dissimilar to a war cry. With a shove, she forces me onto my back, and she's suddenly straddling me. She sits on my cock, rubbing her wet pussy over me, and I hiss from the intensity, from the desire burning through me. Her thighs squeeze my waist, and she reaches down to grab my throat.

"Are you ready for another game?" Her cheeks flush a pink color, her wet hair wild, and she licks her lips, showing me exactly what she wants.

Fuck, I adore this woman.

I reach up and grab the neckline of her shirt and tear it, the fabric ripping down her chest, buttons popping, the latch on the front of her bra unfastening in the move. Those beautiful breasts bounce freely, cherry red nipples tight and calling my name. She gasps but doesn't move to cover herself. While I love my women strong, I take charge.

Grasping her small waist, I thrust my hips up, and I twist us over so that I'm on top. She breathes heavily, and I love the reaction I have on her. I reach down between us and tug her skirt over her hips.

She's tiny compared to me, even if she writhes against me, pushing me against my shoulders. Those small sounds she makes, those heavy breaths, are a song to my ears. She's exactly where I want her—legs spread and my cock sliding over her entrance.

Her body tenses while fury burns in her eyes.

"Ten... Nine... Eight..." I coo, toying with the girl whose hips already rock back and forth over my erection. Elation sweeps through me so hard it takes every fiber of strength to hold back a bit longer. Her arousing scent engulfs me, and I'm dying to sink my tongue into her pussy, to really taste her, but that means giving her a chance to escape. And she's not going anywhere.

"Seven... Six..." she continues, her hands gripping my shoulders, holding on, so ready for me despite her words.

"One." I growl against her mouth as I push into her. She moans, fingers digging into me with anticipation. I drive into her, widening her, fitting so damn perfectly that it's like she's made for me.

Electricity sizzles between our connection.

"First lesson when making a deal with a demon—always spell out everything."

She lifts her pelvis, drawing me into her. A rumble vibrates in my chest.

"Bastard." She cups my face, forcing me down to kiss her.

I take my time with her, making sure she's ready for my size, but she urges me to speed up with her hips, using them to meet my every thrust. Delicious waves of pleasure shudder through me the faster I go. Her thighs cling onto me, her ass off the ground.

Her cries fill the woods. With one hand flat on the ground to hold us, I scoop the other under her back, lifting her off the ground as she protests my pause.

"Don't want the ground to tear up your back," I whisper. She loops her arms around my neck, holding on, her face in the curve of my neck. Hot breath flutters down my back as I plunge into her harder and harder.

The ride is wild, and I can't feel anything but my gorgeous rabbit.

She moans beneath me, her body quivering with each rushed thrust, her soft breasts rubbing over my chest. There's only so much a demon can take when fucking such a beautiful woman.

She shakes against me in an abrupt explosion of her climax, her scream like a howl on a full moon. I grasp onto her, rutting her when my own orgasm crashes through me, diving south and bursting out.

She holds onto me as I pulse inside her, my seed flooding her, and I'm rather proud of how much cum spills into her.

"That was incredible," she breathes.

We're tangled together, lost, and everything about her feels perfect.

She loosens her grip and slides from me, collapsing on the forest ground and staring up at me with a beautiful smile, the battle between us gone. My gaze dips to take in all her beauty, down to her delicious pink pussy, where the first threads of my seed drip from her gorgeous lips. The sight has my cock throbbing with a need to reclaim her, over and over.

Our passion beats on the wind around us, echoing the hungry sounds we'd made.

If I had my way, we wouldn't be close to being finished. I picture myself throwing her over my shoulder and returning to my room where I can keep her all for myself. I almost laugh out loud at what Cain's reaction would be.

"Elias," she murmurs. "What are you thinking about?"

Her sweet voice slices through my thoughts, and I refocus on her. This is where I want to be. I pull at her torn shirt and press the fabric together to cover her chest, attempting to fasten the two buttons I hadn't managed to tear off, while leaning down and kissing the corners of her mouth.

"Thinking about stealing you all for myself," I whisper in her ear before I pull back.

She pushes herself to sit up as I draw her skirt down, drawing her knees together. "Is that even possible?"

Her question surprises me, and I slowly lust over the idea that she wants it as much as me. Except the real answer lies in her gaze. It's curiosity that has her asking, not the prospect of following through on such an act.

I shake my head. "I doubt Cain and Dorian would allow that while, by contract, all three of us own you." I kiss her bent knees, cursing myself for even bringing up such a notion. The moment carried me away to a delusional place where, for a sliver of a moment, I let myself believe I deserved any kind of happiness.

She pats her hair and readjusts her torn clothes to cover herself, and I take a seat next to her.

Before us stands a myriad of trees bursting with bottle green leaves, but amid them the lake in the distance glints through. Back in Hell, I never once desired to live on Earth. No one down there did. It's an abominable location for demons, but after the extended time we've endured here, the place has started to grow on me. Where before I'd seen only land wasted with growing trees and waters too pure to drink, now... there's a shred of beauty I recognize in the landscape. It took me a long time to reach this point, so I can only imagine the agony of being ripped out of here and thrown to the deplorable realm of Hell for an innocent.

We sit in silence for a long while, and there's reassurance settling in my limbs that she hasn't run from me yet.

"I always imagined demons as vile and ugly," she says, taking me by surprise. She hugs her bent knees and looks over at me with a raised eyebrow. "You three have surprised me. Though the jury is still out on exactly how dark your souls really are." She half chuckles, speaking before I get a chance. "You know what I think?"

"What's that?"

"Whether you're a demon, a witch, a human... every one of us has evil and good in us."

I study her for a moment. "If you met some of the monsters down in the darkest pits of Hell, you might change your mind on that."

She shrugs and glances out toward the lake. "Maybe I'm being way too introspective. I blame the amazing sex."

I laugh and blow on my curled fingers before rubbing them down my bare chest in a faux polish attempt. "I have that effect on women."

She rolls her eyes and nudges me. "Don't get a huge head. You still cheated at your game, remember?"

"I need to teach you how to correctly make deals with a demon."

"I'll hold you to that." She pauses, her brow pinching like it does every time she's thinking something. "So, with demons existing, there are angels up in Heaven, right?"

"Yeah."

"Do they ever come down to Earth?"

"Those arrogant pricks? The whole time I've been in your world, I have yet to hear one person talk about seeing an angel."

"But it's possible, right?" she insists.

"I guess. But doesn't mean they do. The queen of England could visit the north pole if she wished, but she never does."

She cuts me a sarcastic look, then pushes herself to stand. One hand is outstretched toward me, palm facing upward, and with her other hand she clutches the torn fabric across her chest. Her entire body trembles from the cold.

"Let's go get cleaned up. And you need clothes." I accept her offer and get up, then in a flash, I sweep her off her feet, an arm under her knees, the other at her back.

She releases a small, startled cry, her eyes wide with shock.

"Let me do the honors, seeing as your shoes are all soggy and you've lost your panties."

She punches me in the arm. "You tore them off! And though it might be hard to believe, I can walk without wearing underwear."

"Not if I'm near." I meet her gaze, and that earlier electricity sparks up between us once more.

Her face scrunches up, but it's all fake. I see it behind her eyes, smell the arousal in her scent. She wants me badly, and I tuck that little memory nugget away to hold onto as a beacon. Something to grasp onto when my mind refuses to forget the past and my world turns so dark, I can't see what's in front of me.

DORIAN

I do a double-take at the folded piece of paper on the small desk in my bedroom and pause in the doorway. I'd spent most of the day driving through town, talking to anyone I knew at Storm's markets, and even cruised in my car through the woods surrounding Glenside. Anything to find out where that fucking bastard, Sir Surchion, went. Not a single clue. The warehouse is burned down, and his hiding spot in the mountain is abandoned.

It's like the dragon just vanished, which would not surprise me. Except he took three of our relics, and I'm not taking that lying down. When I catch him, I'll rip his spine out with my bare hands.

Still, I stare back at the note. Who the hell has been in my room?

I grab the paper and unfold it. Instantly, I inhale the faint waft of sulfur and growl under my breath.

Of fucking course.

Fire burns through my veins as I stare at the few words written across it.

Who is Aria Cross?

Maverick. Demon of Greed. Of course it's him. Of course he's found out about her. Of course he's poking his nose where it doesn't belong.

A tornado of fury and dread twists within me, and I scrunch up the paper and toss it to the ground, seething that the prick has been watching us. But how the fuck does he know her full name when we only just discovered it ourselves?

I pace the room in long strides, going from my window to the fireplace and back. A nerve pulses in my temple that Maverick is paying her attention. His actions all stem from a cesspool of deceit, from Lucifer.

A finger traces the length of my spine at the thought,

a shiver gripping me. Not much scares me, but the devil is a fucking unpredictable psychopath. And if his sights are set on our Aria, we are in deeper shit than we ever suspected.

I jerk my head to the ball of scrunched up paper and grind my back teeth. Maverick's damn words burn through my mind.

Who is Aria Cross?

Fisting my hands, my knuckles turn white, and I swing around, my fist cracking against the wall. Pain punches back up my arm, but I don't give a shit.

Whatever Maverick is up to puts Aria in the line of danger. No matter how much he sugar-coats his unprompted visits to me, a wolf in sheep's clothing is still a wolf.

I march across the room, snatch the note from the floor, and storm out into the corridor. By the time I reach Cain's office, I'm trembling with rage. The scrunched-up paper feels heavy in my hand, like a burden growing heavier by the second.

Without knocking, I charge in, gaining myself a glare from Cain, who's sitting at his desk. He lowers the folder from his hand to the table.

I dump the note on the table in front of me. "We're in big shit."

Cain's eyes narrow at the ball of paper and then move back up to me. "If you're coming in here to dump your garbage, it goes in the fire."

"Just read the fucking note," I snarl, but impatience itches along my spine, so I flatten it out for him, slapping my hand down on the table. "Read."

Picking it up, he stares at it for longer than it needs to be read. It's four words that have put my mind into a tailspin.

"Did you read it?" I push.

"Who's it from?"

"You've already forgotten your brother's handwriting? It's Maverick. That asshole has turned his attention on Aria."

The paper trembles in Cain's hand, and he holds it so tight, his fingers tear through the page. He dumps the note on the desk and gets to his feet, his lips thinning, the corded muscles in his neck pulsing.

"She can't find out about this. I don't want to scare her, but we need to uncover what my brother wants from her." He meets my eyes. "If Maverick is following orders, it seems my father thinks you might be the weak link to get to me."

Weak link? I glare at Cain but bite my tongue. This has more to do with there being only two of us working with Cain, and everyone knows Elias is an unpredictable fuck. So who else are they going to try to go through to get intelligence? Not that I'd give anything away, but I know how to play the game.

"Hate to break it to you, but I get a feeling this note has nothing to do with you," I say with a chirpy cadence, which gains me a wry frown.

"Don't be too quick to dismiss their intentions." Cain huffs. "We need to keep a tighter watch over Aria. My decision to have her join me on my trip is sounding like a better idea by the second."

I stare at Cain as he marches out of his office before

I can remind him it was me who suggested he take Aria with him.

Half the time, I struggle to remember how I ended up expelled to Earth with him. But what surprises me more is that we haven't killed each other yet.

CHAPTER THIRTEEN
CAIN

*T*he Town Car stops in the middle of the private airstrip in front of the jet, and the driver gets out to open Aria's door. I don't wait for him to come around to my side. I climb out myself, needing the icy morning air to fill my lungs and clear my head. The entire journey here, Aria refused to talk to me. Refused to so much as glance my way, even when I tried plying her with questions. At first, her rejection annoyed and angered me, but soon, that turned to uneasiness.

I don't know why it bothered me so much, but after she ripped off the winged necklace I gave her, threw it at my feet, and told me to fuck off with glossy eyes, I couldn't help the hurt I felt and still feel now. In that moment, I realized I've become soft for her. We've always liked to play this back and forth game, but I've taken it a step too far this time and I don't know if she'll forgive me for using her this way.

Dorian would tell me I need to let go and open up

more, and maybe I do. The time Aria and I spent together in my office had been the most unchained I'd felt in a long time. I shouldn't be pushing her away by forcing her to go to Missouri with me. But what other choice do I have? We need her to find the relics. If she isn't going to go willingly...

I glance over the top of the car to where she stands on the other side, arms wrapped around herself in a long wool coat. Even shivering and wanting my death, she's still the most beautiful creature I've ever seen. Maybe I can find a way to salvage whatever is between us. I have an idea in mind, but I'm not sure how she'll take it. I'll just have to wait and see.

Her gaze flicks my way before she strides across the blacktop to the plane. I follow far enough behind to give her space, but not enough for her to try making a run for it. Of course, I hope she's learned by now that trying to escape is a wasted effort, but one can never be too cautious.

After climbing the steps, we enter the plane's cabin. It's a thing of luxury with white leather seats, plush carpets, and dark wood accents. I've travelled this way numerous times, but Aria's gasp is loud, her amazement and excitement infectious. I smile as she takes in the spoils having that having money grants us, spinning in circles and running her fingers over the interior in awe.

"Do you like it?" The question slips from me without thought.

Silence answers, and really, I don't expect her to respond after the stiffly quiet car ride here. Why should

I? She's obviously perfected the art of giving the silent treatment.

Instead, I sigh and take one of the oversized chairs by the window. My temples throb with a budding headache. I don't know how I'm going to survive this trip with her—let alone get her to help me find the spine—if she won't even look at me for more than two seconds.

The cabin door closes with a loud whooshing sound and seals shut, and Aria looks around, suddenly paler than before. Moving slowly, she reaches for a chair on the opposite side of the plane and sits down. Her trembling hands don't go unnoticed.

She's afraid. Deathly afraid, I realize. Her throat works to swallow over and over, and she presses her head into the cushions with her eyes squeezed shut.

The engine rumbles to life, shaking the floor under our feet, and she grips the armrests so tight, she might puncture the leather. We haven't even taken off yet, but she looks like she's about to pass out any moment from lack of oxygen. Or worse, vomit.

"Are you okay?" I whisper her way, even though I already know the answer.

"Never flown before," she manages to squeeze past her clamped lips.

I should have known better. Aria lived in poverty and foster care all of her life. She wouldn't have boarded a plane before. Possibly never seen one, besides ones that flew overhead. This is an entirely new experience for her.

The plane starts to glide backward, and her entire body stiffens.

"Is-Is it happening now?" she squeaks in panic. "Are we taking off?"

A short laugh escapes. "No. The pilot is only getting us ready to depart. We're taxiing onto the runway."

"It's not funny," she snaps back. She's still too scared to open her eyes.

As amusing as this may be, I do feel a bit bad for her. Even though I'm no stranger to flying, it took me some time to trust these metal wings over my own demon ones. I can understand where the fear comes from.

I stand up, walk over to her side, and take the seat directly across from her. She peeks one eye open to see me now facing her and grimaces. "I prefer to suffer alone, thank you very much."

Leaning over, I grasp her arms and yank her out of her seat. Being in a private jet, the stewardesses will overlook the lack of seatbelts. She half-cries out before landing, knees spread, in my lap. Her eyes snap fully open, and she stares at me for a long moment, mouth agape.

I glance down to see that under her heavy coat, she's wearing another low-cut shirt and skirt ensemble, similar to the tempting little number I'd found her in yesterday on the staircase. Only this time, she knows work is off the table, so is her outfit choice simply to test me?

Because it sure is working.

To make things even more tantalizing, her breasts are just inches from my face, begging me to bury my face in between them. Taste them. My mind conjures the most delicious images of us sitting like this, naked, her bouncing up and down on my cock as she rides us both into the mile-high club. My grip on her arms strengthens as my thoughts run away with me.

Her gaze narrows, but under the facade, I can see her own deep-seated arousal. I'm sure her thoughts have followed mine.

"What are you doing?" she asks. Even her tone, low and breathy, is tinged with desire. The sound of it sends electric pulses straight to my groin.

I don't answer, because in all honesty, I really don't know what I'm doing. My intention had been to try and comfort her, but things quickly took a left turn. Whenever I'm close to her, all my common sense seems to fly out the fucking window.

"Cain," she says a bit more forcefully, but right then, the engine roars and the entire plane shakes. She yelps and wraps her body around mine—arms around my head, chest pressed against me, face buried in my neck. Every muscle in me tenses at her closeness, and for a moment, I'm unsure what to do.

Hesitantly, I slide my hands up her back and press her closer as she trembles. I can't help but think how perfectly she seems to fit like this in my arms, how good she feels. I inhale the sweet scent of her as she clutches me, my head whirling with her and only her—my Aria. And when the plane lifts into the air, she squeezes me deathly tight as if she's clinging on for dear life.

"It's alright," I mutter gently near her ear. "I have you."

The smallest whimper is her only reply.

We hold each other like that as the jet ascends higher and higher. Soon her shaking stops, but she doesn't move from my embrace. Nor does she say a word. Time passes, and the *ding, ding* of the pilot's radio sounds from the speakers.

"It's safe to walk about the cabin now," he announces. "The weather is clear. Minimal cloud coverage, and wind speeds are normal. We should arrive at our destination in just under three hours."

The *ding, ding* chimes again to signal the end of the radio transmission, and only then does Aria lift her head to look at me again. This time, her cheeks are kissed with pink from embarrassment, and she rubs her glossy lips together.

"Sorry about that," she whispers as she starts to climb off me and takes her seat across from me again. The second her warmth of her body is gone, I frown.

"Nothing to be sorry about," I say. "Take-off and landing are always the most troubling parts. Especially if you've never flown before." And sudden turbulence, but hopefully we won't experience any of that on this trip.

She nods and leans back in the chair, her spine still uncomfortably straight and rigid.

"How are you feeling now?" I ask, knowing I still need to tread lightly with her.

She says on a long exhale, "I think I'm okay... For now, at least."

"Good."

Her gaze drops to her lap, and another tense silence

stretches between us, reminding me of our dreadful car ride. I'm not sure I can endure another three hours of tense nothingness like that.

Ask her something. Something about her.

Glancing around the plane, I scramble for something else to say to keep the conversation going. But the only thing that comes out of my mouth is, "How are you doing?"

She looks up, brows pinched in confusion, and I want to punch myself for my stupidity.

"You just asked that..." she says, still eyeing me.

I rub a hand over my face. "Yes, well, I meant in regards to things in general. With your shadow and what happened with Sir Surchion."

I grind my teeth and wave for one of the attendants to come over with a drink. I need it. But as obvious as my blunder was, Aria doesn't seem to notice.

"Oh." Hesitating, she licks her lips. "I have nightmares still, mostly about falling into darkness... but I'm sure those will go away. They usually do." She trails off, but her words aren't lost on me. She's used to traumatic things happening to her. She's lived a hard life—that's obvious—but like always, she's come out of it on the other side. She's survived. She doesn't dwell on it, and that takes a great deal of strength.

"I haven't let Sayah out—willingly—in a while," she continues, her gaze focused on something beyond me, glazed over by her own thoughts. "After what happened in the warehouse, I've... I've been afraid to."

"Sayah?"

"That's the name I gave her, my shadow, when I was

younger. We've always been like friends. Helping each other. At least, until recently..."

The stewardess comes over pushing a cart. She hands me my whiskey and asks Aria if she wants anything. She politely turns the offer away.

Once we're alone again, I say, "Because she's been escaping on her own." I take a quick sip of the whiskey and instantly relax at the familiar, silky fire that races down my throat.

Aria nods, and her lips twist into a frown. "I used to be able to control her. She's always listened to me. I don't know if I've lost control of her, if she's gotten stronger, or if I never had control over her in the first place."

I can see where her fear comes from. This shadow creature does appear to be living inside her. Living through her. To find out she has no control over it...

Aria lifts her hands and stares at her palms. "When she manifested in the warehouse, my body started to glow, and it felt like I was covered in pins and needles, like when your foot goes to sleep."

She glances at me to see if I can relate, which I can't, but I have an idea of what she means so I wave for her to go on.

"She was draining me and getting more and more solid. I don't know how else to explain it, but I got so weak. Then I blacked out."

"That's when we came in," I say. "We saw you fall. Unconscious."

"I'm terrified it'll happen again," she confesses. "I'd rather not let her out if I can help it."

"What happens if she slips free? Like before... in my office." *When we were wrapped in each other and riding the high of our orgasms.*

As the need rekindles within me to relive that moment, I take another sip of my whiskey, hoping to quash the fire. When it comes to this girl, I'm not sure anything will ever truly be enough.

She glances down again, color hitting her cheeks. She knows exactly what I'm referring to. I don't know why, but her moments of innocence like this make me want to grab her, crush my body against hers, and kiss her shyness away. Draw that ravenous hunger that I know she's capable of back out.

Heat prickles across my skin, and I'm suddenly uncomfortably hot under my jacket. Shifting in my chair, I drain the rest of my whiskey in one final gulp and place the empty glass on the table beside me.

Her gaze drifts out the small window where crystal blue skies and white clouds race by. "She's never been able to leave my body without my command. Whatever's happening, I don't see how it's good," she says.

I have to agree.

"We'll figure it out," I tell her. It's something I've promised her before, and it's a promise I'm willing to keep. I'm not exactly sure how, but I'll find a way.

She sighs, still not looking at me. Her shoulders slump as her worry takes hold. "I don't see how. I've been searching for any clues to who I am for years..."

My heart clenches knowing this is affecting her so. I hate seeing her full of turmoil over something she can't control.

Before I realize what I'm doing, I lean forward, reach out, and rest my hand on her bare knee. Her gaze snaps my way, her entire body stiffening from my touch.

Shit. I've made a mistake. I pull away, instantly regretting my poor attempt to comfort her.

Why am I so terrible at this? To claim her on my office desk comes with no doubt, but the idea of bringing her ease when she's distressed has me blanking.

If Dorian were here, he'd be laughing at how much I'm struggling. I've never tried to form a deeper relationship with another person before. Especially a woman. Sex and souls were all that mattered once we were cast to Earth, and I've gotten both in abundance and without challenge. There was never a need for anything else.

But with Aria, I want more. I have her soul. Our sexual chemistry is hotter than an inferno, but I'm still unsatisfied.

I want all of her.

A small smile flickers across her lips. "It's okay, you can leave your hand there," she whispers, and then adds, "your touch is just so warm."

"It's the hellfire," I reply, glancing at my hands and settling my hand back on her thigh. "It runs through my veins."

"Is it like that for all demons?" she asks. "Dorian and Elias, too?"

I nod. "Yes, but more so for me, since I am an original sin demon and…"

"The son of Lucifer," she finishes for me, carrying no judgement in her tone.

I clench my jaw. Even though it's true, I still despise hearing it out loud. It's a part of myself I wish never existed.

"Sorry, I know you guys aren't really on the best of terms," she says.

"That's an extreme understatement."

"I just can't see Lucifer, ruler of the underworld, as daddy dearest with seven kids…"

I gesture to the stewardess for another whiskey. "That's because he wasn't. And we also were never children."

Mouth agape, she waits for me to continue, but I wait for my drink and take another mouthful when it arrives. It slides down my throat, but it's strong enough to settle my unease.

"I never had a mother, like other souls do," I decide to start with. Our lineage is a complicated one, so simplifying it for Aria will be a challenge.

"No mom? But how were you born?" she asks. A legitimate question, considering.

"We… weren't."

Her brows pinch as her confusion grows. I continue. "I don't know what Lucifer's reasons were for creating us. Maybe to help expand his kingdom and have someone to watch over all seven levels of Hell for him. There's no way to know for sure, but my father created us by splitting his own soul into seven pieces. He ripped us one by one out of his own most sinful attributes."

"Pride, Greed, Lust, Sloth, Wrath…" She struggles to remember the others.

"Gluttony and Envy. Yes," I begin. The next part I hate to admit. "We are pieces of him."

"But you aren't like him," she says quickly.

I run a thumb along the rim of my glass, my attention drifting past her to the back of the jet. "I wouldn't be so sure."

I know what she's trying to do. She's trying to make me feel better, but she doesn't understand the workings of Hell. Or how dangerous Lucifer really is. She can't even fathom the power he possesses. There's a reason God threw him out of Heaven and imprisoned him down below. But Lucifer then turned around and made Hell his kingdom instead.

Remembering the letter Maverick sent to Dorian, my gut twists with anger and worry. If my brother knows about Aria, there is no doubt in my mind my father does, too. And if he discovers the power she holds, he'll either see her as a threat and kill her, or worse—take her for himself. Demon contracts mean shit to the Lord of demons. She isn't safe.

I don't want to scare her, of course, but Lucifer's ruthlessness and drive to get what he wants knows no bounds. He'll do whatever it takes, destroy whoever he has to, and I suspect it won't be long before his prison of Hell won't be strong enough to hold him anymore. If he manages to escape, then we are *all* doomed.

"I don't believe it," she says, but I catch the hitch in her voice that reveals her uncertainty. "I don't."

"Then you're hopelessly naive." I lift my glass to my lips again. I've tried for so long to separate myself from my father, to be my own man, but it won't change the truth of my creation. As much as I despise it, Lucifer will always be a part of me. "I am Lucifer's greatest sin made flesh."

"Yeah, but you're not vicious. Or cruel. A royal pain in my ass sometimes, but not totally heartless."

"I very much am all those things."

"Not with me."

I pause. Her words shock me, taking a moment to fully sink in. "You have no idea what I'm fully capable of."

Being on Earth has definitely changed me and shifted my views of the living, but Aria has softened me in other ways. There's no denying it. I tell myself I've kept her alive this long because of her mysterious gifts, but that's not true, now is it? Deep down, I know it isn't. I've let her stay around because I wanted her to. Because I wanted *her*. Plain and simple.

I've known it all along but didn't want to admit it. It's just like with this trip. I told Dorian it was to find the spine, but the idea of being alone again with Aria was just too tempting.

She's my weakness. I can see that now. Which makes me vulnerable.

And that's one thing my father could never say. He never felt a thing for anyone else besides himself in all of his existence. Not for any of his mistresses, not for any of his subjects or his children. He never loved a soul.

I look up at Aria, who's sitting quietly across from me with big, dark eyes full of concern and a small, hopeful smile. My chest instantly warms. It's such a strange and unfamiliar feeling, that my lips curl up on their own.

Maybe she's right, and I'm not an exact replica of Lucifer like I've always feared.

Because there's something I've realized I have that he never will.

CHAPTER FOURTEEN
CAIN

"Where specifically are we going?" Aria asks while staring out of the window of the pearl white Jaguar. The moment Aria and I landed, I hired a car that would make Dorian jealous. It roars each time I shift gears, and we glide down the road.

Now we're heading as far from the city as possible. Woodlands flank both sides of the road. We left the freeway thirty minutes ago, and with fewer cars on the road, Aria's curiosity piques. She's been asking me where we're going since we left the airport.

"It's a surprise," I answer and glance over, expecting her to meet my gaze. She doesn't disappoint, and I can't help grinning at her. Her eyes widen with expectation that I'll tell her everything.

"I love surprises. Tell me more."

It's tempting to drag this out, to tease her until she begs me, given how much fun I can have. Those are the times to make deals with people, as they are most likely to agree to anything. I've always been curious about humans' inquisitiveness and the trouble it gets them into.

But as I veer left and turn down a dirt road, the liberty of time has vanished for such luxuries. "You'll find out soon enough," I assure her, which sends her back to staring outside the window at the wild forest with overgrown shrubs and lofty pines.

"Give me a clue," she insists.

"I think you are going to really like it."

She glowers at me over her shoulder. "That is not a clue."

"And I never agreed to feed your curiosity. We're almost there."

She stiffens. "See, now that's a clue." She swivels in her seat to face me. "Could be a number of things. Nod if I get it, okay?"

I don't respond, but she continues. "A picnic? We're staying in a cabin in the woods? There's an exclusive, fancy hotel out here? A zoo?" She huffs when I remain silent. "Am I getting close?"

Smirking, I can't help but admire her tenacity. I pull the Jaguar off the dirt road and kill the engine. "We're here," I say in a victorious voice, which I know will only push her to ask more questions. Something about her eagerness has me smiling.

My little Aria straightens, chewing on her lower lip, staring at me, then outside into the woods. All I can see around us are trees, though it's getting darker outside. "There's nothing here. I can't believe you brought me to the middle of nowhere."

"You need to learn patience."

She rolls her eyes as she swings open her door. "Yeah, yeah."

"Here, take this," I say before she gets out, grabbing a flashlight.

She purses her lips, staring at it. "What's that for? Are we hiking? Is that what this is all about?"

I can't help but laugh as we both climb out of the car.

By the time she shuts her door, I've strolled ahead to where the dense trees thin out. The dirt track ahead has long been overtaken by the forest. I trample through overgrown grasses, and all the while Aria fiddles with the flashlight, not looking where she's going. She bumps into me, then lifts her head.

Except it's not me she sees. Her gaze swings to the clearing in the trees before us, at the building I brought her to, suffocated by woods. But it's still intact.

Her mouth drops open. "Holy shit!"

ARIA

I stare at the enormous, dilapidated hospital. Four floors of gray walls stained by years of running water and dirt. Metal bars cover the windows, some of which are shattered. From inside the building, there is nothing but darkness. The only saving grace about us going inside there is that the sun hasn't fully gone down yet.

"You don't like your surprise?" Cain asks me. When I glance over, he's waiting expectantly, and I blink back, unsure at first how to react. His idea of a surprise is bringing me to the hospital I was born at? Yeah, it's great, but when he said he had a surprise for me, I was envisioning going to a movie, or driving to a cliff to overlook the sunset, and maybe chocolates. Definitely chocolates. Not visiting the Amityville house.

"It's… different. And probably has ghosts."

I finger the flashlight he gave me. I am convinced I need more than one measly light to enter the place that belongs in a horror movie. And to think—this is where I was born, yet it freaks me out.

"We'll be lucky if ghosts are all we find in there," Cain answers. It's like he's trying to reassure me, but he does a terrible job.

"Can you sense anything in there with your demon feelers?"

He looks over at me with an arching brow. "'Demon feelers'? What are those?"

"Your spidey senses, you know. Since you're from Hell, can you sense other creatures from the underworld? Better we don't walk in with any surprises."

I chew on a hangnail. I watched way too many horror movies growing up, and now my imagination is on overdrive. You'd think with the shadow living inside me and dealing with demons, I'd be impervious to a scary building.

You'd be wrong. I am shaking like a leaf because I hate the idea of anything jumping out at me in the dark.

Cain's hand slips into mine, our fingers interlacing, his warmth spreading over me. "You don't have to fear anything while you're with me. I thought after I caught you researching this place, you might want to come and see it personally. Never know what we might still find."

"That's actually a really nice gesture. Thank you." It's also a tiny bit creepy, but the good factor of his deed far outweighs the scary factor. I won't deny, there is a reassurance in having a demon of sin in your corner. But does that also make him a target for benevolent spirits?

Taking a deep inhale, I follow his lead as he steps over wild grass and approaches a small gap in the wire fence surrounding the closed-down hospital.

As Cain pulls the looped wire aside so I can step into the grounds, I ask, "We're trespassing, aren't we?"

"As long as we don't get caught, we are fine. I will get us inside," Cain says as he slides in after me. "Then I can let you know if I pick up anything with my *demon feelers*." He smirks, and I can't help but laugh.

"I see what you did there, and I'm super impressed you tried to make a joke."

"Tried?"

I shrug. "Well, it could use some work. You're a bit stiff."

His mouth drops open in a sarcastic response, and there is something refreshing about having Cain lower his guard. I can tell he's trying to be more approachable and less bossy, which I appreciate. Maybe Dorian said something to him about his demeanor? Whatever the answer, I don't care as long as I'm dealing with Mr. Flirty here and not Mr. Control Freak.

Once we reach the front entry, we climb up the

three steps to the two metal doors. They're barred with a thick chain and lock threaded through the handles.

"Stand back," Cain commands, placing his hands on the metal chain. In moments, the thread of black veins wriggle under the skin of his hands.

The once gray metal now morphs into colors of oranges and reds. From my spot, I feel the radiating heat he's generating. With his mere touch, the metal starts melting, falling in globs to the ground until the lock falls to the ground with a clang. The hellfire again.

Cain pushes the doors open, which groan in protest like their hinges have forgotten how to work.

I lean forward, peering into the gaping mouth of darkness waiting for us. I swallow hard and follow Cain, stepping over the threshold to enter the hospital.

Grabbing my flashlight, I flick it on and sweep the beam of light over a very old and sad waiting room. There are no seats, only a counter with a large crack in the middle, like the earth has shifted underneath. Dust and cobwebs cover everything, and dried leaves that must have blown in through the shattered windows cluster in the corners.

Cain doesn't have a flashlight, but it doesn't stop him from strolling straight ahead toward the double doors that head deeper into the hospital. He pushes one of the swinging doors open and waves for me to hurry up.

Shivers creep over the back of my legs as I stride closer and enter a pitch-black corridor. I bounce my light across the shut doors on either side of us.

"Where to now?" I ask.

The door shuts behind us with a swish, and I jump

in my skin. My heart is pounding in my chest. I hate this feeling.

"The doctors' offices were located on the second floor," he informs me.

"How do you know so much?"

He taps the side of his temple with two fingers, and I roll my eyes at him. "You checked out the old schematics of the place, didn't you?"

Half laughing to himself, he murmurs, "Smart girl."

I nod—even though Cain isn't looking my way—and run to catch up to him, sticking to him like glue. Our footsteps echo around us. If the movies are right, doors will be opening and shutting on their own. Shadows moving. Abandoned wheelchairs creaking forward.

Oh god, I am already hating this surprise. My skin crawls, and I press myself closer to Cain's side.

I hear his quickening breath, which has nothing to do with fear, but he better get his mind out of the gutter. Right now I'm so tightly wound I feel like I'm going to snap like an elastic band.

"This way," Cain says, pointing to the faint green glow of an exit light. Once inside, we find the stairwell, and we hurry up the flight. I'm huffing already and can't stop looking over my shoulder at the darkness chasing after us.

On the second floor, a few of the doors sit open, allowing a stream of minimal light to pour into the corridor. I scan the hall we enter, left and right, the walls, the doors, checking everything and everywhere for ghosts. Right now, all I find are way too many spiderwebs, and I feel itchy just thinking of walking into a web.

"Aria," Cain calls.

I swing back around toward him and rush right into something in my path. Oh shit, is that a wheelchair?

Panic slams into me, and I'm stumbling forward, losing my footing before I know it.

Fear catapults through me. I hit the ground, the flashlight is thrown from my hand, and a horrendous terror sweeps over me that something has caught me. I'm plunged into darkness, and in a flash, my instinct has me screaming like a banshee with fear.

Scrambling to my feet, that moment of utter chaos and dread consumes me. In my mind, I'm in a horror movie and Freddie Kruger is coming down the hall for me, his long nails scratching across the walls.

I shudder and run, only to bump into someone. I scream louder.

"Calm down, it's only me," Cain coos, gripping my shoulders. "You tripped over a chair."

"Cain," I murmur and press myself against him, burying my face into his chest. My breaths still race as he holds me, rubbing my back. He's so warm, and in his presence I feel nothing but protected.

"You are safe. Nothing is going to harm you while I'm with you."

Gradually, my breaths slow, and the earlier panic dissolves. When I glance up to look at Cain, I suddenly feel stupid at how quickly I spiraled out of control. My cheeks flush.

"I'm sorry," I whisper. "I got myself all worked up, and then I freaked out once I fell."

He cups my face and leans in to kiss me, a soft, quick kiss that comes with comfort and reassurance. I raise myself on tippy toes to reach him easier, to stay attached to him. Right now, I want nothing more than to crawl into his arms and forget about this stupid hospital and how dumb I reacted.

"I never realized you were so afraid of the dark," he says against my lips, still holding onto me, his fingers digging into my back.

I half laugh and shrug. "It's more creepy places like this that freak me out. I watched too many horror movies growing up."

He pushes a loose lock of hair out of my eyes and behind an ear. "Ninety-nine percent of the time, they leave you alone if you don't go out of your way to contact them. Those movies you watched are all exaggerated for shock value."

"Yeah, try telling that to my panicked side while in a scary hospital."

He straightens, his arms falling away from me, and a coldness takes their place. "It was a mistake bringing you here. I never wanted to terrify you. Maybe we should leave and go somewhere nicer. How does that sound?"

My chest clenches. Cain went out of his way to do something nice for me, and I'll feel like the world's worst person if I don't at least spend some time here.

I reach over and take his hand in mine. "We're here

and on the second floor with the offices. Let's at least look around."

It's too late to back out, especially once I see the disappointment vanish from Cain's expression. I'm a big girl. I've faced a damn dragon. What are a few cobwebs and dark corners? I refuse to let that earlier darkness swell inside me again.

I turn on the spot, studying the fallen wooden chair I'd tripped over. The hallway remains covered in shadows, but nothing is coming out for me.

"Aria?"

Sucking in a deep breath, I point to the nearest office door. "Let's start there."

Cain smirks, and he doesn't have to say it, but I feel a sense of pride emanating from him. That only fuels the extra kick in my step, and I wander down the hall, braver than I had been minutes earlier.

I push the door with a hand, and it creaks open.

An explosion of dim light pours in from outside, showing a room with a desk on its side, no chairs, and the filing cabinets all open. Papers and folders litter the floor.

"Looks like someone else has already been here," Cain says over my shoulder.

"Guess I might not be the only person wanting answers about this hospital." I step inside, the crunch of paper filling the silence, and I pick up several documents from the floor. Flicking over the dusty pages, they all show a patient name on top, the date, and a number of signatures in squares underneath. It looks like a health chart located at the end of the bed for patients in hospital. The more I search, the more inclined I am to believe this place has been used by squatters who had fun pulling out these useless records.

The next few offices we check are in similar states, but then Cain makes a surprised sound from the room across the hall.

Curious, I hurry out and join him. He's leaning a shoulder into the wall near the window, using the last threads of sunlight to read the bundle of papers in his hand. I raise my flashlight and head over to him.

"What'd you find?"

His gaze meets mine, and by the tightness around his eyes, I can instantly tell it's about me. I accept the top sheet from his pile, which I hold the light over.

The top reads 'Abandoned Children' in thick, bold print. Beneath the heading is a list of handwritten names that cover half the page.

The notion of what I'll find flames over me like a blazing fire, and I frantically scan the page until on the right-hand side, I find my name in cursive writing.

Aria Cross

Unease grips me, squeezing as the words on the page swirl on my mind.

"Why does this say I was abandoned?" My pulse races, beating with a thunderous beat.

Thoughts crash through me, but nothing is making sense. "The invoice I found from Murray means I was born here, right? So…" My mouth dries at the prospect of what this paper insinuates. "My mother abandoned me after she gave birth to me?"

My knees threaten to buckle as a horrible sensation

bleeds through me. One where my mother didn't want me, where she gave me up.

"Aria, you don't know that. There are so many reasons."

As flames swallow me, I jut my chin up to face him. "Like what? She died in childbirth? And my father had abandoned her. Or me. Whichever way you look at it, my family didn't want me."

Cain reaches for me, but I brush his hand away and head out of the room, my insides splintering. Tears don't come, though—I'm way past that. I cried too many times growing up, wishing I had parents, though part of me always imagined there was a special reason they couldn't be with me. But years ago, I told myself they were dead so I could finally move on and not hold onto empty hope.

The paper shakes in my hand.

Strong hands grasp my waist, and Cain draws me back against him, his arms holding me tightly.

"Nothing changes about how special you are to me, to Dorian, and to Elias."

I inhale, each breath shuddering all the way down to my lungs, and I grasp onto his arms, holding onto him like I can no longer stand on my own feet.

"I've got you, Aria. You will never be alone ever again."

Those few words break me. Tears spill down my cheeks, and I cry for all the things I never got to experience in life. For the times when I was so young and fantasized that my parents would come back to me. For when I prayed so hard that they didn't abandon me. For the years I held onto a thread of possibility…

But now I knew the awful truth. And they might as well be dead.

My family is never going to come looking for me. Because they never wanted me.

Sobs shudder through me.

Cain holds me against him, the back of his hand caressing my cheek, stealing the tears away. His tenderness surprises me. My heart flutters in the way he makes me feel both adored and wanted.

I don't know how long he holds me, but for a while, I enjoy melting against him. I'd always laughed in romance movies when the female loved being snuggled, how they made a big deal about it. As far as I was concerned, it was overrated.

Except I think I made a mistake. To have someone so powerful look out for me is the most empowering and exhilarating sensation. Strong arms wrapped around me like a security blanket, as stupid as it sounds, are everything to me in this moment.

I shuffle and turn in Cain's arms to face him, his hands lowering on my back, ensuring I stay close to him.

"Why are you so beautiful when you cry?"

I scrunch my nose, blinking at him. "I'm a mess. That's the opposite of beautiful."

"You're wrong. It's the first time I've seen your real emotions. There's no bravado or joking around, you are just being the real you. And it's stunning."

He leans in and kisses a loose tear that runs down my cheek.

Under his embrace, his reverence, his admiration, it's easy to lose myself. He makes me believe his words, that maybe I'm so much more than the girl rejected by her parents.

His fingers gently trace the curve of my neck, then run over my collarbone. The hairs on my nape shift. He ignites desire in me with a simple touch.

Before we make a move to leave, his mouth is on mine. He pulls me even closer, drawing me with him as he walks backward. In a swift move, he swings us around, and I gasp.

Suddenly we're kissing again, our bodies crushing together, the wall at my back holding me up. His passion, his roaming hands over my ass, send delicious shivers over my body. Everything about him is all-consuming, and he leaves me breathless.

He abruptly breaks our kiss, pulling back, his chest rising and falling with each rapid inhale. "Tell me to stop, Aria, before I rip your clothes off and claim you right here."

I try to respond and tell him we should leave, but only a whimper spills past my lips as his fingers graze over my breasts, finding my erect nipples. Any attempt at protest dissolves.

Flames burn behind his eyes, and my body betrays me as I run my hands down his chiseled chest.

He's kissing me again, our tongues battling, and I marvel at how easily he wins me over. My knees go weak, but I remind myself we're in a creepy hospital. And right now, we're going down the path seen in all horror movies... making out big time in the spooky building.

"Let's not do it here," I murmur against his lips, my voice soft. I'm struggling to find more words when my body pulses with arousal.

Cain moves his mouth to the corner of my lips, across my cheek, then pulls back. Jolts of molten pleasure flood my body, and I cling onto his shirt, fisting it.

"You're right," he answers, and even though I asked him to stop, a sense of disappointment settles in my chest. His brow rests against mine, and he smiles. "You're a temptation I struggle to resist."

I don't remember anyone making me feel this way before I met these demons. "Around you, I forget myself," I admit.

He laughs and grabs my waist, holding me close to him. A quick kiss, and he draws away. "We have a few more hours to kill before our next plane, and Dorian told me about an amazing diner nearby that makes the best apple pie."

His drastic change of topic tells me that pulling away is a struggle for him. Granted, I barely have any self-control around the demons either, but I still bathe in the notion that I make him lose control.

"I'd love pie." The idea of stuffing my face with food —along with a distraction to keep myself in check— sounds heavenly. Though it occurs to me then that another reason Cain kissed me so passionately may have had a lot to do with distracting me from my earlier tears.

Well, his plan worked wonders. And now I just want to leave this hospital.

"Shall we?" he asks.

"Yes please."

His arm around my back tightens as he brings me in closer to his side, and the only thing I can think about is how, suddenly, things between Cain and I feel a lot more complicated.

CHAPTER FIFTEEN
ELIAS

"Do you see this?" I growl, shaking a torn pair of sweats in Dorian's face as he lounges sideways on a chair in the library, book in hand. Unlike Cain, he's not much of a reader, but his selection today is all about dragons and their lore, something to help us track down Sir Surchion while Cain and Aria are away tracking down the spine. "That fucking lynx has torn up another pair of my pants!"

Dorian snorts a laugh without looking up. "The animal is marking his territory, it seems."

"*His* territory?" I fume. "I'm the alpha in this house."

"Not anymore."

I throw the shredded pants on the ground. It's the third pair I've lost since the little furball moved in. Finding clothes for me is difficult enough with my height and size.

Dorian slams the book shut and tosses it on the coffee table. "Elias, I'm surprised at you. Intimidated by a little pussy."

"Fuck off." There's no way I'm going to let a *kitten* challenge me in my own territory. "If it wasn't Aria's pet—"

"And if you didn't care about her," Dorian interjects.

I clench my jaw. He's an expert button pusher, and the sly smirk on his face proves he's proud of the fact he's got me pinned. I want to knock that cocky smile right off his face. Working with him to find Sir Surchion without Cain to buffer is going to be a one hell of a challenge. We always butt heads. Mostly because Dorian doesn't know how to keep his fucking mouth shut.

"Oh, come on now," he goes on, swinging his legs to the floor and grasping the arms of the chair. "There's no need to lie about it. You've had sex with the girl. It's no secret. At least to me."

Usually, I wouldn't care if Dorian commented on my recent conquests. Sensing sexual energy was his "thing," or whatever, but for some reason, knowing that he knows about what me and Aria shared makes me tense.

Denying it is pointless, though, so I pull my shoulders back and decide to face his nonsense head on.

"Sex and caring are two very different things," I say through a stiff jaw.

"Yes, I suppose you could say that. But why else would you not roast the lynx over an open fire and serve it for dinner?"

Taken aback by the truth of it all, I only stare at him, blinking.

"Ah, there it is," he says. "You *do* care. Even if it's just a little."

How does he do that? He knows how to entrap people with mere words. He gets me every fucking time!

He suddenly lets out a long, defeated sigh, his gaze drifting to the shelves surrounding us. All the mirth leaves his eyes, and instead, there's a weighted concern there. "There's nothing to be ashamed of. We're all feeling it. Somehow, the girl has put us all under her spell. Even I'm finding myself caring more than an incubus should. Feelings are starting to mingle with sex. I never thought I was capable of such a thing."

I study his expression for a long moment, wondering if he's still screwing with me. But when his mouth tugs down in a frown and his joking demeanor doesn't return, I realize quickly that he's not. He's doing quite the opposite, actually. He's confiding in me. Something I never thought I'd see.

Then, his head swings my way, and he says, "I know you're still hurt by Serena."

The sound of that traitor's name lights a fire, and fury engulfs me. "Don't say her fucking name."

He holds up his hands in surrender and stands. "Look, I get it. She fucked us all. I know that. But you loved her. You can't deny it. You were willing to give up everything for her, and she used you and tricked us all. We're all guilty in some way."

A growl rumbles in my throat. I've been trying for nearly a century to push that bitch out of my mind, but her betrayal still stings. The moment Lucifer revealed she'd been working for him all along, listening to our plans to overthrow him and using the information to help him keep one step ahead of us… If I ever see her again, I'll… I'll…

"I know you don't want to get your heart involved again," Dorian says, interrupting my vengeful thoughts, "and I don't blame you. It's messy shit. But hear me out here. What I'm proposing is for… fun, more or less."

"Out with it, Dorian."

"To prevent us all from turning into Cain's green-eyed brother, Lorcan, and competing with each other, let's simply play nice and share. If Aria's on board, of course," he explains. Still unsure where he's going with this, I wait for him to go on. He does. "We're going to be spending a lot of time together searching for the relics to get back into Hell, and instead of fighting each other, let's all just enjoy what Earth has to offer instead. That's what I've been saying all along, isn't it? Why wallow and squabble? Where's the fun in that?"

I think about what he's proposing. Aria can be with whoever she wants—no strings, no commitments, no jealousy or rivalry—and we just enjoy the ride. Sounds picture-perfect in theory, but sharing a mate with another man, let alone two, goes against all my baser instincts. I don't know about incubuses or the original seven demons, but shifters, specifically hellhounds, choose one mate for eternity. It's near impossible not to see any other male as competition or a threat.

But then again, this isn't for a life-long commitment, as Dorian says. This is just fucking around. Aria obviously wants us all, so why not take advantage of our contract with her and let loose? Like we used to in Hell. Before Serena mucked things up for us.

Remembering Cain and how possessive he was over Aria when he saw me through the window as he was fucking her in his office, the notion of this working out quickly deflates. We need all of us to be on board.

"Cain's not going to like this," I reply with a shake of my head. "He'll never agree."

Dorian's smirk returns. "I wouldn't be so sure about that."

"What?"

"Cain and I used to share many a girl back in the good ol' days. Sometimes at the same time, if you know what I mean."

There's no way. Cain? Mr. As-Much-Charisma-as-a-Walking-Statue, Cain? I don't believe it. I *can't* believe it.

"You're shitting me."

"Oh no. Scout's honor." Grin widening, he holds up three fingers like he's pledging something. "It was before you joined our little group, of course. Cain was quite wild."

I can't even imagine Cain as anything other than tight-lipped and proper, the model of what a person would expect Pride incarnate to be.

"I'll believe it when I see it," I say and huff a laugh.

Dorian joins in, his head tilting back as laughter bounces through him. "You leave it to me. I'll talk to him."

And we all know Dorian has a gift with words. If he were alive, he could be a lawyer... or a used car salesman.

The merriment stops abruptly, and Dorian becomes deathly quiet. With his face turned toward the high ceilings, he squints as if seeing something above us, and his spine straightens.

"What? What is it?" I know an alert pose when I see one. Like when in the woods and a sudden sharp sound captures your attention.

My gaze snaps up, and I see it, too—a smear of black across the skylight's frosted window. My hackles rise. The hellhound within me snarls as the inky spot moves, growing larger as it spreads what looks like wings...

Wings.

Dorian and I look at each other at the same time, knowing exactly what is spying on us.

"Crow!" we say in unison.

Startled, it squawks and almost slips off the roof. Its talons scrape across the glass, unable to grab on. Frantic, it flaps its wings and swoops lower, appearing in another skylight a second later before picking up a gust of air under its wings and rising out of sight.

Shit!

"Follow that bird!" Dorian commands, as if reading my mind.

Immediately, we're both off and running for the back doors of the house, tearing off clothes and changing into our demons mid-stride. As my hound, I burst into the frigid, early afternoon air and throw my nose into the wind. On the breeze, the scent of bird mixed with sea salt and gasoline lingers. An odd combination, definitely new.

Gotcha.

Dorian's right by my side, shirtless, with his horns, pointed ears, and tattoos on full display. "There!" he shouts, pointing one of his sharpened nails to the sky. And sure enough, there the little fucker is, heading east toward a thick patch of trees. He's going to try and use the canopy for cover.

With our eyes trained on the black speck in the sky, we barrel into the thick brush. This time, there's no way we're letting Sir Surchion's crow get away.

DORIAN

We run for miles with Elias on four legs and me on two. Eyes always trained on the skies and the distant black speck flying ahead of us. Now that we got sight of the collector's little pet, there's a good chance it's going to lead us straight to the very man we need to see.

Or should I say, the dragon.

Elias must have caught on to the creature's scent, because even when it temporarily disappears in a cluster of clouds or behind the forest's thick canopy, he's still hauling ass, snorting and panting like a rabid animal. It's not long before the crow pops back into view again and we're closing the distance once more.

The crisp scent of water hits my nose, followed by the strong, toxic smell of gasoline. Soon, the ground underneath our feet turns to asphalt. We've reached a city… but not Glenside. We're closer to the water now. Possibly the next town over. Dawson most likely. Factories, both in use and abandoned, rise on either side of us, and in the distance, black smoke billows from colossal stone pillars. The streets get smaller, causing me and Elias to weave around tight corners, dodging piles of crates and heavy machinery, just to keep up with the crow's pace.

We pass a billboard with a picture of a cartoon captain character holding a thumbs up and the words 'Choose Captain Seabox for all your packing and shipping needs!'. Elias makes a sharp left, causing me to skid to a stop and change directions. The saltiness of the air becomes sharper, and I know it's leading us toward the harbor.

This fucking bird must be smarter than we thought. It's brought us to a dead end.

"Elias!" I call and slow down. Glancing around, I realize we've run straight into a shipment yard with stacks of giant metal cargo boxes that humans use to store and ship items overseas. The name 'Captain Seabox' is scrolled across every one.

Oblivious to anything but his baser instincts, Elias rushes ahead, blind and deaf when it comes to the need to chase, hunt, and kill. He's already on the long strip of dock, heading straight for the end.

Ah, shit.

Let him run straight into an icy water bath and possibly freeze to death? Or save him?

As funny as it may be, I call upon my power, knowing I don't have much time to catch him. The runes across my chest and shoulders glow blue, and I push against the ground. I'm flying at top speeds, my feet a blur under me, and I reach Elias in no time. As the pesky bird soars further across the water, Elias launches off the pier, realizing too late that there are no more boards beneath him. I snatch him by the scruff of his neck and dig my heels in, our momentum wanting to lurch us both off the ledge.

Fuck, he's heavy. It takes all my strength to stop us from falling off the edge and heave us backward. I land hard on my ass, pain jutting up my spine, while Elias rolls sideways before colliding with one of the pilings with a grunt. He quickly sheds his fur, shifts back into his human skin, and shakes his head clear.

"You're welcome," I say as I hop to my feet, but Elias ignores me and hurries to the end of the dock, butt-ass naked. Sir Surchoin's crow caws manically, as if laughing at him, before flying across the rough waters and disappearing.

For a long moment, Elias stands there, muscles stiff, like he's debating jumping in and chancing the swim.

I grab his shoulder. "Woah, there. Let's not do anything stupid, now."

His gaze snaps my way. Every muscle in his body is tight with rage. "He got away," he says, pushing each word through clenched teeth.

"I know how much this must sting your ego, but let the bird go," I say, trying to reason with him. "This is where having Cain here would've been handy, but neither of us have wings, and if you die, Cain'll think it was me. I promised him not to off you this time."

As usual, he doesn't find my joke funny. But he does spin around and trudge back up the dock, mumbling obscenities the entire way. I don't blame him. It's hard to believe a fucking bird with a brain the size of a peanut somehow outsmarted us. Talk about a confidence kicker.

Striding between the rows of metal boxes, a thought strikes me. They aren't caves, but they're dark spaces just the same... portable, but a safe place to store a large amount of items... or a dragon's treasures.

Maybe the collector's pet didn't trick us. Maybe I am giving him too much credit. What if he led us exactly to Sir Surchion's hiding place after all?

I stop on the spot and pat down my pockets in search of my cell phone.

"What are you doing?" Elias asks, annoyed.

When I find it, I yank it out and dial the phone number on the billboard across the way.

"Dorian!"

I wave him off as it rings. "Shhh!"

He throws his hands in the air, exasperated.

When a woman answers "Captain Seabox, how may I help you?" I put on the friendliest voice I can muster and say, "Hello, I have a few storage containers with you guys going out on the next ship. I can't seem to remember the date of departure or arrival?"

"Name?" the woman asks.

Here goes nothing.

"Surchion."

Some clicks of a keyboard as she looks up the information on her side. Seconds pass.

"Your twenty containers will be on the next cargo ship," she says finally. "Docks Wednesday and departs Friday. Arrival will be Le Havre, France in thirty days."

Jackpot.

He's trying to flee but wants to bring all his stuff with him.

That means one of these boxes has our relics in it. But which one? "And do you happen to know the numbers of my containers, by any chance? I'm a bit absentminded nowadays."

"Absolutely. Can you tell me your security password, please?"

Shit. Of course it couldn't have been that easy.

"Uh, I'll have to find where I wrote it down and call you back," I lie. "Thank you, dear."

I hang up the phone to find Elias staring at me blankly.

"What the heck was that all about?" he asks, brow creased.

Grinning broadly, I walk over to the closest storage container and rap my fist on the metal. The bang echoes loudly. "Elias, my boy. I believe we just found the dragon's lair."

It takes him a minute, but I can see the gears turning as he puts the clues together. When he reaches the end, he says, "There has to be hundreds of these containers. We can't search every one. That'll take weeks. Months."

He's right. But what he hasn't realized yet is that there's no need to search them all. Not when we have a relic-detector living in our house.

"We need Aria."

ARIA

The Milo Swamps aren't exactly a skip and a jump away from civilization. More like a Jeep ride through the hills and mud and an airboat trek later. The place smells like sewage and rotting eggs, and the water is green and more like slush than liquid. How anything can live here is beyond me, but Cain assures me there are poisonous snakes, spiders, and other things that bite if I don't stay close to him. But even a prince of Hell can't protect me from mosquitoes, and they're the ones tearing me up right now.

Did I mention it's somehow ungodly hot here, despite it being so close to winter? Oh, and the smell is strong enough to make my eyes water?

I definitely won't be looking for any vacation rentals anytime soon.

Once we reach an area surrounded by skinny trees with tall, octopus-like roots standing out of the water, our guide slows the airboat so it glides over the water, making little noise. It's much darker in this part of the Milo Swamps, since the sun is blocked by the strange water-forest's twisted canopy. Barely any light shines through at all, and the guide is forced to turn on a spotlight and more lanterns around the boat.

Cain is as still as stone beside me, rigid with anticipation. He's ditched his suit jacket and has his sleeves rolled up to the elbows. Sweat makes the fabric stick to him.

"How much longer?" he asks, his tone tinged with frustration.

The guide, an older man wearing rubber pants and a

wide-brimmed hat, points into the darkness up ahead. "Nah much farther now," he says in his thick southern accent.

Despite the wide range of creatures singing their songs, the place is pretty quiet. No sounds of men, as far as I can tell. Wasn't a group of them supposed to be camping out around here? At least that's what Cain told me. But so far, there's no sign of anyone but us. Uneasiness snakes up my spine.

I'm not sure I like this.

Cain must be thinking the same thing because he says, "Are you sure we're going to the exact coordinates I told you?"

The man nods.

"Shouldn't you have a compass or something? A map?" I add in. Even with those tools, I didn't know how anybody could navigate in this place. It was like a maze of green slime and sticks. Everything looked the same after a while, and this guy was leading us with nothing but his instincts.

"No ma'am. I've lived in these swamps since I was a youngin'. I know it like the back of mah hand."

I glance at Cain. He looks unsure, too.

"Can you call someone?" I offer as a solution. "See where they are?"

"Won' get any phone service 'ere," the man says with a near-toothless smile. "But yer can try."

Cain pulls out his cell and checks the screen before shaking his head and confirming the guide is right.

He lets out a wheezy laugh. "Told ya."

Cain leans in closer to me, and like always, his nearness sends delicious shivers throughout my body. I try my damndest to ignore them.

"Do you feel anything?" he whispers. "Anything from the relic."

I want to tell him I don't like being used like this, like some supernatural relic detector. I'd even planned on fighting helping him find the spine after he'd told me I had no choice coming here with him for that very reason, but after what he'd done for me in the hospital, I couldn't bring myself to resist anymore. Even though it'd been clear he'd been out of his element and uncomfortable, he'd tried to connect with me in some way, and it had meant a lot. I wanted to return the favor.

Maybe that had been his plan all along. I really don't know and probably never will. But for now, I would help him find the spine. Then, hopefully, I'd find my way out of the demons' contract and make a clean getaway before they find all the relics and drag me to Hell with them.

That's my plan so far, and I am sticking to it.

I close my eyes (more for dramatic effect than anything else) and try to feel any twitchy movements from my pinky toe. Nothing. Completely stiff and normal in my sneakers. Even Sayah is silent inside me, coiled away like usual lately.

I crack one eye open and look Cain's way. "No, sorry."

"Not a thing?" he prompts again, as if I must be wrong.

Annoyance pinches. "It's not like I'm not trying here," I say. "I feel nothing."

"We must be in the wrong location," he snaps and straightens, but the old man guides the boat around a bend, and a few tents and hammocks come into view on a thin strip of land.

"There," he shouts. "Is that what yer lookin' for?"

"Yes." Cain's on his feet immediately and walking to the edge of the boat. "You can drop us off here."

Carefully, the man steers us closer to the shore. Cain climbs out first, as graceful as can be, while I stumble across the deck like a newborn giraffe on wobbly legs. Cain snatches my wrist before I can topple overboard and half-hauls me onto solid ground.

"Thanks," I breathe and smooth down the front of my shirt. My shoes sink into the spongy moss, and I wipe the sticky sweat from my forehead. Gross.

"And you weren't even in heels this time."

I snort a laugh, but despite his attempt at a joke, Cain's expression is deadly serious. His focus is clearly on something else—the spine relic. His gaze is already sweeping the campsite, but as it first appeared, the place seems to be abandoned. There's no movement from the tents. Only ash sits in a firepit, the fire long since extinguished, and various gadgets and high-tech location equipment have been just tossed to the side, as if someone had to drop it all and make a quick run for it. There has to be at least two million dollars' worth of devices here.

I gnaw on the inside of my cheek, my nerves coming back with a vengeance. I don't like this one bit. Even without Sayah, I know warning signs when I see them.

"Freeman and his men should be here," Cain

mumbles mostly to himself as he strides across the campsite and kicks one of the tents. As expected, no one's inside to protest or come out.

"Do yer want me to stay? Take yer back?" the old man asks with a frown.

"Maybe they just went back inland for some local food?" I try to inject some hope into my voice, for Cain's sake, but he doesn't seem to be buying it. Rubbing his jaw, he continues to walk around the tents, examining the equipment and whatever else was left behind.

"All righty. I'll give y'all an hour before I come back for ya," the guide calls.

"That won't be necessary," Cain replies sharply. "We won't need it."

I suspect he's planning on flying us out of here in his demon form, but since the old man couldn't possibly know that, he hesitates.

"There's no other way back—"

"Thank you for your services," Cain cuts him off. Even though his words are pleasant, his delivery is harsh and aggressive. He reaches into his pocket and pulls out a wad of money as big as my fist. He throws it to the man, who catches it against his chest. When he sees how much money he's been given, he gasps.

"Oh, I can't take this—" he starts, but again Cain stops him.

"Of course you can," he says. Then his voice drops to that guttural rumble that comes whenever his demon is close, and his eyes darken a shade. "Now go."

The guide has a bit of a harder time finding the gear

shifts, but when he does, he slowly backs the airboat—and our only sure way out of this hot, soupy, godforbidden place—out of the channel. Within seconds, it disappears into the fog, and the sound of the motor dissipates into the local wildlife's noisy and chaotic song.

Besides the creatures who live in this place, I can't help but feel like we're completely on our own.

CHAPTER SIXTEEN
ARIA

I don't like this. I don't like this one bit.

What if the camp had flooded and all the team members drowned? Or some wild animal ate them all? Like an alligator or... a creature from the black lagoon type deal?

Okay, that may be a stretch, but the setting certainly fits.

Cain is as cool as a cucumber as he continues to search the place. Well, as *cool* as Cain can be. He's still highly aggravated the men we were supposed to meet aren't here and has resorted to fiddling with his cell phone in hopes of finding some reception. By the deep scowl on his face, I'd say he isn't having much luck.

"How did they contact you?" I ask as he begins to pace, gaze still focused on his screen.

He doesn't even look up. "Freeman called me," he says distantly.

I'm assuming Freeman is the man who was supposed to be leading all this.

"And he said he was here?" I go on.

"Obviously."

Damn. Touchy much?

I cross my arms and glance around the abandoned campsite again. Looking it over this time, I notice the tents appear new. If they've been sleeping in the marsh for days and days, you'd think there would be some wear to them, right? Instead, creases are still visible in the fabric, as if they'd just been taken out of the packages and thrown up for show.

Am I just being paranoid now?

Another anxious shiver snakes down my back. Something isn't right here.

Rubbing my lips together, I swallow past the tightness of my throat. "Wait, how did Freeman call you if there's no service here?"

Things just aren't adding up.

Crunch. When I look over to Cain, the cell phone in his fist is now a mashed mess of plastic and shattered glass. His palm glows red, and the sharp scent of fire rises. Then he throws the smoldering remains of the phone deep into the swamp, farther than I can see. A distant splash sounds when it hits the water.

Panic begins to crawl along my skin. I really don't want to be here a second longer. "Can we go now?" I rub the back of my arms. "This place is giving me the creeps. More than the hospital, believe it or not."

Cain's head whips my way, his eyes still black from anger. "You're sure you can't feel the spine." It's supposed to be a question, but it comes out too short and aggressive to be.

"I already told you I can't," I bite back. "What, do you think I'm lying or something?"

"There is no way for me to know whether or not you are."

What. The. Actual. Fuck.

Fury bubbles up inside me. I glare at him. "I'm here, aren't I? I let you drag me all the way to west bumble-fuck and get eaten alive by mosquitoes, and for what? My health?"

He stares at me for a long moment, his expression unreadable, his jaw tight. For some reason, it only annoys me more.

"I know you don't want to hear it, but there's no relic here. Nothing. Nada. Zip. You've flown us across the country for *nothing*."

Cain's mouth opens to say something, but something whistles by my ear, brushing so close, I feel a breath of air against my cheek. Cain flinches back, his brows pinch, and it takes me a second too long to realize the handle of a dagger is sticking out just below his shoulder.

My stomach plummets, my brain struggling to catch up with the sudden danger we're in. Cain grips the dagger and rips it out with a grunt. He chucks it into the ground, his rage immediate. Black blood oozes through his wound and soaks into his shirt.

I whip around to find five men rappelling down ropes from the treetops, dressed in camouflage and faces smeared with green and black paint.

Heart racing, I spin back to Cain, whose eyes are wild with fear. But not for himself. For me.

Behind him, three more men appear on the water in kayaks. It doesn't take long before they beach them, jump out, and start creeping up on Cain's turned back.

Terror seizes me. We've been tricked. "Cain!"

Just as the men reach him, his wings burst from his back, tearing through his clothes, the change to his demon form instantaneous. His wings knock two of the strangers into the water, while the other is speared through the chest by one of the taloned claws at the very tip of his wings.

I cringe on the inside at how much it must have hurt.

Rough hands grab me from behind, yanking my arms behind my back hard enough to make me cry out. My first instinct is to thrash and kick, but when the cool and sharp edge of a blade presses into my neck, I freeze.

Pain pinches as the knife cuts into me, and I tilt my head back as far as I can and hold my breath. Heart beating frantically, a shiver races down my spine.

Cain's entire body vibrates on the spot, his anger and fear coupled with the power of the change rushing through him all at once. He wants to murder every one of these men, and he probably could in a blink of an eye, but there's one thing holding him back.

Me, in danger.

He doesn't want to risk my life. And right now, that means everything to me.

"Let. Her. Go." He punctuates each word with an unnatural and terrifying growl.

The man at my side responds by pressing the blade

harder into my neck. The pain slices through me, making me whimper.

"A ssstep clossser and I'll disspatch her," the man beside me practically hisses. From the awkward angle of my head, it's hard to get a good look at him, but when his gaze flicks back to me, I catch a look at his eyes. They're the brightest shade of green, with black slits for pupils.

A snake shifter. Shit!

I've met plenty of supernaturals at Purgatory, not to mention there was one snake shifter in a past foster home. It's hard to forget those eyes and the strong hiss-like accent. Oh, and the venomous bite. The most important one to remember.

The man gripping my arms wrenches them back further, and I curse.

Cain is about to take a step towards us but stops himself. "What do you want?" he demands instead, standing tall, looking like a force to be reckoned with. "If it's me, here I am. Let the girl go. She has nothing to do with this."

"Oh, but ssshe doesss," the man with the knife says. "She'sss the one we're here for."

Cain's eyes widen. He was obviously not expecting them to say that. And neither was I.

Me? What could they possibly want with me?

My pulse races wildly. My heart's beating so fast, I'm shocked I haven't keeled over on the spot from a heart attack yet.

"Although, I will sssay. Having you here isss alsso a plusss." He lifts the blade away from me only to gesture to the others to close in on Cain. They move slowly but gracefully toward him, like snake shifters do. I can see the conflict warring in Cain's gaze. He wants to kill all these fuckers, but the two men holding me hostage make him hesitate.

I want to tell him not to worry about me. Fight, dammit! It's the only way we can possibly both get out of here alive. It would be easy for him to take them down, too, I'm sure. With the amount of power he possesses, the hellfire, and the wings, he could cut through these mediocre supes in a flash. But when the three shifters surround him, he only folds in his wings, pulls his shoulders back, and lets two pin his arms behind him while the other stands by with another long knife. With shaky hands, he points Cain's way.

We're doomed.

My gaze flicks back and forth, searching for something to save us. Anything. A desperate idea strikes, and I suck in deep breath, knowing that what I'm about to do is absolutely bonkers and is going to hurt like hell.

No other choice.

I stomp on the shifter's foot with the heel of my sneaker. I hear the crack, but I throw my head forward and then back, hearing the resounding pop of his now broken nose. My vision blurs for a second, and pain spikes behind my eyes, but it did the trick. He releases me and stumbles back, clutching his face and cursing madly.

"Aria!" Cain shouts. There's genuine fear in his voice —something I never thought I'd hear from the prince of Hell himself. He throws out his arm, flinging one of the men across the ground. The man collides with a tree with a hard thud and doesn't move again.

The snake shifter beside me swings his knife at me, but I drop to my knees and he misses the top of my head by less than an inch. I frantically crawl through the mud for my life, determined to reach Cain. That's when I feel the biting sting of the fresh cut across my neck from the bastard swinging his blade. Not life-threateningly deep, but I can feel blood sliding down my throat and chest. I clench my jaw through the sting and keep going.

Another crash and a blur of green as another snake shifter is tossed like a sack of dirty laundry. When I look up, I see Cain, wings spread wide, black lines slithering down his face. In his hand is the throat of the third man. He holds him feet above the ground, and the man kicks wildly as he tries to get free. Cain's fist glows red as the hellfire ignites. The man screams.

But like before, Cain jerks back, suddenly hit by something. Another knife. This one through the center of his chest.

No!

My heart constricts with dread. He's a demon, and he just had a dagger thrown at him before, but somehow I know that it's bad this time. I see the agony painted on his face.

Stumbling a step, he lets go of the shifter, who drops to the ground and scrambles away. The veins recede, his eyes flickering from black to blue again, and he blinks rapidly as if stunned. Looking down, he grasps the handle, but his legs give out and he falls onto his knees.

Oh my god! No!

I scream. Louder than I've ever screamed before. While on all fours in the mud, terror and fury shake through my entire body. Tears sting my eyes.

He can't die! He can't! He can't!

"You're coming with me," the shifter with the blade-throwing skills barks behind me. I hear him stomping closer, but I don't move. Pain, anger, and sorrow are whipping through me like a torrent, cementing me to the ground. My breathing slows. Everything around me becomes sluggish, and all I can hear is the booming of my heart.

I clench my fists, squishing mud between my fingers, and notice the familiar reddish-orange sparks of power radiating from my hands. Just like in the warehouse when Sayah broke free.

On cue, the shadow underneath me ripples. I gasp, feeling the terrible tugging and suffocating feeling like the last time she manifested, but before I can say anything, Sayah pushes from me and elongates along the ground, covering Cain in her darkness before stretching up to the sky.

The strange sparking light crawls along our tether as she grows and grows, touching the forest canopy. Slowly, she begins to gain density and become less transparent, and I feel the change immediately. My lungs squeeze and nausea rolls through me. I'm trembling under my skin, and when Sayah's two ruby-red eyes blink down at me like a nightmare come to life, I become locked in place by sheer terror.

"Sayah, come back!" I yell desperately in my head, too

weak to form the words out loud. I can't move, and black spots dance before my eyes. She's draining my life away again. Even forming a coherent thought is becoming too difficult. *"Sayah... you're... killing me."*

But she continues to ignore my pleas and crawls along the canopy, blotting out the sunlight and cloaking us all in darkness.

Cain stares, mouth agape, while any remaining snake shifters stand paralyzed with fear.

There's a loud sucking noise, as if Sayah is drawing in a gulp of air, and then there's an explosion of sound.

"RUNNNNNNNN!" she bellows in a deep, monstrous voice. Wind rushes through the swamp, like a gust at hurricane speed, and the ground quakes.

I sway on the spot, fighting against unconsciousness. Time seems to crawl, and all I can focus on is continuing to breathe and stay awake. My body feels so heavy that I'm forced to lock my elbows to stay upright.

Gentle hands are on me suddenly, scooping me up and pressing me against something hard and warm. Cain's cologne fills my senses, and my body sags against him with relief. I don't know how he's alive right now when he just took a dagger through the heart, but he's holding me tight, and I relish in the knowledge that he's okay. At least for now.

"Stay with me, Aria," he whispers into my hair.

Exhaustion weighs me down. I can barely keep my eyes open anymore, but I fight to stay awake.

What about the shifters? Are they gone? And Sayah...

Through my hazy vision, I can see the giant shadow

creature begin to shrink, descending down the tree trunks and slithering across the muddy ground. The less solid she becomes, the easier it is for me to breathe. The strangling feeling eases, and my eyes struggle to refocus again. Sayah's red eyes blink one last time before disappearing, and she slinks back inside me, my shadow returning to normal under me and the red sparks dissipating.

It takes a moment, but my senses eventually return. There's a dull ache in my temples and behind my ribs, and no matter how hard I try, I can't seem to stop the tremors rocketing through me.

Time passes, although I don't know how much. We sit like that, with Cain's arms wrapped around me as the after-effects of Sayah's power leave me. With my head tucked under his chin, he strokes the hair over my shoulder, every gesture full of a softness I didn't think he was capable of. My gaze is glued on the dark blood stains on his shirt, and I remember how close I'd been to losing him only minutes ago.

It takes a while, but when the last of the shaking disappears, I ask him, "What happened? The snake shifters..."

"Gone," he replies, tone low. "Your shadow chased them off."

She did? Sayah actually saved us?

I pull back a little and peer up at his handsome face. His blue eyes are full of concern, and his skin looks a little paler than it should. "Are you okay? I saw you fall... I thought..."

His finger runs along my cheek and down my jaw. "I'm fine now."

"But didn't the blade pierce your heart?"

"Just nicked it." He lets out a short laugh. "Besides, I'm surprised you think I even have a heart."

Any other time, I would've laughed or joked, but after everything we've just been through, I can't even seem to muster up the strength to smile.

"He just missed it," he says to assure me, but despite the confidence in his tone, something is still off with him. "And I was able to heal quickly enough."

But how?

As if reading my mind, he shifts us and nods toward the unmoving body feet away from us. Even though his skin is grayed and severely sunken in, I recognize him as the man who'd been leading the ambush. The shifter with the knives. Cain drained his soul.

"Are you all right?" he asks, drawing my attention back to him. He may have regained some of his strength from killing the shifter, but it's clear it wasn't enough to heal him a hundred percent.

I nod and turn away from the dead body. As disturbing as it is and as scary as it had been to witness the first time Cain had done it, knowing he'd devoured his soul doesn't bother me as much as before. It probably should, but it doesn't.

"Do you think you can stand?"

I nod again and start to lift myself off him. His hands find my waist to help me, and even when I'm on my feet, he doesn't let go. Probably too afraid I'll tip over if he does.

His gaze drops to my neck, and his lips tug down into a frown. That's right. The cut there. I almost forgot.

"It's not deep," I say, trying to ease his worry. "Just a scratch, really."

He doesn't respond, but I can see the lingering turmoil on his face. He's always been so good at masking his feelings, but it's getting harder for him, it seems. Or maybe it's getting easy for me to read him? I'm not sure.

"We'll get it bandaged on the plane," he replies stiffly.

"Speaking of," I begin, glancing around the swamp. After being ambushed by snake shifters and almost kidnapped *again,* it's looking like my theory of the staged campsite was accurate. "How are we getting home? Are you well enough to fly us both?"

"I can take us to shore."

That's a relief. I want to get the hell away from this place, and I'd be happy if I never return.

Finally, he steps away from me, putting space between us.

"Do you think Freeman had something to do with this?" I ask the question that's still left unanswered.

"I'm not sure," he confesses.

"Do you think the spine was ever here?"

His gaze darkens. "No. I don't."

It would explain why I can't feel anything around here.

"It all must have been a ploy to get us out here," he goes on.

"Or *me.* Snake-eyes did say they wanted me."

He pauses and straightens his spine, his body tensing with anger, but he doesn't answer.

"But why?" I press.

He doesn't reply right away. After a few silent moments, he finally says, "I don't know."

He's *lying...*

I push for more. "Maybe Sir Surchion sent them? Or do you think someone else knows about me and Sayah?" Honestly, I don't know what's worse.

He turns and strides away from me. He stops in front of one of the tents, clenching and unclenching his fists. "I don't know."

Another lie...

I'm about to call him on it, but his head snaps up as if he's caught sight of something, and my body ices over. Another surprise attack? Have the shifters returned?

"What? What is it?" I ask, throat tight.

He walks over to a nearby patch of thick brush and vines and pushes them aside with a swift swipe of his arm. Hating being left in the dark, I hurry to his side and peer through the weeds. What I see sets my heart back into a frenzy.

Another dead body. This one also sunken, wrinkled, and grayed. Soul drained. Unlike the snake shifters, this man has blond curly hair and waterproof overalls and boots on. Not camouflage gear and face paint.

"Oh... my..." Acid climbs up my throat, and I swallow it back down. In these past few weeks with the demons, I've seen more corpses than I'd like to. Personally, I've reached my limit.

I glance at Cain. His expression is contorted in fury, his lip curled in a silent snarl.

"Freeman," is all he says.

Guess he hadn't been in on this ambush after all. Or if he was, he was double-crossed and got what he deserved in the end. But only demons can drain souls like this, as far as I know. And that means another demon had been here and taken his soul. Not Cain.

Another demon...

Not good.

"Cain—"

He cuts me off by turning sharply, snaking his arms around me, and snapping back into his demon form. The second his wings expand, he lurches us both into the air. I yelp with surprise and cling to him, wrapping my legs around his hips and my hand behind his neck.

"Shit!" I cry out, my heart jumping into my throat.

As we ascend, I peek down at the swamp, which gets smaller and smaller as we spear upward. We're moving so fast, my stomach does an excited flip-flop. It's an exhilarating feeling. Nothing like take-off in the plane had been.

Nearing the canopy, I catch a glimpse of something ghostly pale against the dark greens and browns of the Milo Swamp below. Something unfamiliar but familiar at the same time. But soon, we burst through the treetops. The brightness of the midday sun whites out my view, and I'm forced to close my eyes against the harshness of it.

Wasting no more time, Cain tightens his grip on me,

shifts directions, and flies us both toward the safety of the mainland.

CAIN

*A*s the jet readies to take off and bring us home to Vermont, I become lost to my thoughts. I'd been tricked, led into a trap that almost cost us our lives, and for what? Because I have been too preoccupied with Aria and her gifts? Because my obsession of finding these relics has blinded me to the everyday dangers we face while on Earth?

Being leaders in a supernatural underground enterprise has always been a risky job. Being demons has put other targets on our backs for decades. It's no secret we're unliked and unwelcomed here, but we've always managed to stay one step ahead of our enemies.

That is… until Hell decided to step up to the plate.

A demon devoured Freeman's soul. No other supernatural is capable of leaving a corpse like that behind. I know the signs when I see them, and if my assumptions are right—and they usually are—the snake shifters were hired by a demon. A demon who is looking for Aria.

Maverick.

He's the first person I can think of. Is it a coincidence he's been trying to recruit Dorian and Elias to Lucifer's side and just sent Dorian a note asking who Aria is, only for us to run into an overly complex trap with bounty hunters and one of my workers dead? Doubtful. This has Maverick written all over it.

My own brother. I knew he'd do anything to get what he wanted—it's in his nature, after all, as Greed—but I never thought he'd turn on me. Especially after I saved his life after our father suspected him of treason during our coup attempt. He *had* been helping us, of course, but to spare him, I took the blame. Elias and Dorian stood by my side, and we took the punishment together. Maverick was a coward and ran the moment he was free.

I'll never understand why Lucifer was so eager to kill Maverick but gave us banishment. A prolonged torture, I suppose. It's impossible to try and find reason with that demented mind of his.

But for whatever purpose, it's clear Maverick is now under Lucifer's thumb and is searching for Aria. She isn't safe. And he apparently knows about the harp, too, which means things are about to become a lot harder and more dangerous. For all of us.

If only I could speak to my brother, maybe I could convince him to stop this useless effort to gain our father's approval. He doesn't care about anyone but himself, and he never will. And if I can't make him see reason, I can always just beat sense back into him. I don't want to kill him, but I will if I must to keep everyone safe. Especially Aria.

And what of Aria's shadow, Sayah? The way she grew to a monstrous size and was able to speak was astonishing. But unleashing that kind of power comes at a cost. The creature steals Aria's life every time she manifests. She's becoming more and more uncontrollable. But Sayah may not be doing so purposefully. She did save us in the swamp, after all, so what her true intentions are, I really don't know.

I'm not sure what to make of any of this yet. I need more information.

"Are you sure you're okay?"

Aria's voice snaps me out of my mental spiral. I look over at her, finding her forehead wrinkled with concern.

"Yes," I lie, a bit too quickly for it to be believable. So I sit up straight and let out a long sigh to settle myself. "I'm fine."

"You know, I probably shouldn't be condoning this, but..." she drops her tone and glances around nervously for anyone in earshot, "...maybe you should *eat* again? It makes you feel better, doesn't it?"

She's right to speak cryptically about it. The stewardesses are human, after all. She's also right. Once we get home, I'll have to take another soul to replenish my strength. The shifter missed the center of my heart by centimeters. I've never felt that weak before in all my existence. I know being on this plane hinders our powers, but I never considered to what extent. When that blade struck my chest, I swear death touched me, as if it was letting me know it can still come for me in this world.

We are going to have to start being more diligent about feeding to keep our energy up. Especially with what is coming our way.

"Don't worry about me," I tell her, but that only increases the worry lines between her brows.

"I thought you'd died," she says, emphasizing the last

word. The pain on her face surprises me. My death would make it easier for her to break free of her contract, and she knows this. Yet I heard her scream when I fell.

For all our bickering and the hateful words we spew, it seems she does care about me. Somewhat.

I think back to the broken necklace I still hold in my shirt pocket. The one she ripped off her neck and threw at me on the staircase. If I offer it to her again, will she accept it? Has this trip changed anything between us at all? I want to think so, but I truly don't know.

The rumble of the engine grows louder as the plane starts down the airstrip, quickly gaining speed. Like the previous take-off, Aria grips the chair's armrests and squeezes her eyes shut. She holds her breath, puffing out her cheeks, and my eyes land on the freshly bandaged spot on her neck. Anger stirs, knowing I couldn't prevent it from happening, but I'd been impressed by her courage to do what she needed to break free. It only makes me admire her more.

As the plane lifts into the air, I reach over, grab her by the wrist, and tug her close to me. Her eyes fly open, and when she realizes she's sitting in my lap, her cheeks blush pink.

"I don't need you to hold me again," she says, but her arms are already gripping onto my shoulders and her eyes are locking with mine. The fear she held a moment ago is now gone, replaced with a lustful hunger she's trying desperately to hide from me. When she speaks again, the words come out in a breathy whisper. "Like you said before, the take-offs and landings are the worst part."

I don't know if it's the fact that we almost died in the swamps, or if the idea of having her is just as intoxicating as the painful thought of losing her, but I can't help myself anymore. I crush my mouth against hers, the need for her taking over all common sense.

As if a switch has gone off inside her, her tongue sweeps into my mouth, and she's kissing me back with the fervor I crave. The beast unfurls inside me, and like in my office, we begin wrestling for dominance through our kisses and wandering hands.

I can't get enough of her. Her scent. The feel of her. Her little moans as my fingers wander over her shoulders and along the curves of her breasts. I can never seem to get enough.

Typically, when I'm with a woman, my goal lies primarily with satisfying my own needs, but with Aria, her pleasure heightens my own. Just seeing the hunger in her eyes, hearing my name on her lips and knowing I am the one fulfilling her desires makes me want to serve her for the rest of eternity.

I've never felt like this before. The power she has over me is overwhelming. Commanding. Unnerving. I fear I'll never escape it.

Grabbing her by the waist, I spin her away from me and open my legs wide so she can sit in between them. Since I've broken our kiss, she's about to protest, but once she feels my erection pressing into her back, a gasp escapes instead. We've barely done anything, and I'm so hard it hurts.

She peeks up at me and murmurs, "What are you up to?"

I answer by letting my hands drift down her arms. Goosebumps rise under my palms, and she trembles against me.

Her head rolls back. "Cain..."

If the last thing I hear before my death is my name upon her lips like that, I'll die a happy man. I begin to leave a trail of kisses along the curve of her neck, and my hand glides to her right breast, which I squeeze greedily. Another moan escapes her.

"Do you remember our limousine ride the first night I took you to Purgatory?" I whisper in between kisses. The night she'd brought herself to orgasm in front of me and I was left dazed by her beauty but furious for being unable to indulge.

"H-How could I forget?" Her voice has turned into nothing more than breathy pants now. Despite the lace bra she's wearing and the fabric of her shirt, I can still feel the beaded tip of her nipple easily. My finger traces it, and she squirms.

"You don't know how badly I wanted to have you then." My tongue swirls below her earlobe. "To have you like this..."

I find the hem of her skirt and slowly, torturously, pull it up along her thighs.

Suddenly, Aria turns rigid in my arms. "Cain, wait," she says. "The stewardess..."

Peering across the plane, I see one of the attendants in the back room looking our way with wide eyes. Having realized she's been caught spying, she quickly glances away and pretends to busy herself with something else. I, for one, have never cared about onlookers. If they wanted a show, I'd give them a show, but it's clear Aria is still uncomfortable with the idea, so I reach over to the controller and press the privacy button. The automatic curtain closes, blocking us from the attendant's work area, and a red light blinks ahead.

"There. Now no one will bother us," I say.

Still unsure, Aria remains stiff against me.

I begin pressing my lips down her neck and shoulder again. That seems to help her relax a little. With my other hand, I pop the button on her shirt. "Now, where were we?"

"I think you were about to show me what you wanted to do to me in the limo that night?"

"Ah, yes. That's right." I fist her skirt and wrench it up. She gasps.

I slide two fingers up and down her panties, right along her seam, and find them drenched already. Perfect.

Pulling the fabric to the side, I repeat the action, but this time, her entire body twitches in response. I smile.

"Spread your legs for me," I say. Without hesitation, she does. I take the opportunity to push my fingers inside her, two at once.

"Ah…"

I pump them in and out slowly, stretching her, letting her become accustomed to my presence without hurting her. Soon, I'm sliding into her heat easily, my fingers coated in her wetness.

Pulling out, I direct my attention to her clit instead,

rubbing the sensitive little nub and loving the way her muscles jump. Her breathing picks up.

Her hands find mine—one on her breast and the other between her thighs, and she grips both, encouraging them to keep up the torture.

Hellfire erupts in my chest, and my demon surges forward. My spine tingles as my power pushes through me, but I hold back. This is not the place to release my wings. Instead, I channel all my energy into pleasing the irresistible woman in my arms.

I increase my pace, stroking her faster and faster. Her head falls back again, pressing into my shoulder, and when she groans loudly, I know she's close to reaching that high.

Her nails bite into my flesh. She's gasping for breath, and I'm entranced by her all over again, just like in the limo.

"Come for me, Aria," I growl and nip along her jaw. She's moving her hips in time to my strokes, grinding against me at the same time. If she keeps it up, I'll end up coming, too.

She cries out, her entire body shuttering as her climax peaks. Her thighs squeeze together, capturing me in between them, but I continue to play her through it, not really wanting it to end.

The second her muscles relax a little, I sink my fingers inside her again. I imagine it's my cock plunging into her over and over, knowing just how good that tight little pussy of hers feels.

This time I'm relentless, using my fingers to fuck her hard and fast as she rides out the last of the orgasm. Her screams of pleasure are music to my ears.

I hold her tight as her back arches, her body convulses, and her pleasure slowly starts to unwind. When she finally relaxes against me, a smirk forms across my face. Of course, if I were at my full strength, this would've just been the beginning for us. I would fuck her right here in the middle of the plane's cabin until her screams could be heard from Heaven itself, but I'd have to settle for this for now. At least until I can drain another soul and heal myself more.

As I withdraw from her, Aria brushes her skirt down before twisting to face me more on my lap. Her brilliant smile is all my pulse needs to pick up speed again. Before I know it, I'm cupping the side of her face and leaning in for another kiss. Nothing aggressive this time, just the softest brush of the lips.

When I ease away, her gaze searches my face, the smile fading.

"What is it?" I ask, afraid I might have made some kind of mistake.

"Don't scare me like that again, okay?" she replies softly.

It takes me a minute, but I realize she's talking about what happened in the Milo Swamp with the shifters. The worry and hurt in her expression should have given it away.

"Promise me that you won't die," she insists.

It's a foolish thing to promise her—I'm a demon, after all, one with very deadly enemies and some very dangerous deals on the horizon—but I hate seeing her fearful like this. I want to ease her anxiety, and the only way I can think to do that is by feeding into the lie.

"Okay," I say, "I promise."

"Good."

It seems to have done the trick, because she leans into me and rests her head against my chest. Unsure what I should do, I take a chance and wrap my arms around her. She sighs contently and closes her eyes, telling me I made the right choice.

CHAPTER SEVENTEEN
DORIAN

The moment Elias hears Cain and Aria's car turn into our driveaway, he leaps to his feet. "They're here," he says anxiously.

We've been trying to contact Cain for hours, ever since we learned where Sir Surchion's been hiding his treasure, but the phone's been going straight to voicemail and his texts have been left unread. I know I encouraged him to enjoy his time with Aria, but shit. I hadn't meant for him to cut off all communication with the outside world. It's so unlike him.

Something must've gone wrong. That's the only logical explanation I can think of, and it only makes me even more thankful they've returned home.

The sound of tires crunching on gravel grows louder and then stops. Footsteps and then the turn of the doorknob. Elias and I walk into the foyer to greet them the moment they step foot through the door.

Aria steps in first, looking a bit disheveled with her shirt undone at the top and her hair a bit tangled at the ends—all good signs at first… until I see the bandage taped across her neck.

My stomach drops. "Holy shit," I gasp.

Elias must have seen it too because he glances between her and Cain, gaze darkening. "What the fuck happened?"

"Uh…" Aria turns to Cain as he strides inside.

"In the parlor," Cain says shortly, and with his command, we all move into the front room.

No one sits. The air is buzzing with unsaid words, and I can tell by the way Aria's shifting side to side on her feet that she's itching to tell us what happened to them on the trip, just as we're anxious to tell them our news.

I can't wait a moment longer. It's been so long since we've had a bit of good news, and if Aria's wound gives any hint as to how their excursion went, I'm guessing Cain needs a bit of a spirit lift.

I'm about to open my mouth when Elias steps forward.

"We found the collector's new lair," he says with a wolfish grin.

Motherfucker beat me to it.

"Well, really *I* found it," I retort. "Elias almost ran straight into the harbor and froze his balls off chasing a bird."

He growls at me, but I shrug it off.

Like always, Cain is unamused by our antics. "And? Did you get the relics?"

"No. Not exactly," I reply and instantly see annoyance flash in his eyes. "But we know where they are," I add quickly. "They're in the next town. Dawson. In some of Captain Seabox's storage containers."

"The place by the harbor?" Aria asks.

Elias nods. "We found Mordecai spying on us. We chased him there."

"And after some clever recon work by yours truly, I found out that he rented twenty of those big metal boxes to ship his treasures to France. A mobile lair this time, more or less."

Cain walks to his favorite spot near the fireplace and leans against the mantel, lost in thought. He's so predictable that way. "When does the ship depart?"

"Friday."

"That gives us some time," he muses.

"Time?" Elias repeats gruffly. "What do we need time for? Aria is here now. She can help us find the relics and—"

"No." Cain's reply is quick and sharp, taking everyone off guard.

Cain's been obsessed with finding the harp's pieces since we stepped foot on Earth, and now that we have three of them in our sights, he wants to wait? What the heck happened in Missouri? The Cain I know would never turn down a chance to hunt down a relic. It's almost like he came back a different man.

His head swings Aria's way and his expression softens. It's then that I realize, in the light of the fireplace, that there are shadows under his eyes. His cheeks are sunken in, and there's a hunch to his normally pulled back shoulders.

Yeah. Something definitely happened in Missouri.

"Aria, maybe you should go rest some," he suggests. "We both had a bit too much excitement."

Even his tone with her has changed. Eased.

Something unsaid seems to pass between them.

"I'll tell them," he assures her. "You don't need to worry yourself about it. It's okay. Go."

I expect her to protest as usual, but instead she sighs and says "Okay." With that, she turns and leaves us without a fuss.

What in the world?

I walk over to the doorway and peek out. I wait until she disappears up the second flight of stairs before spinning around and confronting Cain again.

"Okay, please explain to me what's going on here. What did we miss?"

Cain lets out a long breath and rubs his forehead. "I don't even know where to start."

"At the beginning would be best," I say. "Come on. Out with it."

Elias leans back against the wall across the room, waiting.

Cain waits a long moment, and then, looking grim, he starts. "We stopped in Illinois, at the hospital written on the receipt Aria had found at her foster father's. I meant for it to be an olive branch of sorts, but what we found wasn't as consoling."

Cain would think of going to an abandoned hospital as a romantic gesture. I fight the urge to roll my eyes. The man is hopeless.

"What did you find there?" Elias asks.

"Her name on a list of abandoned children," he replies. "She was devastated."

"So she was born there and then later abandoned?" I question.

"It appears so."

"Sounds familiar," I grumble under my breath.

"Anyway," he says, trying to get us back on topic, "that wasn't even the worst of it."

Elias runs a hand through his tangled hair. "Shit."

Cain turns fully to us, his entire figure darkened by the fire at his back. "The entire mission for the spine was a plot to steal Aria."

My breath freezes in my chest, and I almost choke on the pure shock of his words. For a moment, I wonder if I even heard him right.

"A trap?" Elias asks before me as I sputter and try to regain myself. "Was it Freeman?"

"No," Cain replies. "We found him dead in the bushes. Drained."

When I can finally speak again, I say, "Blood drained, like from a vampire? Or…"

"Soul drained," Cain says.

Elias and I exchange confused glances.

"But that means… a demon," Elias says.

Cain nods before turning to me, and my veins ice over with dread. Not just any demon. "Maverick."

Elias's eyes widen. "Aria's in serious trouble."

"We all are," Cain replies.

"Did you tell her?" I ask. "Aria?"

"I don't know if it's my brother for sure," he says, "but that's the only conclusion I can come to at the moment. Once I find out more and am absolutely sure, I'll tell her. There's no need to cause her more panic and worry than she already has."

I guess that is true, although keeping things from her when her life is on the line doesn't seem right, either.

Elias snorts. "Sending you halfway across the country on some wild goose chase has Maverick written all over it to me."

"A hundred percent," I agree. That slimeball was always overcomplicating things just to enjoy the show. "I should have been tipped off by it being supposedly found in a swamp. That's the snake's natural habitat."

Cain continues to rub his forehead like he has one bad headache brewing. Honestly, I wouldn't be surprised if he did. "Funny you put it that way—he hired snake shifters to ambush us."

I pretend to shiver to show my disgust of their kind.

Snake shifters. Creepy fuckers.

"I assumed the ambush had been for me, but they wanted her," Cain goes on. "Once it was discovered I was bringing her along, whoever it was must have changed their plans."

"I hope you tore those slithering assholes apart," Elias growls.

"Aria got hurt, as you saw. There wasn't much I could do without endangering her life further."

I pause, a smile forming. "Look at you. Caring about a living soul. A woman, no less."

"We need her," he says immediately, but I've known him long enough to see through his tricks.

"Uh huh."

He clenches his jaw.

Elias doesn't care about any of this. He wants to know about the fight. "How did you get out of there?"

"Sayah saved us."

"Sayah…" Elias's brow wrinkles in confusion.

"Her shadow," he explains. "That's the name she gave her."

"It's… a 'her'…?" Elias asks.

Cain's gaze hardens. "We're getting off topic. The fact of the matter is her shadow escaped her again without her control. Sayah rose like a monster, as tall as the trees, and spoke somehow. It was enough to scare off the rest of the shifters, but Aria was almost left unconscious from it."

I run a hand over my face. "So some escaped."

His body stiffens with anger, and it's enough to answer my question.

"So that means Maverick knows about Aria's shadow," Elias says. It's what we're all thinking.

"And about the harp," Cain adds.

"Fuck!" Elias punches the wall hard enough to rattle the picture frames.

This is bad.

"What do we do now?" I ask Cain, unsure where we're supposed to go from here. Looks like our good news wasn't good enough to overshadow the shitshow Aria and Cain experienced on their trip.

"We ready ourselves for another potential showdown with a dragon," he replies. "We'll worry about Maverick after."

"The ship leaves in three days," Elias reminds us. "It needs to be before then."

Cain nods in agreement. "Yes. That should be enough time to collect some souls and build up our strength. This time, we won't be taken by surprise. We can't fail."

"And what about Aria?" I ask, thinking of the mysterious woman staying in the bedroom upstairs.

"She needs to rest now. She's been through a lot."

I blink and switch on my power. Like an infrared detector, I can see a person's sexual energy. If a person has been intimate recently, it will come back the strongest. A brilliant shade of red. Virgins or people lacking in the sex department are a cool, sad, blue color, and there are different colors for everything in between. I can sense a person's hunger, their desire, as well as the overall sexual tension of a room.

On Cain, a deep red surrounds him. Not the brightest it can be, like when I saw him after his and Aria's little romp in his office, but a sexually charged aura just the same. He might not have gotten his rocks off during their trip, but he definitely came close.

Ever since Aria walked through our door, he's been sporting a lot more reds than ever before. It's a good color on him, if I do say so myself. Although he hates when I read him like this. Does that stop me? Absolutely not. I enjoy teasing him too much.

But it seems like each of us has taken a liking to our little guest, and more than in a contractual way. We've each spent time with her, intimately or not, and, I daresay, *cared* for her at some point. I know I talked to Elias about keeping this fun and civil between us four, but it's strange that each of us are feeling things other than lust. Elias may have been in love once, but I never thought it possible for me to want anything from a woman besides her body. As an incubus, it isn't in my nature.

It makes me wonder if Cain or Elias have ever considered the same thing.

"Do either of you think it's strange that we all care about Aria in one way or another?" I ask against the tense silence clogging up the room.

From both Cain and Elias's stunned expressions, it's clear they weren't expecting me to say such a thing, but when that surprise turns to deep thought, I know I've struck a chord.

"I mean, besides the sex," I clarify. "Is anyone else liking the idea of her being here? Her being with us?"

Tensing, Elias looks over at Cain, hoping he'll be the first to answer.

Cain hesitates, choosing his words carefully. Like always. "I… think her being here will be beneficial, yes."

I give him a bored look. "That's not what I meant, and you know it."

"I told you already," Elias replies through clenched teeth. "I will never make that mistake again." He's talking about Serena, of course.

I wave my hands and shake my head. "I'm not going that far. I'm merely wondering if it seems odd to you that we've all taken an interest."

"I don't think so," Cain responds in his normal stand-offish way. "She's been with us for some time now."

"And she's beautiful," Elias chimes in.

Cain agrees. "And the darkness inside her reminds us of home, too—whatever it really is. It's like having a piece of Hell here on Earth with us."

Well, when they put it like that...

"It's just another sign that we've been living too long together on this plane. Our tastes are starting to overlap," Elias says with confidence.

I bark a laugh. "Now that's a disturbing thought."

"Let's not think too hard into something that doesn't matter in the long run," Cain instructs and heads for the door. "I'm going to call Ramos and see whose soul contract is up so we can feed and be ready for whatever fight is coming our way."

"Good idea," I reply. "Because it's sure to be a doozy, and no offense, but you look like shit."

He doesn't comment, only walks out, leaving me and Elias behind. I glance at him, see the conflict warring on his face, and I know he's thinking the same thing I am.

Is there something more to us being enthralled with Aria? Or is it truly nothing, like we want to believe?

Honestly, I really don't know.

ARIA

It's hard to not wonder if what happened between Cain and I means as much to him as it does me. I'm sitting on the edge of my bed, stroking Cassiel, unable to sleep. I've been up since dawn trying to figure out what I am doing by letting myself have feelings for these demons.

They are unlike anything I expected. Don't get me wrong, they are still assholes and dominant, but I'm starting to see a side to them that makes me rethink the whole 'leaving them' thing. And that there is a massive mistake when I know what's at stake.

Me ending up in freaking Hell.

I set Cassiel on the floor, and he pounces on the bouncy balls Dorian arranged for the little boy. I pace, unsure what the right thing to do is. An unease coils in my gut at the attraction I have for the demons.

On top of that, I feel a rising pressure deep inside me… Sayah's been stirring ever since she came out at the swamp. She is terrifying, and to have her inside me, being so unpredictable, scares me.

Unable to stand another second in my room and needing fresh air, I slip out into the corridor, leaving Cassiel inside to keep playing. Most of the time he sleeps anyway, seeing as he's still a kitten.

There are no guards, which makes me ecstatic, and I hurry down the hall on silent steps. Past the paintings of devilish acts, I rush downstairs and make my way to the back door where I'm less likely to be spotted.

The door creaks when I open it, and I cringe, glancing over my shoulder. No one is rushing after me, but I realize that if I were to run away on foot, I wouldn't get far. Not after I've seen how remote this mansion is, and then there's Elias tracking me down. Maybe that's why they no longer have guards outside my door.

A cool breeze finds me as I step outside and onto the grounds. I walk deeper across the yard, the grass still wet with dew, birds singing in the distance. It is beautiful out here so early in the morning. So peaceful.

I close my eyes for a moment and take a deep inhale, trying to calm myself, to drive all the thoughts out of my head so I stop feeling like I'm suffocating from the inside out.

The sun warms my face when a faint tickle crosses my nose. The touch is as delicate as a cobweb. I slide open my eyes when something white catches my attention from the edge of the woods to my right. I twist around to find the white figure standing where he'd been the last time I saw him from my bedroom window. A shiver runs down my spine that I didn't see him there before.

There's something startling to be this close to him. He's wearing a white sleeveless tunic and pale blue jeans, arms hanging by his sides, and he's looking at me. Like the last time I saw him, there is an almost ethereal aura about him as though he's glowing... or maybe that's the effect of the sunlight rising behind him. His white hair is short around the sides and back of his head, longer across the front, sweeping over his brow.

I'm stunned, frozen on the spot, and for the life of me, I can't help but feel like maybe he *is* an angel. It's ridiculous, but an excitement stirs in my stomach to meet such a celestial being. But what is he doing here of all places?

He inclines his head in my direction and waves for me to join him.

I stiffen, my heart thumping in my chest. Something inside me is drawn to move closer to him, but as tempting as his invitation is, I shake my head and turn to head back to the house. I've learned my lesson of trusting strangers.

The crunch of foliage behind me has me turning around quickly.

He's there, feet away.

I flinch with the shock shuddering through me, recoiling. "W-who are you?"

He doesn't move to grab me, but shoves his hands into the pockets of his jeans and leans on one leg, the corners of his mouth curling upward. So close to him, I am completely taken off guard by how fast he moved… then there's his sheer beauty. That's what I notice first. It's not a word I'd often use to describe a man, but he has an interesting look that is both rugged and beautiful. Sharp cheekbones with a delicate nose, a strong jawline, and dark brown eyes with golden flecks in them. He has the longest lashes, making me jealous, as I can't even achieve that look with mascara. He reminds me of a prince from an old fairy tale, too perfect to be real.

"Delicate little thing, you don't need to fear me," he says with a voice so sinfully dark I'm not sure it belongs to the angelic figure before me.

"Are you an angel?" I murmur, unable to stop looking at him in awe. He may not be as broad in size as the demons, but he's tall and still powerful, his strong muscles flexing across his thick biceps. Who the hell is he?

"I want to help you control the darkness inside you." His gaze glimmers with an anticipation that echoes within me.

I blink at him, letting his words swirl on my mind. Sayah? He knows about her? Curiosity floods me. If he's offering some insight into what Sayah is, how to control her, I am all ears.

"I'm listening." I swallow the boulder in my throat, torn between stepping farther away from him and grilling him with questions. Why is he here? To save me? Is Sayah so dark that an angel feels the need to approach me about her?

A strange trepidation crawls up the back of my legs, and I hate that feeling. Hate how my pulse races. Hate that I can't make myself leave him when he promises me answers I crave.

"I feel the darkness staining your soul. I can help."

The way he says that makes me partially wonder if he's referring to the demons in my life and the influence they've had over me. Is that his intention? Finding out more about them?

When I don't respond, he says, "You want help or not?"

A strange sensation washes over me when he looks at me so deeply—he might very well be staring into my soul. With it, a fear bubbles deep in my core, a trepidation that if I don't stop Sayah, she will be the end of me and everyone close to me. And here I am, not even giving the possibility of saving myself a chance.

Fear dances down my skin and wraps around me tighter. His gaze deepens, and he never blinks. I could easily get lost in the depths of those eyes. The longer we remain this way, the more flashes of dread slash through me. Urgency drums in my veins that my time is running out.

Panic clings to my insides.

My arms tremble.

Coldness grips me with its touch.

I can't let Sayah out... I need to control her. I'm gasping for air. I stare into his eyes and lick my lips, temptation just within reach. "And if I do?" I breathe.

He takes a hand from his pocket and stretches it out toward me. He doesn't have to say anything. My hand reaches for him of its own accord.

Fingers touch.

A spark jumps up my arm so fast, I don't have time to react. Instead, flashes of light ignite in my mind. And for a long pause, I can no longer feel my body. It's like there's no weight to me, no heart pounding ferociously, no fear. Only a darkness lingering at the edges of my mind.

It consumes me, swallows me.

"Don't fight it." His deep voice streams over my mind.

Except I'm shaking and terrified. It doesn't feel like Sayah is backing away, but shoving forward inside me, growing and growing.

His lips are moving, and I want to listen to his words, but it's too hard. Only the sharp swishing sound in my ears finds me... the sound of grating sandpaper, scraping raw.

I grip his hand, my fingers digging into his as my knees buckle.

Darkness rolls over me like undulating waves, crashing into me, dragging me deeper.

A sudden thudding of boots hitting the ground echoes around me, pulling my attention away from the angel and to the woods to my right. Light flashes in my mind, and I stumble before I fall to my knees.

Frantically, I glance back, but the angel is gone.

Instead, a hulking figure rushes toward me.

In seconds, Elias emerges from the shadows in the tree line, his face contorting with distress. "Aria," he calls to me, alarm lining his voice. "Are you alright?"

My thoughts are thick, like molasses, impossible to flick through.

Elias is at my side, and I'm off the ground and in his arms in seconds.

The angel. Where is he? What has he done to me?

"Talk to me," Elias insists, drawing my attention to him.

"I feel like I'm falling," I manage.

"I've got you."

"No," I persist, my mind slurry. "In my head I'm falling."

In moments, I'm in my bed, and Elias sits next to me. "You fell and must have hit your head. Why were outside on your own?"

His questions muffle when I try to make sense of them. All I know is that I shake off the torrent of darkness in my head, the sensation of Sayah hovering just below the surface, waiting for her turn.

Elias strokes my hair. "Everything will be okay," he reassures me. "You need to rest."

Maybe he's right. I lay my head on the pillow, closing my eyes as he keeps running his fingers through my hair. There's something soothing about his presence, and I let myself slip under his hypnotic touch.

CHAPTER EIGHTEEN

ARIA

My knuckles go white as I hold the hairbrush, staring at myself in the mirror. All I can think about is the angel. His touch did something to me I don't understand. He said he'd help with my darkness, but it doesn't quite feel that way. Unless it takes a while?

I slept most of yesterday, which has made me feel better. Though something inside still feels odd, like I don't quite fit together. And I can't shake it off. I've always held control over myself, but ever since Sayah went AWOL, I've struggled to shake off the strange sensation that something isn't right with me. Except now it's like she's awake all the time inside me, like I've opened up a door I don't know how to shut. Normally, she's in the background.

Dropping the hairbrush into the sink, I huff with frustration and head out of the bathroom. I've checked the woods from my window most of the morning, but there's no sign of the angel. I want answers, but he's not there.

On top of everything, I had a dream about the 'abandoned' list we found in the hospital. And now the need to uncover what happened to me as a baby presses on my mind. Maybe it's for the best that I focus on something other than the darkening cobwebs clinging to my insides.

Cassiel pads across the bed and headbutts my arm, so I lift it so he can crawl onto my lap. I swoop him up into my arms and press him close to my chest. He rubs the side of his head against me, and I adore how soft he feels, how affectionate he behaves. It's exactly what I need right now... a hug.

"You're so cute, you know that," I whisper, gaining myself a faint purr as he remains attached to me.

I sit here, unable to stop my mind from whirring or the feeling that I'm balancing on the edge of a cliff I'm about to plunge off of.

Except, I can't think like that. I won't let it get the better of me. So I focus on Cain taking me to the hospital. He didn't have to do that, but he did.

How can I overlook such a meaningful gesture?

That last thought has me climbing to my feet. I know exactly how I can dig deeper into my past, and it's something I should have done earlier. I step into my sneakers, still cradling Cassiel, and we head out into the hallway to search for Cain.

It isn't long before I track him down in the parlor, staring aimlessly into the fireplace.

He glances my way when I step inside to join him,

raising a questioning eyebrow as his gaze falls to Cassiel, who has his head propped on my shoulder.

"He loves snuggles," I confess.

"I thought we agreed it stays in your room," he responds. "And how are you feeling?"

"Much better." I lie a little because if I admit there's still a weird sensation in my head, he won't let me go anywhere. "Also, this is Cassiel's home too, and he should be allowed to roam freely."

As I round the couch, I find Dorian lying on his back, legs crossed at the ankles and his hands behind his head.

"Ahh, my two favorite felines," he teases, and I roll my eyes.

Then I set Cassiel down on his legs. The lynx quickly leaps up onto the back of the sofa and arches his back.

Dorian reaches over and scratches him under the chin, which Cassiel adores, pushing himself against Dorian's touch.

"Why are you encouraging that thing?" Elias sneers as he saunters into the room. Seems the whole gang's here, which doesn't deter me from asking them my question.

"I've always had a way with felines. What can I say," Dorian answers and winks at me.

"Didn't we say it was staying in your room?" Elias says, and I cut him a hard stare. "And Aria, are you okay to be wandering around? You fell over yesterday."

"I was just telling Cain and Dorian I'm feeling brand new," I say chirpily. "And I don't agree with Cassiel being locked up. Maybe we need to get him a few scratching posts around the house." I shrug.

Elias gives a fake laugh. "What next? A cat flap in our door and milk bowls all over? For all we know, it has fleas or other bugs."

Dorian pushes himself up from the couch. "Really? You're worried the cat has fleas when you spend days sleeping out in the wild in hellhound form?"

"Fuck you!" Elias snaps. "I take showers when I get back."

The air thickens, and my intention isn't to create a storm due to my new pet.

"Look, next time we go shopping, one of us will pick up flea and worming tablets. I'm sure the cat ones will work the same on Cassiel. Problem solved," I say.

"Is there also something to stop it from tearing up my clothes?" Elias huffs. "Without making our house look like a cat cafe? Goddammit, we'd become a laughingstock if anyone from back home saw us sharing our home with a tiny fluff ball. Seriously."

I ignore his impatience with accepting Cassiel because he isn't going anywhere, which is only confirmed when no one responds. I take the moment to change gears while smiling at them. "I was hoping we could talk about something else," I say, sweeping my gaze to each of them, settling on Cain.

"Go on," he says as Dorian sits on one side of the sofa while Elias moves to stand near the wall with the bookshelves, arms folded over his chest.

"Ever since Cain and I found that note in the hospital in Illinois, I feel like I'm missing something major about my parents. And I'm thinking that I need to check everything again, including talking to my friend Joseline. She lived at Murray's the longest of us all. She knew him the best. There's a chance he might have said something to her. Even the smallest thing might help me find out why my parents abandoned me." I finally take a breath.

"So you want to visit your friend?" Cain asks, which I thought was pretty obvious. "I'm not sure it's a good idea. You haven't been well."

I straighten my shoulders. "She should be home unless her work schedule's changed. Like I said, I really am feeling better. I miss her, and maybe that's part of why I haven't been great. I just need a small getaway." Part of me thinks if I return to the familiarity of my friend, it might also help shake off the strangeness in my body.

Cain blinks at me, and I see the wheels spinning behind his gaze. Softness sweeps over his expression when he says, "It might be a good idea."

His smile reminds me of our time away when he showed me a side of himself I've never seen before. A side I adore.

Dorian narrows his eyes at Cain. Apparently even he is taken aback.

"Elias," Cain states. "You will accompany Aria. While you're out, buy some cat tablets, or whatever will ensure our house isn't infested with fleas."

When I turn to Elias, shadows gather under his eyes as he stares at Cassiel, who is prancing toward him along one of the bookshelves. Elias's upper lip curls upward, a growl rolling out.

Cassiel suddenly catapults himself at him, claws first.

I freeze on the spot, same as the others, as we watch the spectacle. Elias jolts away from the shelves to escape Cassiel's grip, but it's too late. Cassiel has latched himself to his arm, claws digging into his clothes and skin to hold on.

Dorian howls with laughter, while Cain just shakes his head.

Elias hisses and snatches Cassiel by the scruff, plucking the cat off him. Tiny holes appear in the sleeve of his tee, along with spots of blood. "It just attacked me! You all saw that! It needs to be locked up."

I hurry over and collect Cassiel into my arms. "Don't be so dramatic. He just wanted to snuggle you."

He gives me a deadpan stare. "Yeah right. Snuggle me with its claws." He pulls at the sleeve of his shirt, now punctured, and sighs heavily. "I'm going to change. Meet you out front in ten, and don't bring that thing with you," he snarls.

"Geez," I say, watching him storm out of the room. "Someone's in a crappy mood. It's only a lynx."

Dorian sidles up to me and collects Cassiel into his arms. "Ignore him. He's not a pet person."

"There's just one thing," I say to him, gaining his attention. "I need to borrow a phone to message Joseline. I don't know exactly where she lives."

Dorian doesn't waste a moment and hands me his

phone, and I hastily punch her a quick message about me visiting.

Two seconds later, his cell phone pings. Joseline sent half a dozen lines of excited emojis followed by her address, which I memorize as I smile at her response. "Thanks." And I hand it back to him.

Cain approaches me as Dorian heads over to sit by the fire with Cassiel. "Just a quick trip. There and back, understood? Tonight, we're all going out somewhere, and I want you rested beforehand."

"Where are we going?"

He exchanges a knowing glance with Dorian and looks back to me. "You'll find out once you return with Elias."

In ten minutes, Elias and I are sitting in the back of the limousine, the driver taking us farther from the mansion. Lofty trees with leaves already yellowing from the colder weather approaching pepper the landscape. There is literally nothing out here but wilderness.

I turn to Elias, who stares at me rather than at the landscape. He's changed into a long-sleeve blue button-up shirt that pulls taut over his chest. The fabric curves over his biceps, and well, there is absolutely nothing small about Elias. And I mean nothing. The thought of us in the woods heats my cheeks, and I swallow hard, steering my thoughts elsewhere.

"So, the limo, hey. You didn't feel like driving? I mean, I'd be happy to give it a go."

He eyes me without a single reaction. Is he still pissed about the whole 'Cassiel pouncing on him' thing? "I don't drive."

"Don't like to drive or can't?"

"Latter. Never saw the need. I only go into town when I'm on one of Cain's errands."

"Me too. Well, not the Cain part. I didn't get my licence because it costs so much and I never had the money, or access to a car, for that matter." I half shrug. "Public transport did the trick back in town."

He leans forward, bent arms resting on his thighs. "What are you really hoping to uncover from your friend?"

I sit back in my seat and lick my lips, curious about his question. "You make it sound like I have an ulterior motive. You were there when I explained why."

"I heard, and Cain informed us about the list you found at the hospital. But I'm curious why finding out about your past is suddenly so crucial. Makes me wonder if maybe you have other questions for your friend."

I narrow my gaze in his direction. "You don't trust me?"

"That's not what I said." He blinks a couple of times, his gaze slicing into me. I was grossly not expecting this grilling from Elias.

"Why are you all grizzly today? Are you angry at the cat shredding your sleeve?"

His face scrunches up as if that's the last thing on his mind. Okay, so it's not that.

He suddenly pulls back and reclines in his seat.

I lean forward, reaching across to place my hand on his. After our time in the woods, I know we have a connection, so I hope to tap into that. "Did I do something wrong?"

"No," he responds instantly. "I just don't want any surprises—I'm trying to keep you safe. And I'm worried about you and how you've been recently. I want to ensure you are feeling one hundred percent in doing this."

His answer is not what I expected. "Oh, you're worried about me."

He places his hand on mine, trapping it against his thigh as he pulls in closer to me. "Is that so hard to fathom?"

Tingles rush up my arm from where he touches me, and now, no matter how hard I try, I can't stop thinking about him claiming me in the woods. His dominance, his obsession. I can't deny that his presence alone leaves me buzzing with a rising desire. Suddenly, I'm studying the curve of his mouth, remembering his rough kisses and how incredible they felt. Somehow, that earlier fog in my head clears up when it comes to everything Elias.

His thumb strokes the back of my hand, and my body tingles. "I adore the way your body reacts to me. Your pupils dilate, your nipples press against the fabric of your dress. It's beautiful."

Fire streaks across my chest, and a flash of arousal clenches between my thighs. A single touch, a few words, and I'm putty in his hands. How did we even get to this point when moments earlier he seemed to be brooding?

Despite the unbearable need coursing through me, I slide my hand from his. Yay for me in having a semblance of self-control.

"Around you, I lose my thoughts and control," he admits, his fingers curling around my hand, having no intention of releasing me. "I don't know what's come over me half the time, but aside from being unable to stop thinking about grabbing you over my lap and fucking you right now, I want to keep you safe. That's why I asked earlier. I *am* on your side."

My thoughts glide back and forth between thinking straight and the cobwebs blurring my thoughts. Every inch of me hums under his attention, and his words seem genuine. The thing is, I don't for a moment doubt he wants to keep me protected. The issue is more about his true intentions. Does he see me as a means to an end, a way to get relics? Or are his actions spurred by his motivation to return to Hell?

I hate that such doubt swirls in my head, and I wish for things to be simple. Except there is nothing straightforward when it comes to these demons, is there?

"You still carry doubt," he says, pulling me forward by my hand. "Come to me."

"Umm why." My voice trembles, but it doesn't stop me from leaning closer. Large hands fall to my hips, and he practically lifts me off my seat, bringing me to him. My hands snap to his shoulders, and his legs are pressed together, forcing mine to straddle him. Our chests press together, and my insides tighten. I glance to the black glass between us and the driver.

"You were too far from me." He chuckles, and I lower my gaze to meet his. "Do you have any fucking idea how irresistible you are?"

I struggle to believe him. My track record with guys is almost non-existent, yet around these demons, I feel like a goddess. "I don't think that's true," I say. "You three are the hottest men I've ever laid eyes on, but I don't quite understand what you see in me."

With one hand, he cups the side of my face and brings me closer so our lips graze. The heat from him envelopes me, and a growl rumbles in his chest.

"Hear that?" he asks.

I nod. "I even felt it in your body."

He takes my hand and places my palm flush with the center of his chest. "Hellhounds connect with others through their animal side as well as their human side. My hound has been drawn to you from the beginning. He's claimed you. That is why I won't let you out of my sights, why you will always be mine, why I will hunt you down if you ever run. I've already bonded with you."

I've lost the ability to talk. The cocktail of arousal from the hardness in his pants rubbing over my heat and the fire in his words short-circuit my brain. He has this way of turning me on while sharing heartfelt words that leave me dumbfounded.

His hands are on my thighs, sliding upward. "When I look at you, I see everything I am not, everything I long to claim and connect with."

I gasp as his fingers inch under the material of my dress.

"Do you see now why you mean so much?"

The pad of his finger strokes the edge of my underwear.

"Yes," I breathe heavily, shaking against him.

"You are stunning when you're turned on."

I can't stop myself, not when I'm shivering with building need. I press my mouth to his, and he kisses me instantly, savagely, his tongue sweeping into my mouth. He licks my lips as he pulls aside my underwear, teasing me with touch, his fingers roaming over my drenched offering.

He pauses and pulls back from our kiss. "Just triple checking—you are okay with this after yesterday? I don't want to make it worse for you."

"Just shut up and kiss me." Arousal soars within me as he fiddles with his pants, unzipping himself. Seconds later, the tip of his searing hot erection glides over my entrance.

"Is this what you want?"

"Please don't stop," I whisper against his mouth. Without ceremony, he thrusts into me, his hips jutting upward, filling me completely.

I moan, throwing my head back as my hips rock up and down to match each of his movements. He plunges in and out of me, the intensity heightening.

Shudders of pleasure flare over me, and I'm groaning louder now, the beautiful ache he brings driving me insane. Pleasure and pain tangle into a beautiful dance of him kissing me passionately as he fucks me like a demon.

His growls rise to meet my own. He grips my hips and moves me to a faster tempo as he surges closer. He fills me, stroking my insides, igniting an inferno between us. In moments, my orgasm breaks free, tearing through me like powerful waves, crashing into me over and over.

"Oh, Elias," I cry out as he pumps into me, his body convulsing along with mine as we both explode with climaxes, almost in unison.

My breaths rush in and out of my lungs as I cling to him, both of us wrapped up in each other, pulsing and moaning. Finally I collapse against his chest, drawing in ragged breaths.

"That was everything," he whispers in my ear, breathing heavily as well.

"It was pretty amazing."

When I pull back, he's smiling wildly. "I have no control around you," he admits as he leans over and pulls out a packet of tissues from the side of the door.

"That's two of us." I laugh at how similar we both are.

He makes short work of pulling out of me and wiping me clean, lifting me to sit across from him. His strength is extraordinary.

I adjust my underwear and glance outside as I lower my dress over my legs, noticing we're already in town and parked on the curb.

I jolt forward and stare outside at the sidewalk, where people are wandering in and out of stores.

"Oh shit! We just had sex on the side of a busy road!" My heartbeat escalates, and it has zero to do with arousal. "Can people see through the windows?"

Elias chuckles. "I thought you were into being an exhibitionist?"

My mouth drops open. "You knew and didn't tell me?"

Still laughing, Elias pushes open the door, and a flurry of air rushes in, cooling my burning cheeks. He heads over to a trash can to throw away the ball of tissues.

I hurry to climb out, suddenly feeling like everyone is looking my way, judging me. My head spins, and I steady myself until it stops. Being out of the car and off Elias's lap, that earlier unease creeps forward. I lick my lips and tense up, hating the foggy sensation.

I can't help but feel eyes on me from people on the sidewalk. I pat down my skirt frantically. God, was the car rocking with us humping? I look over to see our driver is sitting with his window open, blowing out smoke from a cigarette like he's the one who's just had the most incredible sex.

Embarrassment strikes me like hot pokers. He had to know what we were doing.

Elias shuts the door. "Are you ready?"

Shaking off the nerves, I glance around to the road packed with cars and people everywhere. Storefronts in every direction. "Where are we? Joseline doesn't live here."

Elias offers me that brilliant smile that weakens my knees. "We're making a pit stop for supplies for your cat." When I follow his gaze, I find a small grocery store right in front of us.

Right!

He leans in quickly and kisses me. "You are unusual."

I narrow my eyes at him. "How so?"

"You didn't bat an eye to having sex with me openly in the woods, but here you are blushing over *maybe* being seen? You should be proud of enjoying sex."

"Are you even listening to yourself?" I say, unable to even fathom his reasoning. "Let's just do this. It feels like everyone is staring at me."

He laughs again, louder, drawing more attention our way.

Head low, I hurry alongside him and into the store. We're barely a step inside when a staff member, a blonde with long legs and the reddest lipstick, pins her attention on Elias.

She's strolling toward us with an extra swing in her hips, her gaze taking all of him in, pretending I'm not standing right there next to him. Next thing I know, my earlier embarrassment has dissolved into a surge of jealousy, rising through me like a beast.

CHAPTER NINETEEN
ARIA

"Welcome to Gracy's Groceries, GGs as we like to call it." The staff member smiles like a mad person toward Elias, batting her eyes. "Is there something I can assist you with, sir?"

I don't even hear his response. I'm not sure what's suddenly come over me. Fire burns across my chest at the way she laughs and reaches over to place her hand on his forearm. It mingles with the confusion knotting in my body and makes me feel unfocused. It's the only way to describe it.

"Flea tablets for a cat," Elias responds, completely and utterly oblivious to the flirtatious woman. She must be in her mid-twenties, her red knee-length skirt super tight, the white button-up shirt following every curve—and she is definitely sticking her chest out at Elias.

"I will personally show you," she insists, pouting her lips. "I am a huge fan of cats."

Gag.

"No, we're fine, thank you. And he hates cats," I

interject curtly. I loop my arm around his and nudge him to move away from the praying mantis and into the first aisle, which is filled with canned soups and beans.

"I don't hate cats," he says. "Are you sure we don't need the lady's help?"

"How hard can it be to find cat tablets? We don't need anyone's assistance." I release Elias and march down the aisle.

I feel creepy inside by acting so stupid. What is wrong with me? Still, the inferno in my chest rages each time I think of the way she practically threw herself on him, while a blanket of darkness coats my mind. I'm a walking mess.

"Are you jealous?" he asks as he catches up to me near a display of chocolates.

I turn toward him, then scan to see if there is anyone around. "Do you want me to get you the microphone? Pretty sure the people out on the sidewalk didn't hear you."

The corners of his mouth curl upward while I toss daggers at him from my glare. "Oh, rabbit, she does not interest me. There is nothing she can offer that you don't have. Just looking at you, I get a hard-on." He reaches down and gropes himself to prove his point just as an old couple pushes their cart past us, the woman gasping at the sight. "But I will be honest, I love seeing you all fired up over me. It's hot."

He's smiling wickedly and gloating.

"Don't kid yourself. I am not jealous of that stick. I-I j-just didn't want her to trick you into buying the most expensive tablets for Cassiel. He is no ordinary feline."

Why do I suddenly feel like I'm burning up? "I don't need to explain myself to you."

I whip around and march from aisle to aisle, doing my best to look as normal as possible— even if I seem to be walking at an angle—until I find the one for pet supplies. Perfect. Now I can get this and we can leave. I feel stupid for my earlier reaction, and worst yet, I don't want Elias to rub this in my face. He seems the kind to remind me of it every second he can.

Halfway down the empty aisle, strong fingers curl around my wrist and haul me backward so abruptly, I stumble on my feet and crash right into Elias's chest.

His hands clasp my waist, and before I can protest, his lips are on mine. He drives me back, still attached to me, until my back hits the shelves. Small boxes of things fall to the floor, but neither of us stops.

A delicious shiver races down my spine. A moan escapes my lips as my nipples tighten at the way he kisses me. It's rough, like he's trying to prove I am the only one for him, his tongue surging into my mouth. I'm panting. It seems I have no control, and the moment he kisses me, I'm instantly addicted. I feel like a soft porn star, ready to go at the drop of a hat.

His mouth leaves a trail of kisses over my cheek and licks the tender spot under my earlobe. "Seeing you jealous makes me so fucking horny, I want to strip you here and now and eat your pussy."

I might have just had a tiny orgasm just hearing him whisper those words. When he kisses down my neck, a wave of desire pulses through me.

But a sudden clearing of a throat has me pushing Elias aside.

I stand rooted to the floor, iced over as I stare at the woman who was preying on Elias earlier. She's at the end of the aisle, eyeing us like she might erupt into a volcano of rage. I elbow Elias, who's gone back to nibbling on my neck, and shove him off me. My cheeks turn scarlet.

I want to die.

Quickly, I reach over to the shelf and pick up the first cat flea box within reach.

"Ah, found it. Okay, let's go," I say, loud enough for her to hear.

As we pass the woman, Elias gives his farewell, which seems to sate her fury and turn it into another obsessive staring event.

Using the self-serve machines, I scan the box and Elias pays, then we're out of there so fast, I'm practically running to the limousine. I want to be away from so many people.

"I swear, that woman was going to either kill me or hump you right in the aisle," I say as I climb into the back seat.

"I would have preferred she watched *me* hump *you*." He shuts the door before I can respond, but I have no doubt he meant every word. Along with realizing Elias is into voyeurism, it makes me wonder—what else turns him on?

In no time, we're are driving through the city, and Elias is grinning, well aware of the influence he has over me and that I'd just morphed into a green-eyed monster back in the store. But what sits on my mind is that I might not be doing as well as I first thought.

To distract myself, I glance down and read the packet in my hands. "Says here we just have to give the cat one tablet every month to keep him clear of fleas and worms."

His jaw tightens. "Great."

I look out and see we're right outside my friend's apartment. A sudden explosion of excitement floods me.

I shove open the door of the limousine and rush outside, an overwhelming sensation billowing inside me. Excitement. Nerves. Anticipation.

By the time I reach the front steps of the lofty apartment complex, a shadow falls over me.

"I will accompany you to your friend's front door and wait outside," Elias says behind me, and I twist my head to look at him.

"Thank you." Does he understand how much such a gesture means to me? That he offers me trust and alone time with Joseline means a heck of a lot.

He tilts his head to the side, eyeing me. "You're looking at me like you want me to carry you back into the car for another round of fun."

"Actually, this is a look of admiration for your gesture, but you've just lost that brownie point." I turn, smiling at his fallen face, and hit the button next to Joseline's name on the panel near the door. Only then do I realize I hadn't called Joseline to let her know I'm coming over. Not that I have a phone to do so. Well, too late for that now.

"Hello," her crackly voice responds over the small intercom.

"Hey babe, it's me."

"Aria!" she squeals over the speaker, and seconds later, a beep sounds at the door. "Come up, girl."

I shove the door open and rush toward a closing elevator. Elias is on my heels, and we're lunging through the metal doors where an elderly couple stands inside. A quick smile to them, and I jam my finger into the fifth floor button.

Elias stands behind me, his hands on my waist, drawing me closer to him as the doors shut. Then we lurch upward.

The older woman makes no effort to hide her gaze. She is studying us, when her husband clears his throat. He leans closer to his wife and says, "Remember when I was as big as him?"

My heart melts at the way she smiles at him as if she is falling for him all over again. That's how I want to be when I get old... then I think of the demons in my life and don't even know if they do get old. With it comes a myriad of questions about me getting old and dying before them, and why the heck I am even having such thoughts? As if the demons were long-term anything with me.

The elevator shudders as it stops, and the doors open. The old couple head out just as the woman glances over her shoulder at me. "Climb that tree every day." She smirks, eyes Elias, then heads out with her husband.

My mouth drops open that she just said what I think

she said.

"What an odd couple," Elias murmurs as the doors shut. "And that is one crude old gal."

I burst out laughing that time. Once we head out and walk down the dimly lit corridor that smells like a new car, I pause in front of number 502. Before I can even turn to Elias, the door swings open.

"Oh. My. God. I can't believe it. I miss you!" Joseline throws herself at me, speaking in her usual Joseline way —so fast I can barely understand her.

She's hugging me so hard, I can't breathe.

"This is the best surprise ever!" She jumps and squeals some more before she pulls back, holding my hands, studying me. And only then does she realize we aren't alone in the corridor.

The moment she turns her head to look over at Elias, her demeanor stiffens. "You brought him? The demon eye candy?"

Last time I saw Joseline was out on the sidewalk near Murray's, and well, even then, Elias didn't make a good impression.

Elias's eyebrow raises, but he manages to hold a stoic expression regardless. "I'm going to be out here waiting," he reminds me.

Joseline doesn't need to be told twice. She loops her arm around mine and hauls me into her apartment, whispering, "He's not a people person, is he?"

"You have no idea."

I glance back just as she shuts the door behind us and catch Elias looking at me with a deadpan expression. Like nothing in the world could be more boring. Joseline takes my hand and drags me inside.

Her place is vastly different from what I expected. It's filled with brand new furniture, paintings on the walls, new light fixtures, and shiny floorboards. There's a curved leather sofa in front of a large TV mounted on the wall, a cabinet with glass doors displaying crystal animal figurines, and the sliding door that leads to the balcony shows a small barbecue outside. The kitchen sits to the right, and the hallway leading to the bedrooms—which I somehow suspect are decked out as well—is on the left. I had plans to get an apartment with Joseline before the whole 'Murray selling me to demons' debacle, but those plans obviously got thrown out the window.

It seems like she's doing well for herself. Without me.

"You like it?" She beams with pride and hurries onto the plush white rug in the middle of the room. "You need to feel how soft this is under your feet."

"Did you get a promotion at work?" Don't get me wrong, I am ecstatic for her, but she didn't have much money.

"Got something better." She flicks her mousey blonde hair over her shoulder. "A rich roommate, but she's out with her boyfriend right now. It's nice to have the place to myself today."

"Damn, she must be loaded. This is amazing for you." I kick off my shoes and rush over to sink into the rug. "Oh, this is heaven."

"Right? So, tell me everything. How did you get the

demons to allow you out? You're not their prisoner? It sure seemed like they were holding you captive last time I saw you. What's it like living with them? Are they all hot like that one outside?"

She talks so fast, it's hard to keep up with all her rapid-fire questions. I try to sort through them to answer each.

"Hmm, let me see. I asked them to bring me here. Living with them is the most surreal thing ever. They have major issues and don't fully understand humans, so it's like I'm in the twilight zone most of the time. They're actually surprisingly nice to me… sometimes. Other days, they have their devil horns out."

I head over and flop down on the couch. Joseline does the same, then turns to eye me. "You totally slept with them, didn't you?"

Heat crawls over my cheeks. "He can probably hear us, you know."

Her eyes widen, and she glances toward the door. I have no clue if I'm right, but I prefer not talking about my crazy sex life with my best friend when I still don't get how I can be so madly attracted to three demons. Or do the things we've done together.

"Anyway, what have you been up to?" I reach over and take her hand. "I've missed you so much."

"Me too, babe. Mostly just working." She keeps telling me about her work as a sales clerk, how the girl she lives with might be secretly running a video porno program from her bedroom based on the sounds she hears at night, and general, normal things like clothes shopping and sales.

"I don't miss shopping," I admit. "Never had the money for it anyway."

She jumps up on her feet. "Geez, how rude of me. I didn't even offer you coffee!"

"Yes, please!" As she busies herself, I recline and let my mind wander to what life might be like if I lived here.

Freedom.

Not being watched every day or needing permission to leave the house.

Probably scraping by on some meager dead-end job to pay the bills.

I push off the couch and go stand at the kitchen door, propping a shoulder against the wall. As I guessed, all the appliances are new, the stainless steel shining still like it's just been unwrapped.

"I got a job," I say.

"Really? They let you work? Where?" She spoons coffee granules into two cups as the kettle heats up. She's never been a fan of filter coffee and loves her Nescafe.

"At Purgatory."

She drops the empty spoon in her hand onto the tiled floor. "At the sex club? Isn't that place by invite only? Don't tell me they are pimping you out, or I will seriously kick their asses."

I snort a laugh, loving her protectiveness. "Cain, one of the demons I live with, owns Purgatory, and he gave me a job taking orders and delivering drinks. I get a bit of pocket money and it gets me out of their mansion. Anyway, I work with this girl who's dating a master vampire, and she's really kind to me."

She collects the spoon and tosses it into the sink, the metal on metal clanking loudly. "I heard there are rooms where guests can go and have sex."

"They're called the Red Rooms, and it's pretty accurate. On my last shift, Man Swell was there, and women booked private sessions with them in the rooms. Did you know they are dolphin shifters?"

"Shut up! They are not!"

I nod as her surprised expression reminds me how much I've missed just gossiping with her about anything and everything.

"I suddenly feel dirty having drooled over fish. Tell me more." As she pours hot water into our cups, I take the chance to give her a quick rendition, remembering Elias waits outside.

By the time we sit down and sip on the nutty coffee, I turn to Joseline. "Hey, listen, I wanted to ask you something about Murray."

She drinks her coffee, looking at me over the rim of her cup, and nods with her dazzling hazel eyes.

"Recently I got ahold of some paperwork showing I was abandoned at the hospital after I was born."

Her eyes widen. "Oh, shit. I'm so sorry." She reaches out and places a hand on my thigh.

"I've been trying to find out a bit more about my parents. Maybe get an idea why they did what they did? So, I thought, you and Murray were close… Did he ever mention something to you in passing about my background?"

Her lips purse and pinch to the side of her mouth. "Geez, half the time I didn't listen to his waffling. I know he did his best to look after us, but he was a selfish bastard. He once tried to convince me to visit someone's house and take" —she pauses to put her coffee cup down so she can curl her fingers into air quotes—"'something from their personal belongings' so he could trade it for his gambling habit."

My stomach twists. "Oh wow. I didn't know."

"He backed off when I told him to go shove it where the sun don't shine. Anyway, aside from that, the only thing I can think of is he once made a strange comment about you I ignored."

I lean in close. "What was it?"

"Something about being paid well to take you under his care. I just assumed it referred to those measly government paychecks he got for fostering us. Though in hindsight, it was strange he only mentioned you, not me."

I sink into my seat, lowering my gaze to my lap, trying to piece it all together. He was paid to foster me? That didn't make sense.

"Anything else?" I ask.

She shakes her head. "Sorry, babe."

"It's fine. Just another piece of the puzzle I'm working on." I smirk and set my cup down on the coffee table, then get up. "Just need to pee. I'll be back," I say, heading down the corridor to the bathroom.

"Cool. I'll get us some cookies," she calls out.

My mind swirls with uncertainty, disappointment sinking through me that I didn't find more information.

That's another reason I should come back and visit her. I'm sure Elias is getting antsy outside.

Strolling past Joseline's room, I can't help but glance inside. She's always been a mess-maker back home. Clothes strewn on the floor, drawers open, bed covers a tangle… except that's not what I find.

My feet stop moving and lock in place in the doorway of her bedroom. I am staring at a damn pentagram painted on the wooden floorboards, sticking out from a rug that hasn't been fully rolled flat. Something in my stomach tightens. Since when has Joseline been into dark magic? She was born a witch and practiced white magic mostly… the small stuff, like putting positive energy around her. But I've never seen her use any symbols like this before. Unless she'd hidden it from me.

A quick glance over my shoulder shows she is in the kitchen with her back to me, so I slide inside. A huge four post bed fills half the room with dark mahogany wood and satin blue sheets. Fancy. Expensive. Like the rest of the apartment now. Did her friend buy her a new bed as well?

I scan the rest of the room. Bookshelves crammed with books and black candles, including a skull-shaped crystal ball. That is totally her. The table by the window has several parchment papers and scrolls, and curiosity draws me closer.

I examine the flattened-out scroll, running my finger over words I don't understand. At the top is a circle with another inside, the letters surrounding it too faint to make out. And in the middle is a strange shape, almost like an obese slug with no head curling around an arrow. No wait, there's an eye. Whatever it's meant to be, it's freaky. Nearby is a bowl of small bones, and my skin crawls.

What is Joseline doing with this stuff? She once told me she never uses bones in spells, as it draws negative energy. Ice fills my veins that maybe my friend is messing around with something dark.

"Hey, what are you doing?" Joseline's abrupt voice has me jumping in my skin.

I jerk around, fire scalding my cheeks as panic sets in. "Just wanted to check out your new furniture." I curse myself for sounding so lame, and she looks at me with a stoic expression like she sees right through my lie. I might as well come out with it. "What's with the pentagram and bones? Are you going into the dark stuff?"

She huffs and strolls in to join me. "Most of it is my roommate's. She swapped rooms when her other roommate moved out—she wanted the other since it's attached to the bathroom. But she hasn't moved all her crap yet."

"So she's a witch too?"

She nods. "She's in a new-age coven. Super secretive, but they're into some exotic stuff. I try not to judge." She simply blows it off and smiles, heading out the room. "You coming?"

I'm not sure what to make of her response, but now I worry that her new roommate is leading her into the dark arts. "Listen, if you want to talk about anything, I want to be here for you. I'm going to ask the demons to bring me over so we can catch up more often. What do you think?"

"Yes. I'd love that. But seriously, babe, I'm all good, and in fact—"

A loud knock at the front door steals her words. I sigh, well aware who it is. "I think that's my signal to leave."

She frowns, her lips pinching. "You need to come back, and for longer next time. Promise me?"

"Of course." We make our way into the living room, but the unease of what I found in her bedroom doesn't leave my thoughts. She opens the door as I slip back into my shoes and look up to Elias, who fills the entrance doorway.

"Time we left," he says, his expression serious, even as Joseline stares up at him.

"I'm Joseline by the way," she says to him, extending a hand in greeting.

He just stares at it, his lip curling slightly. "Elias."

Silence.

"Okay, well I better be off," I say and hug Joseline amidst the budding tension. "Please take care, and I'll try to call soon."

"You better." She smiles, and with a final wave, I head down the corridor with Elias.

"We need to work on our social skills," I say.

"Why? I said hello back. It's more than I normally do."

I roll my eyes at him. When we reach the front of the apartment, I glance back and look up to Joseline's window. I hope she's not doing something really stupid.

CHAPTER TWENTY
DORIAN

The moment the limo pulls up in front of the mansion, I breathe easier.

"They're finally home," I holler and thump the top of our car to let Cain know. He's been waiting inside, but my excitement for a possible fight has me bouncing on my toes.

Ever since Elias and I found Sir Surchion's hideaway, I've been ready—ready to take back what's ours and taste some sweet, sweet revenge.

Cain hopes we don't run into the collector this time. He doesn't want to make a fight out of nothing, which surprises me. Cain's always loved getting his hands dirty, but I know what's changed this time. Aria.

She took quite a beating with Sir Surchion and the Full Mooners the last time they crossed, and then again with the snake shifters in the swamps. As much as he tries to fight his feelings for the girl, he doesn't want to risk her safety again. He'd leave her behind if he could, but we need her. So, the goal this time is to go to the harbor, sniff out the relics, nab them, and get out. Dragon free.

The window rolls down, and Cain's glare finds me immediately. "Is there a reason for all that banging?"

Aria and Elias get out of their limo and stroll over to us. The smiles on their faces tell me two things—they had a *good* time, which I can confirm by the bright red color surrounding them both, and they forgot we're on a tight deadline here.

My insides are buzzing with too much pent-up energy. All the extra souls we ate in preparation for this isn't helping either, I'm sure. "Let's get this moving, people! A little more pep in that step."

Smiles fading, they glance at the Town Car, confusion wrinkling both their foreheads. But then the answer seems to come to Elias. His eyes widen.

"Oh shit," he says.

"Yes, exactly," I say. "We've been waiting on you. Now get in."

The idea of a pending fight has Elias's wolfish amber eyes flashing.

"Stand down, big boy," I remind him. "Remember. We are just taking back our stuff, not killing the bastard."

Elias curls his hands into balls. "I don't see why not."

"Wait," Aria cuts in, her voice trembling slightly. "*Where* are we going?"

Oh man. I'd forgotten we hadn't told her of our plans yet. I glance at Cain for backup.

She wraps her arms around herself and shivers.

"We're going to kill Sir Surchion and get the relics back, aren't we?"

"Hopefully it doesn't come to that," Cain replies from inside the car. "The relics are the most important thing. That's our main objective."

And keep Aria safe. I can hear his unspoken concerns, even though he doesn't utter them out loud. He doesn't need to. I know him well enough.

Cain opens the car door and slides all the way in. I wave for Aria to climb in the back with us while Elias takes his place by the driver.

Once inside, I close the door. The Town Car is larger than a normal sedan and much more roomier than any of my sport cars, but between me, Aria, and Cain, it's still a bit cramped. I don't understand why we couldn't have just taken my Audi, at least. It was faster if we needed to get out quick.

The driver pulls away from the house and heads toward Dawson. Everyone is anxiously quiet, all preoccupied with their own thoughts. Aria's mouth is twisted into a sickened grimace, and she looks a bit paler than before. I'd bet money she's thinking about her last run-in with Sir Surchion, too. I know I am. I still have the burn scar on my face from the bastard.

"So, what's the plan?" Aria asks, trying to break the stifling tension. "I just… walk around and try to feel for the relics?"

Cain nods and answers without even looking at her. "Elias and Dorian will scour the perimeter and ensure Sir Surchion isn't around so there are no surprises."

Aria swallows. She tries to put on a brave face, but I

can see the uncertainty lying underneath. I want to tell her not to worry, but would that help any? I doubt it. Not when she's been through so much already. We just have to do like Cain says and protect her if things go sideways. Show her that with us, she can be safe.

The drive into Dawson is faster than I anticipated. It isn't long before we park in front of a locked gate in front of the shipping yard. We definitely did not come this way on our last visit here. There's even a guard station and cameras overlooking the fence.

"Go around, toward the abandoned buildings there," I direct the driver, leaning forward and pointing toward the docks on the left. "Park in one of the small alleys. There isn't a gate there."

Wasting no time, the car swings around toward the more quiet and secluded part of the harbor. We all pile out. The salty and crisp water smell in the air fills my nostrils. Elias leads the way, using his nose as a guide, while Cain and Aria stay in the middle with me holding up the rear.

Passing rows and rows of huge cargo containers, we scan the area. The place seems deserted, besides the random seagull flying overhead.

"Damn. This place is enormous." Aria keeps her voice low as we walk closer to the water.

"Let's be quick," Cain instructs. "As soon as you sense anything, let us know."

She hesitates but eventually gives him a subtle nod.

We pass more metal storage containers, some stacked on top of each other, two or three high. If Aria senses anything at the top, it wouldn't be too hard for me to climb up. But when she continues to pass by them without so much as a second glance, my hopes of having some fun are quickly dashed. Dammit.

"Does merchandise just sit around until someone collects it?" Aria asks.

"My guess is that most of these are empty. Only the ones closer to the docks are filled and ready for shipping," Cain replies.

"Then let's head that way first," she suggests.

Elias lifts his nose into the air, his nostrils flaring. Spinning on his heel, he turns right, down another slender aisle between containers. "This way," he grumbles.

We follow, rounding another long row and emerging closer to the water. A single row of containers lines the pier near a massive, rusty crane. Must be what they use to load the ships, but the thing's definitely seen better days.

I do a quick count. Twenty. Just like the woman on the phone said would be added to the next shipment.

Cain encourages Aria to step closer. Seeming unsure, she hugs herself, shivering against the cold wind, and moves to the first box.

"Anything?" I ask, my nerves getting the better of me.

"Be patient," Aria snaps. "It doesn't work like that."

"Maybe you need to get closer," Elias adds.

She glares at him. "Can you just give me a minute? All this pressure is stressing me out."

Elias and I step back, giving her some space to… well, to do whatever it is she does for this kind of stuff.

Cain turns to us. "Why don't you two do a quick sweep for anything suspicious? When you come back, we'll open the container together."

"Fine. I'll take the left. Elias, you're right," I say.

He smirks at me. "Yes, I am."

What an awful joke. Just *awful*.

Cain shakes his head. "Go."

"Roger that." I fake salute him. Elias and I are off and running in opposite directions in the next second.

ARIA

When Elias and Dorian disappear from sight, Cain gives me a reassuring dip of his head. "Go ahead, Aria. Take your time."

Heaving a sigh, I stare down the long line of containers. I really don't want to do this.

"Would it be better for you if we walk past them?" Cain asks, his tone surprisingly gentle despite the importance of the situation. His gaze, though, pierces through me. What is he thinking? Is he wondering if I'll let him down or if this will end up like the swamps somehow?

Maybe I'm overthinking things, but on my last encounter with Sir Surchion, I almost died. A few times. And let's not forget that the last time I tried tracking a relic for Cain, we ended up ambushed and—to no one's surprise—almost dead. *Again.*

My only hope is that this time won't turn out like any of those other ones. Maybe I shouldn't say anything and end up jinxing it. That would be my luck.

I turn toward the first container and wait for the familiar weird vibrating sensation down my leg and into my pinky toe. It stays undisturbed. Not so much as a twitch. So it's definitely not there.

We keep going down the row, yet my mind is miles away. Part of me is torn between wanting to take the artifacts back from Sir Surchion and not letting the demons get them back. If they find them, then they're three relics closer to going back to Hell, and that means taking me with them. That thought is like a pebble in my shoe, constantly nagging at me in the back of my mind. Since my soul is technically theirs, they want to bring me with them. But Hell is no place for me.

"Hey, Cain," I say softly, unsure if this is the right time to bring this up, but it's grinding on my mind. "I know you want to return to Hell once you find all your relics..." I pause as he glances my way, one eyebrow arched, waiting for me to finish. I stop walking. "Except, I don't want to go. I can't go. I don't belong there."

His gaze darkens on me, and my throat dries. I'm realizing now that what I'm about to say could have dire consequences for me, and I stumble through the rest of my explanation out of fear. "So, I hope you understand that I can't help you find the relics again. It'd be suicide, and I can't do that. I just… can't."

He studies me for a long moment, saying nothing. Worry worms up my spine. I don't know what I can do besides refuse. I can't fight him if he forces me, or worse, tortures me, but I'll stand my ground however I can. My soul was taken from me without my consent. There's no way I'm going to go to Hell willingly.

The longer he doesn't say anything, the more my stomach twists into a pretzel, but suddenly, his hand slides across my lower back. I stiffen reflexively. "I understand your concern," he says, his words as surprising as his touch. "It may be possible that we can adjust your contract."

I balk at that and peer up at him. "Wait, what?"

"For helping us track all the relics we need, we can look at maybe releasing you."

I can only blink at him, unsure if what I heard is right. "You'll break the contract you have over me? I'll have my soul?"

"I'll have to discuss it with Dorian and Elias, but it's a potential option."

A surge of excitement rises through me. That is everything, and if all it takes is finding relics, well, shit. Let's do this.

We continue walking again, and I can't help smiling. I never thought there'd be a way out for me. Well, a true way out, since killing all three of them was never realistic.

Ignoring the tingling deep in my chest, I focus my attention on finding these damn relics, and quick.

Cain stays close to my side, the sun on our backs. By the time we reach the seventh container, the thumping of footfalls race up behind us.

Glancing over my shoulder, I spot Dorian jogging toward us. "All clear."

A shadow suddenly falls over us. I flinch out of

instinct, and my stomach drops, expecting danger, but when Elias lands in front of us, all grin, I relax. Show off.

"Clear on my side, too," he says.

Cain gestures for me to step forward. "Let's keep moving then."

We do, pausing at each container briefly. At the sixteenth one, a slight twitch runs over my pinky.

"We're close." I hurry my steps. The intensity grows with each step I take, bringing me right in front of the last container. I roll my eyes. "Of course it would be all the way at the end."

"Are you sure this is it?" Cain asks, standing so close to me his arm rubs against mine. Dorian and Elias are there too, pressed near.

"Hundred percent sure. My pinky toe is doing an Irish dance. This is our container."

Cain grins. "Stand back."

We follow his instructions. He pulls at the metal lock, testing it. Surprisingly, it pops open immediately, making me wonder if it was even locked to begin with. Uneasiness curls in my gut. Could this really be that easy?

"Be careful," I whisper to him.

Tossing the lock aside, he hastily heaves open both doors.

I'm frozen on my feet, curiosity pulsing through my veins. We all push our way forward for a better look inside. Light spills into the darkness. I had expected a mountain of gold coins and jewelry, or a bunch of trinkets like I'd found in the collector's warehouse, but we don't find any of that.

A man sits inside on a plastic chair, in the very center of the otherwise empty container, with a small box at his feet and a very pleased look twisted on his face. A face that makes dread ice over my veins.

Sir Surchion.

CHAPTER TWENTY-ONE
CAIN

A primal growl rips from my throat.

Sir Surchion sits before us, legs wide, wearing a fucking grin that I want to tear off his face. Pure dark eyes pass by me and find someone else, and a fierceness cuts across his face. "Miss Cross."

She steps back.

Fists clenching, hellfire blazes through me. My heart speeds, my demon form snapping forward. Hearing him say her name, seeing the way he looks at her, and seeing her fear, it enrages me unlike anything else.

Elias snarls, while on my other side, the runes across Dorian's chest and shoulders glow blue through his sweater.

"Remember what I said before?" I ask the two of them, my voice deeper and more guttural in this form.

Elias snarls, spit flying, and drops onto all fours. The shift rockets through him, and in the blink of an eye, a massive black hellhound stands in his place.

Dorian's horns curl, and his hair turns platinum as he changes. "To keep this PG? Yeah?"

We exchange knowing looks. My wings stretch open, shielding Aria from the collector's view. "Fuck it."

"Now you're speaking my language."

At the same time, the three of us rush forward.

Sir Surchion lifts his hand from behind his back, grasping a silver cylinder the size of a spray can. The mad man laughs.

Panic hits me instantly. It's a grenade.

Fuck! "Pull back!" I yell at my team.

In a heartbeat, Sir Surchion pulls the pin and tosses it to our feet. It hits the ground, and with it, an explosion of smoke rushes out. It swells so fast, swallowing everything in sight in mere seconds.

We retreat, stumbling backward. The stale gas floods my senses, but there's no hint of bitterness.... no poison that I can taste. My eyes aren't stinging either, so this is a mask to blind us.

I whip around just as Elias snatches Aria off her feet. Smoke swallows them along with everything else in sight, dividing us.

Sonofabitch.

"We do this like we did in Hell," Dorian says from somewhere on my right. "Remember the infernal pits?"

I smirk. Our old hunting grounds where sulfur leaked through vents in the ground, strong enough to stunt a man.

A sudden whoosh of air blasts against my back, driving me forward from the force. Gray gas undulates around us, along with the echo of beating wings.

"He's taken flight," I shout to Elias and Dorian. Wherever they are.

A looming shadow swoops over us suddenly, confirming my fears.

Knife-like claws jut out of the vapor and race straight for my face.

I twist away, ducking frantically, and throw myself into a forward roll.

Burning, sharp scratches rip down my back, tearing fabric and skin alike. I hiss, the agony excruciating, but thank my luck my wings haven't been damaged.

Shoving myself to my feet, my back is on fire, but I push past the pain. I hear Dorian's howl of frustration and pain close by. The dragon's gotten to him, too.

Panic gripping me, I dart in his direction, tearing through the fog.

Knowing I need to find a clear line of sight, I shove off the ground and take flight. My wings beat swiftly, helping me gain altitude, but with each movement, the open wounds on my back sting mercilessly. I grit my teeth as I emerge from the smoke and take note of how much ground it's managed to cover. It's impossible to see anything down there. I curve around just as something slams into my back so violently it drives me toward the ground. Tucking my wings in, I spin, trying to redirect myself away from the ground, but the smoke is rushing toward me fast. The ground isn't far off, but I'm able to gain a draft of wind just in time to lift myself at the last second.

My celebration is short lived, though, because an immense weight shoves into me again. I hit the ground this time from about ten feet high and roll as my momentum continues to drive me forward. Suddenly, the dock gives way, and I'm falling toward the icy water.

Desperate, I whip my wings out. The talons at the ends embed into the boards, and I'm able to grip onto the edge and haul myself up back.

Breathing hard, I kneel there on the dock, trying to regain my bearings. Behind me, I catch sight of the dragon swirling high above us in the sky. Bastard. The wind swirls through some of the smoke, but not enough to make it disperse fully. It does, however, allow me to see shadows moving among the haze.

From the shapes, it looks like Dorian is scaling the containers to get height on the dragon while it swoops low, toward Elias and Aria, whose figures are getting smaller the farther away they run.

I roar and drive my hands to the ground, pulling on all my strength and power. An inferno blazes down my arms, fiery red flames erupting out of my hands, so hot it scorches the wood underneath me within seconds.

Rushing into the chaos, the fire around me casts orange and red lights across the fog. Above me, Dorian leaps container to container, catching up to the dragon fast. He takes a death-defying leap and lands on the creature's back. He swipes his claws across its neck over and over, cutting through scales and muscle.

The dragon falls, skidding across the ground. Elias snatches Aria and hurls them both out of its path in the nick of time.

When Sir Surchion rises, I'm stunned again by the

dragon's size. It's taller than the stacks of metal cargo boxes. He glints like the color of night, his scales a silvery gray, and with bat-like leathery wings that snap outward. Burning smoke rises from his flaring nostrils as he whips his head side to side, Dorian struggling to hold on.

He spins and Dorian flies off, smacking into one of the boxes with a loud thud. He collapses onto the ground, but he jumps up and quickly vanishes behind a container.

The dragon's gaze pins on me next. Then, unleashing an ungodly sound, it takes a deep breath, and I know what's coming.

Tapping into the darkness inside me, my whole body sizzles with power. I propel everything I have behind it, shooting my arms out. Fire streams out of my palms just as the dragon spews out an explosion of flames. Our attacks slam together in defensive combat, each as strong as the other. Flames lick the air, sizzling and crackling.

Heat overwhelms me, but the dragon doesn't seem to be backing down. Suddenly, there's a blur of something swinging through the air. It smacks into the creature, sending it toppling over its own feet, and the blast of fire ends abruptly. Its head slams into the side of a metal container, its neck bent at an awkward angle, and it crumples.

Extinguishing my own hellfire, exhaustion rakes its claws through me. Being on this plane has me so much weaker than normal, and I hate it.

It's then that I realize what collided with Sir

Surchion in the first place. The giant metal arm of the crane.

Even more shocking, it's Dorian who's in the machine's driver seat.

A smirk tugs at my mouth.

But it seems we're not done yet. The dragon is already squirming, trying to get up again. His tail swings unexpectedly, and he uses the spiked end as a battering ram to whack into the crane. Dorian throws himself out as the thing teeters over and crashes into the water.

Even from a height like that, I'm sure he'll survive. Incubuses are very nimble and athletic demons. Hopefully he was able to avoid the arctic waters, though. That's where things could get problematic for a Hell creature.

A terrible cry shakes the air. Glancing over my shoulder, I see Elias's jaws clamped on the dragon's softer underbelly. He's doing all he can to shake and tear, but the dragon rears up, lifting him off the ground, and roars.

But if Elias is there, where's Aria?

I search the dock for her. Through the fog, a flutter of dark hair darts across the alleyway, behind another container, and I sigh with relief. As long as she stays out of the way, she'll be safe.

Another beastly roar erupts, shaking the very ground beneath us, and my gaze whips back to the dragon. Dorian's there already, joining Elias in the fight to bring Sir Surchion down. He's on the creature's back again, this time slicing into the thinner membrane of its wing. Looks like he was able to land the fall and keep away from the water after all.

Knowing that they need me, I rush over. But strong gusts of wind slam into me, forcing me to stop short. The dragon's wings thrash frantically.

It's rising again.

Elias and Dorian both leap off it just in time and hurry over to me. Smoke from the gas grenade curls around the monstrous creature, creating the illusion of it climbing out of the depths of a fiery volcano.

ARIA

A shiver grips my spine at the dragon rising before us. Between the crane, Cain's fire, Dorian's deep slices, and Elias's tears, its injuries should have killed it. But it's still flying higher and higher, disappearing past the smoke.

I've crept closer to the demons, but I'm sticking to the shadows and staying hidden behind the boxes as best I can. I don't want this to end up like the Milo Swamp where protecting me almost cost Cain his life. I need to stay out of the way.

They're demons with amazing, otherworldly abilities, after all. And I'm just… me. Whatever the hell that is.

Standing silently behind Elias, Dorian, and Cain, I can see the severity of their wounds. Dorian's ditched his sweater and shoes at some point during the fight, and dark purple and yellow bruises line his left arm. His one ankle looks painfully swollen, too. Probably from landing that fall before. He's lucky that's all he got—anyone else would have died.

It's more difficult to assess Elias's injuries with all his black fur, but blood is matted along his stomach, so that can't be good.

But neither of their wounds are nearly as serious as Cain's. Deep gashes stretch across his back. The dragon's claws ripped into his flesh and muscle like it'd been nothing more than tissue paper. I'm amazed he isn't paralyzed or dead. Blood drenches what's left of his shirt, yet he doesn't even wince when he moves. His gaze is trained on the dragon's shadow as it moves across the sky, looking as determined to kill the bastard as ever.

I wish I could do more to help, but what?

"We can't let him get away again," Dorian says to the others.

"I know," Cain huffs. I can see his muscles tense and shift beneath the skin as his wings try to reform, but all he manages to do is split the cuts wider and make more blood flow. He gasps, his brow dotted with sweat. Dread grips me. His wounds are so bad, he can't even manifest his demon anymore.

A strip of black glides over me, and when I look up, I see a sharp beak and feathered wings. It's Sir Surchion's damn crow, Mordecai, coming to add to our troubles.

"There!" Cain shouts suddenly, pointing at the sky. The dragon's dark outline becomes more visible as it swoops lower to the containers. It's losing altitude, probably from being hurt. "After it!"

Elias and Dorian are off, but Cain stays for a breath longer. He peers my way, finding me instantly. He says nothing, but his blue eyes swim with concern. Then he dashes off to follow the others.

Mordecai swoops by me again, this time heading down the row of storage containers toward the open one at the very end.

Oh shit!

My stomach flips. He's going after the relics!

I dash after him, but there's no way I'm going to outrun a bird that can fly.

Just then, a familiar tingling races up and down my spine. It's so strong, I'm forced to stop dead in my tracks. My entire body tenses, knowing exactly what's coming next.

"Sayah, no," I bark. "Don't you dare."

But it's no use. My normal shadow trembles as she takes its place, immediately stretching herself across the ground, down the narrow path.

My body is taken over by a terrible tingling sensation, like when your foot falls asleep but worse. It runs through my legs and arms, causing me to lose all other feeling, let alone take another step. Biting the inside of my lip, I try to force myself to lift my foot off the ground, but my muscles aren't listening to my commands. Just like Sayah.

She follows after the crow, expanding out of me rapidly. The further she gets, the more stress she puts on the tether binding us. And the more stress on the tether, the weaker I feel.

She makes a sharp left into the open container at the

same time the crow ducks inside. The orangey-red sparks begin to race over my skin and across her shadow, and I'm smacked with the same terrible suffocating feeling I'm always left with when she decides to go solid.

Already shaky, it doesn't take much to make me collapse. I lean against the cool metal of the closest storage box and try desperately to swallow more air into my constricted lungs. Everything aches, and exhaustion pushes down on me.

I can't pass out. Not here. Not now.

As my eyes glaze over and unconsciousness tugs at my brain, I see a dark figure in front of me. I wonder if it's one of the demons, but then something solid presses into my hands, and like the flick of a switch, my energy snaps back into me. I blink rapidly to clear my vision and see the shadow before me is just... me. Sayah is gone—returned into me all on her own. And in my hands is the box Sir Surchion had by his feet.

The relics.

I can feel their darkness pulsing through the box. And their song... it's muffled, but the hypnotic tune still leaks through the seal.

Sayah helped us? Again? There's so much more to her that I need to understand.

My gaze sweeps the area around me. The distinct shape of a bird glides through the smoke. I watch as it turns and flies farther and farther across the water until it finally disappears. Seems like Sayah scared Mordecai. Good.

Standing slowly, I look out again and realize none of

the guys or the dragon are nearby. I can hear the grunts and snarls of fighting in the distance, but I'm pretty much alone where I am.

Alone.

With the relics.

An idea sparks to life. I can leave. I can get away. The demons are busy, and I have the relics to sell. I can run to the driver and ask him to take me somewhere—anywhere—and then I start my new life.

This is my chance. But do I take it?

I glance down at the box again. The thing vibrates in my arms.

I... don't know.

My thoughts tug me in so many directions, making my stomach ache. I should be helping the demons. Not here hesitating.

A massive shadow darkens the yard, and when I jolt my head up, I see the spread wings of the dragon as it blots out the sun. I grip the box tightly to my chest.

Knowing the creature is descending, I duck between two stacks of containers to hide from sight. The beast lands at the top, right above me. I can hear the metal groan under his enormous weight. Air rushes all around me as he continues to bat his leathery wings, and more dust and smoke rains down. I shield my face to keep any of it from getting into my eyes.

When I peek down the alley, three silhouettes are rounding the corner and racing toward me, emerging from the haze. Cain, Dorian, and Elias.

Seeing them draw near, the dragon bellows again,

but this time, it sounds more like a wounded cry than anything else.

Dorian's mouth opens to call to me, but he snaps his lips shut, realizing that'll only make things worse. So far, Sir Surchion hasn't spotted me yet. Only them.

I hold up the box—my silent way of telling them I got the relics.

Dorian's concerned expression turns to an impressed smirk.

Then the dragon sucks in a lungful of air and spews a stream of fire between the rows. The demons scatter, and I'm smacked in the face with heat like I've never felt before. It makes my eyes water and stings my face, and I'm not even that close.

Panic cuts through me as I watch Elias, Dorian, and Cain split up and try another tactic to get to the dragon. Dorian climbs up the sides of the boxes like a monkey, Elias swings around the back, and Cain pelts the dragon with bursts of his own hellfire. He aims for the wings, mostly, which seems to be the weakest point, but the fire seems to be doing little damage. At least not as much as we need it to be.

How the hell are we supposed to defeat such a thing? Desperation clings to my spine, and my fingers dig into the box.

We just need a small break, some help.

The tingles return and run through me rapidly, the familiar kind that only comes with Sayah. As if answering my plea, she wiggles along my shadow and manages to lift herself off the ground, taking a form identical to my own. The sudden sharpness behind my ribs and the heaviness in my head leaves me shaky and panting.

She turns and gives me a slight nod, as if telling me she'll be quick, and then in a flash, she flings herself against the container and snakes her way up the sides of the pile.

Pain rockets over me, but I ride the agony and force myself to watch her climb higher and higher. Like before, Dorian wrestles with Sir Surchion, doing his best to dodge his swinging spiked tail and claws. Elias has chomped down on the dragon's leg, and Cain continues to throw fireballs its way. Sayah slithers past them all and curls herself around the creature's neck.

Wave after wave of sharp pain runs through me, and I drop to my knees. My lungs are so tight, I'm gasping and choking, desperate to pull more air in. I need to breathe!

Sayah pulls taut, growing darker as she solidifies again. Spluttering sparks of fire, Sir Surchion stumbles as she chokes him without hesitation or mercy. The dragon's claws slash at her, trying to get her off, and with every swipe through the shadow, pain lacerates into me.

Even without oxygen in my lungs, I still manage to scream. The pain is excruciating beyond words.

The box drops from my grip and I hug myself, praying that it will all end. The pain, the feeling of suffocating—all of it. If dying could grant me some kind of relief, I'd take it.

"Hurry!" Cain bellows to Elias and Dorian.

Darkness feathers at the corners of my sight, but I

hold on, grinding my teeth. *Just a bit longer,* I keep repeating to myself.

My insides tighten with each blow delivered to Sayah. She continues to cut off the dragon's air supply, seemingly unfazed, but I feel every punch, slice, and scratch. There's no blood or broken skin, but the agony breaks me just the same.

Then Sayah releases him and slides down and snaps back into me so fast, my body jerks backward into the side of a storage container. As if given the defibrillator, I'm shocked back to life, my body working again. I gulp down air greedily, nearly choking on it, but I can't seem to get enough into my empty lungs.

The metal groans above me, and when I tilt my head up, I see the dragon crumpling and rolling off its perch at the very top.

Dorian and Elias leap to safety while Cain dashes over to me. He throws himself over me, gripping me close and blocking me from the alley just as the dragon slams onto the ground. The earth shakes violently, the boxes swaying from the impact.

Is it... finally dead?

Dorian is beside us in seconds. I know by the softness of his touch on my shoulder. Elias is there, too, changed back into his human form. Slowly, Cain helps me stand, and they all gather around me. They're all battered and bleeding, but they're alive.

Panting hard, no one speaks. The exhaustion of the fight weighs heavily on us all.

After a long moment, Cain steps back from me, and the corners of his mouth curl up. "It's over," he says and glances down at the box with the relics at my feet. "It's over."

I don't know why, but his words give me all the comfort and confirmation I need. My shoulders slump, and warmth floods me.

We did it. We actually fucking did it.

We got back the eye, the hair, and the heart.

Elias lifts his chin and howls—actually *howls*—the sound filling the suddenly quiet cargo yard. Dorian's grinning ear to ear.

"Let's go home," Cain says and holds out his arm so I can join him on the walk back to the car. But before I can take a step, a flash of something dark swooshes between us, just inches from my face. Hands seize me from behind, wrenching me back.

It takes me too long to process what's going on. Even when Cain's being thrown backward, further away from us, my brain struggles to understand. It isn't until the explosive boom of his body hitting the side of one of the metal boxes that the horror of what's happened hits me full force.

With its dying breath, the dragon whipped out its tail and pinned Cain against the metal, the long, sharp spikes at the end impaling him multiple times through the stomach, chest, and shoulder.

Cain!

I scream, my insides shattering like glass.

My head whirls like I'm being held underwater, and all I can think about is the moment I'd seen him drop in the swamps, nearly dead, after being pierced through the chest with a dagger. This time, dark blood soaks the front of his shirt within seconds, too much for any man to live through, and his head lolls to the side. His blue eyes flutter closed.

But… Cain can't die. He can't. He's Pride, a demon, and the Prince of Hell, for Christ's sake. He can't *die*. Right? He can't.

"Fuck!" Dorian throws himself across the yard with Elias right behind him.

Their panic confirms my worst fears.

But he promised me he wouldn't die, dammit!

He promised!

I've lost complete control of my body, and all I can do is watch as the dragon shudders one final time and the spikes slide out of Cain's body.

Then, both the dragon and Cain drop lifeless onto the dock.

THANK YOU

Thank you for reading Hell in a Handbasket

Start reading book 3 in the Sin Demons series.
All Shot To Hell

NIGHT KISSED

I slay vampires... Then why does the master vamp insist I'm his?

When I'm called in to investigate a chain of suspicious deaths across Alaska, I meet three of the hottest, and most dangerous, monsters I've ever seen.

Just one problem.

They're the things that go bump in the night—a vampire, a fallen angel, and a demon. Enemies I must trust with my life if I'm to solve the dark trail of mysteries before more lives are lost.

But just as hard as solving the murders is denying my attraction to them all. And as things heat up in more ways than one, I know I'll never be the same again…

That is, if I survive the evil I'm sworn to kill... and the ones I've let into my heart.

Night Kissed is the first book in the Chosen Vampire Slayer series.

This is your kind of book if you love kick-ass heroines with sass to match, scorching hot monsters who take what they want, and is perfect for devourers of enemies to lovers books. Expect steam, action, and a supernatural world filled with vampires, demons, shifters, angels... and unhinged alphas who will do anything to protect their woman. Lovers of Anita Blake, Buffy the Vampire Slayer, and True Blood, this is your next addiction.

DEATH WISH

Life's a b*tch--but what comes after isn't much better.

Jade Blackwell, a paranormal reaper, helps supernaturals cross over after death. Her job comes with lots of rules--but not following them is kind of her thing...until it ends up involving her in something much deadlier than she ever imagined.

With the protective veil fading away, demons are crossing realms and impregnating humans, and Jade's best friend is among their victims. She's determined to save her friend, even if it means working with Cole Masters, a dangerous demon halfling and notorious gun-for-hire.

But time is running out to fix the barrier and find a demon cure. With supernaturals everywhere in danger, and the balance between good and evil tipped for the worst, Jade must choose between her own eternal afterlife...or the living world she so desperately wants to be a part of.

ABOUT MILA YOUNG

Best-selling author, Mila Young tackles everything with the zeal and bravado of the fairytale heroes she grew up reading about. She slays monsters, real and imaginary, like there's no tomorrow. By day she rocks a keyboard as a marketing extraordinaire. At night she battles with her mighty pen-sword, creating fairytale retellings, and sexy ever after tales. In her spare time, she loves pretending she's a mighty warrior, walks on the beach with her dogs, cuddling up with her cats, and devouring every fantasy tale she can get her pinkies on.

Ready to read more and more from Mila Young?www.subscribepage.com/milayoung

For more information...
milayoungarc@gmail.com

ABOUT HARPER A. BROOKS

Harper A. Brooks lives in a small town on the New Jersey shore. Even though classic authors have always filled her bookshelves, she finds her writing muse drawn to the dark, magical, and romantic. But when she isn't creating entire worlds with sexy shifters or legendary love stories, you can find her either with a good cup of coffee in hand or at home snuggling with her furry, four-legged son, Sammy.

She writes urban fantasy and paranormal romance.

RONE AWARD WINNER
USA TODAY BESTSELLING AUTHOR

Want to read more from Harper A. Brooks? Subscribe to Harper's newsletter and get *Halfling for Hire* for free! http://BookHip.com/MCBDCN

Join Harper's reader group for exclusive content, sneak-peeks, giveaways, and more! www.facebook.com/groups/harpershalflings

Printed in Great Britain
by Amazon